# A pool of dread opened inside Annja

"If you don't come here immediately I'm going to put out a warrant to have you picked up," Bart said.

"That's not very friendly."

"I'm not in a friendly mood, Annja. Get here as quick as you can, okay?" Bart disconnected the call.

"Problem?" Nikolai asked.

"This is where we part ways," Annja said. "I have to go see the police."

"What about?"

"I'm not sure. Bart wants me to come to the Clark Hotel."

"Where Mario is supposed to be?"

"Yes." Annja gathered her things, putting everything into her backpack.

"And this guy Bart. He's a homicide detective?" Nikolai asked.

Annja nodded.

"That can't be good."

**Titles in this series:**

# ROGUE Angel

## Alex Archer

# GOD OF THUNDER

A GOLD EAGLE BOOK FROM

# W💿RLDWIDE®

TORONTO • NEW YORK • LONDON
AMSTERDAM • PARIS • SYDNEY • HAMBURG
STOCKHOLM • ATHENS • TOKYO • MILAN
MADRID • WARSAW • BUDAPEST • AUCKLAND

First edition July 2007

ISBN-13: 978-0-373-62125-5
ISBN-10:    0-373-62125-6

GOD OF THUNDER

Special thanks and acknowledgment to
Mel Odom for his contribution to this work.

# The
# LEGEND

...THE ENGLISH COMMANDER TOOK
JOAN'S SWORD AND RAISED IT HIGH.

The broadsword, plain and unadorned,
gleamed in the firelight. He put the tip against
the ground and his foot at the center of the blade.
The broadsword shattered, fragments falling
into the mud. The crowd surged forward,
peasant and soldier, and snatched the shards
from the trampled mud. The commander tossed
the hilt deep into the crowd.
Smoke almost obscured Joan, but she continued
praying till the end, until finally the flames climbed
her body and she sagged against the restraints.

Joan of Arc died that fateful day in France,
but her legend and sword are reborn....

# PROLOGUE

*Courland*
*Baltic Sea*
*1104 A.D.*

Death slipped into the village with the thick fog that boiled in from the Baltic Sea. It came in on cat's feet, but took shape as a raiding party. The warriors had been too long at sea and too long without seizing a proper treasure. This morning under the storm gathering over them, they hoped to change their luck.

Skagul, called Ironhand, led the way. He was the chieftain. A large man, well over six feet in height, he was massively muscled from a life spent working hardscrabble earth in his homeland for a harsh existence. His dirty blond beard, rimed with sea salt, hung down to his midchest. Tiny figurines carved of wood, stone and ivory hung in his beard and the long hair he wore pulled back in a ponytail.

The reindeer hide he'd added to his tunic to ward off blows and arrows was cracked with age but still supple and serviceable beneath the thick bearskin cloak. A metal helmet covered his head.

He carried a long-handled war ax in his right hand. His left hand was gone, replaced by a cruelly curved iron hook. Sixteen years earlier, he'd lost the hand in a battle with an opposing tribe. His father had been a blacksmith when he hadn't gone raiding. Together, they'd fitted Skagul with the hook. He was short a hand, but he'd added an incredible weapon to his arsenal.

Senses tingling, Skagul trotted through the ice-cold ankle-deep tidewaters. The longship was nearly flat bottomed and could be sailed or rowed in only inches of water. In his years spent raiding, he'd taken his vessel across oceans, as well as upriver.

His heart beat quickly in his chest, warming him against the touch of early winter and the coming storm. The raiding season was almost over. It they didn't take a prize soon, there would be little to show for their efforts when they returned home before winter settled.

Ahead of them, the village sat quiet and still, frosted by the light snow that had come during the night. Most of the houses were wooden one-room affairs much like the longhouses in Skagul's village. Judging by the smoke from a few cook fires curling into the pink-hued sky, only a few people were up.

Goats bleated in small lean-tos behind many of the houses. Roosters crowed to greet the new day. A few dogs lounged in the lean-tos, as well, sharing space and warmth with the goats.

That suited Skagul and met with his expectations. The

animals could be a problem, but men just crawling out of bed were often thickheaded and slow to react. He was gambling everything he had on this effort, wanting to go back to his people victoriously.

Victory meant wealth.

Behind them, the incoming tide lapped at the shore and birds cried overhead as they skirled through the sky. The dark clouds sailed the leaden sky with greater speed. The wind had picked up, buffeting the Norsemen as they hunkered down in the brush at the edge of the village.

Holding up his war ax, Skagul glanced over his shoulder.

There, in the rolling fog under the storm clouds, he spotted the dragon prow of his ship. Snarling and savage, the dragon looked fierce and hungry. Heavy red and white sails lay furled on the masts, ready at a moment's notice. When raised, the mainsail displayed a snake, mouth open and fangs distended.

Skagul's heart swelled with pride. Her name was *Striking Serpent* and she had earned her name many times over. She was a twenty-oar ship with sixty-three crewmen. There had been more, but twelve had died fighting the Finns and others had been lost along the way. Since Skagul had been chosen to command the vessel, he'd always been successful.

This, though, had been his hardest year. Only a few weeks earlier, a band of Finns had attacked them at camp and stolen away with all their goods. They'd lost everything they'd spent months stealing.

Skagul would not return home empty-handed with so many mouths to feed. Nor would he see his young crewmen return without bride-price.

"Archers," Skagul growled.

Twenty warriors peeled away from the group. They nocked arrows to their longbows.

"There." Skagul waved toward the forested low hills ringing the north side of the village. The land and the trees provided a windbreak against the freezing north winds, which was probably why the village had been built there.

The warriors went at once. They were mostly silent, but Skagul heard some of their gear ring and bang as they took up positions along the hills.

No one in the village noticed.

Standing, Skagul hefted his war ax. The storm winds pulled at his beard and hair. He ignored the cold and moved forward. If things went well, the villagers would take one look at them and surrender everything they had.

The dogs started barking, then ran out to challenge the invaders. Their sharp teeth flashed and snapped. The Norsemen growled.

Skagul swung his ax, cleaving the skull of one dog and killing it instantly. Other warriors killed more of them, and they left the furry corpses behind them.

The goats bleated and chickens ran for cover.

*Something was wrong.* The feeling coiled and twisted through Skagul's belly like his ship's namesake. He held up his ax, calling his warriors to a halt.

The Norsemen stopped, forming a ragged line.

No one peered from the windows of the huts or came to the doors.

Skagul pointed at his men. "You three. Check the homes."

Immediately the warriors ran to the nearest hut. They broke down the door with their axes. The sharp crack of splintering wood cut through the whirling air. One of them went inside and returned almost immediately.

"No one's inside," the warrior announced.

"Check them all," Skagul ordered. As the men went to do so, he strode angrily to the center of the village. He cursed violently, knowing that the spying they'd done the night before hadn't gone unnoticed.

"Norseman!" a voice rang out.

Spinning, lifting his war ax, Skagul peered to the east and spotted a man standing almost hidden among the branches of a tall spruce tree. He wore reindeer hide in much the same fashion as the Norsemen but stood empty-handed. His skin was too light to be one of the Curonians, but Skagul knew they were in Courland. The man's beard was fiery red.

"I am Skagul," the Norseman roared.

"I've heard of you, Ironhand."

Skagul waited but the other man didn't introduce himself. "Who are you?" Skagul demanded to know.

"Your death if it comes to that."

Fury possessed Skagul. For two weeks the frustration he'd felt at the loss of his cargo to the Finns had festered inside him. To be addressed like this, in front of his warriors, was intolerable.

"Brave words from a man hiding in a tree," Skagul scoffed.

The stranger smiled, calmly and confidently. "I didn't have to show myself to you at all. I could have put an arrow through your eye." He paused. "Go to the well and draw the bucket. We've left tribute for you. For all your hard work to take what little other people have struggled to gain." His tone at the end was mocking.

Skagul walked over to the well. He nodded to one of his warriors. The bucket was quickly drawn. He'd expected a trick, but the bucket was filled to the brim with chunks of amber.

The material was valuable and could be used in trade in the Arab lands, as well as with the Franks, Saxons and Celts. Fishermen along the coasts of the North and Baltic Seas dredged amber from the seafloor. Skagul didn't know why the amber was only found there, but knew its rarity made it more valuable.

"That bucket contains a fortune," the man in the tree declared. "You're not welcome to it, but it's yours for the taking. Accept it and walk away. That way neither side has to lose a life today."

Skagul gestured. His warrior poured the contents of the bucket into a bag.

"You have more than this," Skagul told the man in the tree.

"Not for you to take," the man replied. "I won't let you strip these people of everything."

These people. The word choice hung in Skagul's brain. "You're not a Curonian." The more he looked at the man, the more he thought that the man was a Norseman.

"I'm not," the man agreed. "I was born not far from where you were, but I'm raising my children here. My home is here."

Skagul nodded and raised his war ax. "As a fellow countryman, I'll stand you to a proper funeral, then."

The man in the tree grinned grimly. "Then I'll extend you the same offer."

At Skagul's gesture, the archers loosed arrows that flew straight and true. The man quickly rounded the bole of the tree, disappearing from sight.

The branches deflected most of the arrows, but some of them pierced branches and the tree trunk. Almost immediately, a volley of arrows erupted from the brush, arcing high, then descending on the warriors gathered at the center of the village.

"Shields!" Skagul shouted, throwing himself to cover next to the well.

The Norsemen reacted quickly, hauling their wooden shields overhead. The Curonian arrows found flesh, as well as the shields, though. Eight of Skagul's warriors went down under the onslaught.

Standing immediately, Skagul grabbed a shield from the nearest dead man and pulled it into place over his head. "Move, you curs! Take the fight to them!" He led the way, pounding toward the huts, slipping through them as more arrows rained death from the sky. He reached the tree line.

The Norsemen ran at his sides as they had always done, axes, hammers and swords raised. They screamed and growled like a wolf pack.

Skagul ran for the tree, not expecting to find the man there, but hoping to catch some sight of him before he was able to escape. Carrying the shield through the heavy brush slowed him only a little.

They climbed a hill, mostly out of sight of the opposing archers, and surged through the forest. Skagul glimpsed the red-bearded man running swiftly through the forest on the other side of a narrow clearing.

"I see him!" one of the Norsemen yelled. "There!"

Skagul surged in pursuit, no longer in the lead because some of the younger men were faster these days. But all of them knew not to range too far ahead so they could be cut into smaller groups.

"Form a line!" Skagul bellowed. "Stay together!"

On the other side of the clearing, the red-bearded man turned and drew a short-hafted war hammer from his back. He stood his ground, glowering at the approaching Norsemen.

A few of Skagul's archers loosed shafts that bit into the dirt at the man's boots, tangled in his fur cloak and hit the trees around him. One of the arrows pierced his thigh. Without looking down, the man snapped off the end of the arrow and pulled the other half through his leg. He kept his eyes on the Norsemen.

"Strike now!" the man shouted, raising the hammer above him.

The storm's fury suddenly increased. Wind whipped through the trees, clacking naked branches against each other and raising gusts of whirling snow. Lightning blazed through the sky and reached down for the hammer in the red-bearded man's hands.

Yellow flashed on the hammer, revealing that it had been inlaid with amber on the sides of the head and the haft. It looked as if the weapon had been forged of lightning.

The detonation of thunder came immediately on the heels of the lightning strike. A blast of heated air washed over Skagul. When he opened his eyes again, he saw a tree near the red-bearded man topple sideways, trailing smoke.

All the stories about Thor, the Norse god of thunder, who controlled storms and lightning, rushed through Skagul's mind. He knew the gods sometimes journeyed from Asgard, where they lived, across the Rainbow Bridge to Midgard, which was what they called the human world.

This is no god, Skagul told himself, and told himself to

believe it. A god would never have retreated or relied on ambushes. For Skagul saw that was what they had run into as shadows shifted in the forest on both sides of the red-bearded man. Man, he told himself again, not god.

Skagul's reactions, honed in dozens of deadly encounters, pulled him up sharply. He opened his mouth to shout a warning. Before he could say anything, a withering hail of arrows from the Curonians drove him to cover.

This time Skagul saw the defenders hiding among the trees and brush. They rose only long enough to fire their bows and drop back behind cover.

Two of the Norsemen went down with arrows piercing them. But the others never broke stride, knowing from past experience that within a short distance they would be too close for the archers to fire again. As they raced across the clearing, the ground gave way beneath their feet. In disbelief, Skagul watched his men disappear as if the earth had opened up and swallowed them whole. Lightning flashed again and freezing rain poured from the sky. Less than twenty of the Norsemen pulled back from the edges of the pit that had been covered with branches and dead grass so that it blended with the landscape.

The trap hadn't been prepared overnight after someone had seen the Norse ship out on the sea. The Curonians had been prepared for an invasion for some time. Skagul thought about the red-bearded man's statement, that he was raising sons who were Curonians.

It was Redbeard, Skagul thought. He was the one who prepared the Curonians for battle.

A Norse warrior clambered up from the pit. With the rain falling, the earth had turned to greasy black mud. The man was stained with mud and blood. Three thin stakes pierced his body, letting Skagul know the bottom of the pit had been lined with them.

A single arrow flew across the distance and struck the Norseman in the face. The warrior stumbled and went down to his knees. The arrow protruded from one of his eyes through the opening in his helm. He reached for the arrow jutting from his face, then he simply rolled over and vanished once more into the pit.

Curonians charged from the trees. Their bowmen fired arrows over their heads that struck three of the surviving Norsemen.

"Back to the ship!" Skagul yelled. "Back to the ship!"

As undermanned as they were, he didn't know if they would be successful in getting away. He ran, struggling through the brush.

Redbeard and the Curonians pursued, but they were temporarily slowed by the pit they'd built for defense. Occasional arrows slipped through the forest.

Skagul never slowed, but he heard the thump of heavy footsteps closing on him and knew who it was. Lightning flashed overhead and thunder pealed. Throwing a foot out in the slippery sand of the beach, Skagul slid forward and managed to twist his body at the same time. He brought the war ax around in a flat arc aimed at Redbeard's midsection.

The amber hammer blocked the ax. Metal clanged as thunder pealed again.

Surprised and more wary, Skagul stepped back and raised his ax in a defensive stance. From the corner of his eye, he watched as Curonian bowmen put shafts into the backs of his men who'd made it to the sea. The Norsemen fell. The survivors of the first wave turned and charged the

Curonians, unwilling to be shot down like dogs or taken prisoner. They were slaughtered one by one.

Several of the Curonians surrounded Skagul. They had arrows nocked back to their ears. At that range they couldn't miss.

Redbeard held up a hand. Blood stained his wounded leg. He spoke in the Curonian language, obviously keeping them from loosing their shafts. To Skagul he said, "I've told them they can't kill you unless I say so."

"You'd better kill me," Skagul replied. He was afraid, but his pride wouldn't let him admit that. He'd always believed he would die in battle, not like a deer run to the ground by hunters.

Redbeard looked at the dead Norsemen lying on the ground around them. "I would prefer not to if I didn't have to. We've already caused the death of too many of our brethren."

"We?" Skagul scoffed.

Redbeard's face darkened. "You chose to be greedy."

"And those men aren't your brethren."

"I've not always lived among the Curonians," Redbeard said.

"Where do you hail from?" Skagul asked. He pushed away the fear and tried not to acknowledge the cold that bit at him with sharp teeth.

"Birka."

Skagul nodded. Birka was an island in Lake Malar. "I've been there. I come from Jorvik."

Redbeard let out a breath. "I could demand payment from your family for your return."

The offer was a true one, and Skagul knew then that his unwilling host was a Northman at heart. *Mannbaetr* reflected a man's value in his tribe, and it was different for each individual. Even if a man killed another man in a fight, he wasn't put to death as he would be in some cultures. Instead, the killer had to pay the *mannbaetr* everyone agreed on.

No one was put to death except for adultery, treason or stealing. But the worst punishment that could be doled out to a tribe member was banishment from the community.

Thinking about that, Skagul thought he had leverage that he could use. "They won't accept a demand from someone who's been banished."

"I wasn't banished," Redbeard stated. "In my home-land, I was a jarl."

The declaration surprised Skagul. What was a jarl, a man close to a king, doing living with the Curonians?

The storm raged overhead. Lightning blazed through the sky and leached the color from the world for a moment. The thunder rolled in over the sound of the waves.

Skagul didn't want to be ransomed back to his village. He wouldn't accept anything less than going back as a champion. Taking advantage of the lull, he threw himself at Redbeard.

Redbeard knocked Skagul's ax from his hand, but Skagul had expected that. He kept rushing forward, planting his shoulder in his opponent's chest and knocking him back. Before Redbeard could recover, two of the Curonian archers had loosed shafts.

Skagul felt the arrows bite into his flesh at his back and side, but he knew from past experience that neither wound would prove fatal. He carried scars from worse encounters.

Wrapping his hand around Redbeard's face from be-hind, Skagul melded his body to that of his opponent.

Skagul lifted his hook, reaching around in an effort to tear out Redbeard's throat.

Redbeard lifted the amber hammer. Skagul thought of Thor's enchanted hammer. It had been crafted by the black elves on orders from Loki, his half brother. The hammer was the most powerful weapon the Norse gods wielded.

Skagul thought the man was lifting the hammer to bring it into battle. It was going to be too little, too late. Skagul had torn out men's throats before. Nothing would stop him.

Then Skagul saw a tongue of lightning reach down from the dark sky and touch his hook before he could sink the tip into Redbeard's throat. Skagul lost his hold and flew backward, paralyzed and in agony. He felt as if he were buried in red-hot coals.

On his back in the wet sand, Skagul tried to rise but couldn't. When he looked down, he saw that the lightning had blown off both his legs. Blood pumped from the stumps and was washed away immediately by the rushing tide.

Redbeard came to him then. Sorrow showed on the man's face.

"It didn't have to be this way," Redbeard said.

Skagul focused on the amber hammer. As he lay dying, he waited to see if the Valkyries would arrive to take him to Valhalla. After all, he'd died a brave death. But he feared they might not because his death hadn't been a wise one.

Only a fool would have tried to kill a god.

# 1

The four men approached Annja Creed like a well-oiled machine. Their actions told her they'd done this before.

She didn't break stride or change direction, heading toward the Mailboxes & Stuff store that she used to mail and receive packages. In her career as an archaeologist, she often received items for study and sometimes for authentication. A handful of museums and private collectors paid her to do certificates of authenticity on items they were putting on display.

Although everything added up, payment for the certificates wasn't much. However, the benefits included free access to those museums and private collections, and the goodwill of curators who were valuable sources of information when she was doing research.

The four men moved with determination, without speaking. They were young and athletic, casually dressed and instantly forgettable. She guessed that they had military training.

Everything's already been planned, Annja thought. Adrenaline spiked within her, elevating her heart rate and her senses. She stayed within the flow of the lunch crowd flooding out of the buildings onto the street. Everyone was hurrying to try to make it back on time.

She knew the four men had been waiting for her, and wondered if they had followed her from her loft. She hadn't been home in weeks. A dig in Florida had consumed her and given her a brief respite from the dregs of winter that still hovered over New York. She'd quickly dropped off luggage and headed back out.

Layered in dark winter clothing—a thigh-length navy wool coat, sweater over a long-sleeved top, and Levi's, with a knitted black beanie and wraparound blue-tinted sunglasses, her backpack slung over one shoulder—Annja figured the team had watched her closely to recognize her. But at five feet ten and with chestnut-colored hair that dipped below her shoulders, she forgot she had a tendency to stand out in a crowd.

Nikolai, the manager at the shipping business, had left messages with her answering service to let her know she had a number of packages waiting for pickup.

So why hadn't they picked her up at the airport? Annja mulled that over and realized that they weren't law-enforcement personnel. Maybe they hadn't wanted to draw attention to themselves.

Then why hadn't they nabbed her at her loft? If they knew about Mailboxes & Stuff, they surely knew where she lived. That thought led to a whole new line of questions.

Although it stunk to the high heavens, the situation made Annja curious, and curiosity had driven her through most of her life.

Annja took her cell phone out of her pocket and punched in numbers.

"Mailboxes & Stuff," a friendly male voice answered. "This is Nikolai. How may I help you?" His Russian accent was charming, but Annja knew it was fake. Nikolai had been born and raised in Brooklyn.

"It's Annja."

"Ah, Annja, it is so good to hear from you." Nikolai lowered his voice to a conspiratorial tone. "You would not believe what has been going on."

Annja stopped at the newsstand at the corner across the street from Mailboxes & Stuff. She waited in line as customers ahead of her picked out newspapers, magazines and snacks.

Checking the reflections in the windows of the nearby coffee shop, Annja watched the four men attempt to lose themselves in the crowd of pedestrians. If she hadn't already made them, she knew she wouldn't have noticed them.

"So tell me," Annja invited.

"A man came into the store," Nikolai said. "He showed me government credentials and claimed that he needed a package that was supposed to be delivered to you."

The newsstand owner dealt with his clientele quickly. The line shrank faster than Annja wanted.

"What kind of credentials?" Annja asked.

"I don't know. I didn't get a good look. They tried to intimidate me. Something with a photograph and badge."

"Do you remember his name?"

"Agent Smith." Nikolai cackled. "I thought it was very humorous. I asked him if he'd seen *The Matrix*."

Nikolai was a die-hard science fiction fan. He spoke

Klingon and was constantly trying to teach phrases to Annja.

"What did he do?" Annja asked.

"He was not amused. Then he threatened me. So I told him he had to have a court order before I gave any package to him. He didn't produce a court order," Nikolai said. "So I called the police."

"You called the police?"

"Sure. I'm not going to play around with them. You get expensive things here, Annja, but you're not the only client I have that does."

"Right. So what did Agent Smith do?"

"What did he do? He *left* is what he did."

"Did the police come?"

"An hour or so later, sure. Evidently my call wasn't very important."

"Did you file a report?"

"I did. But I kept your name out of it. I just told them that someone using government ID wanted to go through the packages."

"What did the police say?" Only two people separated Annja from the newsstand vendor.

"Just to let them know if the guy showed up again. They really don't like people jacking around with official identification and pretending to be police officers."

"Have you seen him today?" Only one person remained in front of Annja.

"No. Why?"

The last customer moved off after buying copies of *Time* and *Newsweek*.

"Hang on a second." Annja asked for copies of *Cosmopolitan*, *Wired*, *National Geographic* and *People*. If she ended up in some government agency's interview room, it would be nice to have reading material while she waited for her attorney to arrive.

"Are you at the newsstand?" Nikolai asked.

Annja paid for the magazines and said thanks. Then she returned to the phone conversation. "Yes."

Across the street, Nikolai peered through the Mailboxes & Stuff window. He had shoulder-length dark hair, beard stubble, a checked shirt under a sleeveless sweater and deep blue eyes.

"Do you see Agent Smith?" Annja slid the magazines into her backpack, two on either side of her notebook computer to provide extra cushioning. The backpack was built around an impact-resistant core case, but it never hurt to be prepared.

Nikolai scanned the crowd waiting for the light. "Maybe. He's wearing different clothes today."

Annja was aware of the four men closing in on her. "Who was the package from?"

"Mario Fellini."

The name surprised Annja and took her back a few years. When she'd finished school, she'd worked at a dig at Hadrian's Wall in England. The Romans had built the eighty-mile-long wall to cut the country in half, walling out the Picts.

Mario Fellini had been on the dig after completing a double major in fine arts and archaeology. He was Italian, from a large family in Florence, with four older sisters determined to marry him off.

During her time there, Annja had struck up a close friendship with Mario but it hadn't gone any further than that.

Annja didn't know why he would send her something. They hadn't been in touch in years.

"Annja?" Nikolai said.

"Yes?"

"The light is green."

Annja became aware of the pedestrians flowing around her, crossing the street. She stepped off the curb and continued across.

"Do you know this Fellini?" Nikolai asked.

"Yes. At least, I did. We haven't talked in years." Annja's pulse quickened.

"Would he send you anything illegal? Like contraband, maybe?"

"If he's still the same guy I knew, then no, he wouldn't."

"This is good," Nikolai said. "Some of my customers, I'm not so sure. I try to stay away from trouble."

"I know. I'm sorry you're caught up in this."

"You're more caught up in it than I am. That *is* Agent Smith behind you and to your right."

Great, Annja thought. She took a deep breath. "Is the package there at the store?"

"No. With all the interest in it, I thought perhaps I could arrange a more private delivery. I've got it put away for safekeeping."

Annja smiled. "Thank you."

"Is no problem, Annja. For you, anything. If you hadn't gotten so famous doing that show, maybe you wouldn't attract strange people, you know?"

Annja knew Nikolai was referring to *Chasing History's Monsters,* the syndicated show she cohosted. During the trip to Florida she'd worked the dig site involving Calusa Indians. Although now extinct, the Calusa had been Glades culture American Indians who had lived on shell mounds.

Doug Morrell, Annja's producer on *Chasing History's Monsters,* had turned up a story of a ghost shark that protected the sunken remnants of Calusa villages. Annja had covered the legend of the ghost shark—which, as it turned out, most of the local people hadn't even heard of—while she'd been on-site.

As a result of the television show, Annja had ended up being known by a lot of strange people around the world. Sometimes they sent her things.

"You remember the shrunken head the Filipino head-hunter sent you?" Nikolai asked.

"Yes." There was no way Annja was going to forget that. It wasn't the shrunken head. She'd seen those before. The troublesome part was that it turned out to be evidence in a murder case against a serial murderer who had liked the show. That had involved days spent with interviewers from several law-enforcement agencies.

To make matters worse, in the end the investigators found out that the head shrinker had intended to send the head to Kristie Chatham, the other star of the television show. Kristie was known for her physical attributes rather than her intellect. Annja had to admit Kristie's enormous popularity sometimes bothered her.

"That was a mess," Nikolai sighed. "I thought I would never get the smell out."

"I'm sure it's not another shrunken head," Annja said.

"I hope you're right."

Annja's mind was racing. She was usually a quick thinker even under pressure. "Can you make a fake package about the same size as the one I was sent?"

"Yes, but why?" Nikolai asked.

"I want you to give it to me when I get inside."

"Wouldn't it be smarter to go to the police?"

"The police would drive these guys away," Annja replied.

"That seems like a desirable thing to me."

"They've made me curious."

"You know what that did for the cat," Nikolai pointed out.

"Cats are also great hunters. I intend to be a great hunter. I'll talk to you in a few minutes."

"Okay. I'll get the package ready."

"Make me wait on it for a few minutes," Annja said. "I've got a phone call I want to make."

"Sure."

"Oh, and put something in the box." It wouldn't do to lug around an empty box.

"What should I put in it?"

"Whatever you want."

"Papers?"

"No. Something with some weight."

"I don't know—"

"Anything that feels heavy, Nikolai. I just want to fool them for a minute or two."

"Okay. I'll find something."

Annja broke the connection and dialed another number from memory as she went through the door to Mailboxes & Stuff. The reflection in the door glass showed that the four men were close behind her.

They split up into two teams of two. Annja knew then that they were going to try to take the package inside the store.

She was curious and they were impatient. She knew it could prove to be a recipe for disaster.

# 2

"You've reached the desk of Detective Bart McGilley. Please leave a message and I'll get back to you. If you need immediate attention, please call Detective Manuel Delgado." The recording gave Delgado's number.

Standing at the counter in Mailboxes & Stuff while Nikolai went into the back to "check" for her mail, Annja dialed Delgado's number.

Two of the men trailing Annja, one of them Agent Smith, entered the store and started looking through racks of mailing supplies. Nikolai kept an assortment of boxes, envelopes and mailing labels. Annja wondered what they would have used for cover if the accessories hadn't been there.

Both men were intense looking. Their winter clothing could have concealed an arsenal. They never appeared to look at her.

"Detective Delgado." The voice was smooth and Hispanic.

Annja switched to Spanish to make it harder for the men to listen to the conversation. "Hi. This is Annja Creed. I'm a friend of Detective McGilley's."

"I know who you are," Delgado said. "Didn't know you were a friend of McGilley's, though. I catch the show every week."

Terrific, Annja thought, a fan. She figured that could cost her a big chunk of believability.

"Seems like McGilley would have mentioned he knew you," Delgado continued.

Maybe he's not exactly proud of it, she thought. That gave her pause for just an instant. She couldn't imagine Bart being embarrassed about knowing her. Then again, she couldn't blame him, either. If *Chasing History's Monsters* hadn't opened so many doors for archaeological exploration for her, she would never have done the show.

Annja chose to ignore Delgado's statement. "Do you know where I can find Detective McGilley? I called his cell phone number but got his answering service by mistake."

"That wasn't a mistake," Delgado said. "Detective McGilley is in court today. He always switches his cell phone to his answering service when he's on the stand."

"Is he in trouble?" Annja thought back to the last conversation she'd had with Bart. They'd caught lunch at Tito's and chatted briefly. Bart's fiancée was pressing him to set a date for the wedding.

"No," Delgado answered. "He's testifying in a murder case. Should be a slam dunk, but the assistant district attorney wanted McGilley there. The ADA is one of the new batch of wonder kids the law school keeps churning out. She just needed a little hand-holding."

"Do you know when you expect him back?"

"Soon. More than that, I can't tell you."

"All right. Can you give him a message?"

"I can."

"Ask him to call me as soon as he has a chance."

Delgado said he would.

Annja pocketed the cell phone. She'd exhausted the number of people she could call for help. In a way, that was sad. But then again, she didn't usually ask for help.

A moment later, Nikolai came back with a package. It was about the size of a hardbound book. The address on the front was written in Nikolai's hand, but Annja doubted the two men inside the store would know that.

"Thank you," Annja said.

"Of course." Nikolai gave her one of his patented friendly smiles. "Be careful out there."

"I will."

"The potato soup at Cheever's Diner is good today," Nikolai added as she walked toward the door.

Looking back at Nikolai, Annja couldn't help thinking that the announcement sounded like some kind of spy code. She couldn't believe Nikolai had just blurted that out. All that was missing was a big conspiratorial wink.

At the counter, Nikolai shrugged and looked embarrassed. "It's warm, you know. It'll take some of the winter chill off. That's all I mean."

Annja shoved the package under one arm, then walked toward the door. That was when Agent Smith made his move.

THE MAN WAS SMOOTH—Annja gave him that. But he was working on the presumption that he was dealing with someone unused to violence. Most people would have frozen when a strange man grabbed them by the arm. An uninvited touch in polite society usually elicited a blistering look of disdain, followed by a command to release the arm or a demand to know what was going on.

By the time all that happened, it was usually too late for the person who was accosted.

Annja had expected the touch, had desired it, in fact, because it made everything easier. The move put the man in reach.

Gripping her backpack straps with her left hand, Annja turned inside the man's grip. He stood flat-footed, never expecting her to turn like that. Or, at least, not expecting what followed.

Agent Smith opened his mouth to speak. Annja didn't know what he was going to say. Maybe he was going to say her name, or maybe he was going to give her his fake name.

Before he could utter a word, Annja jerked a knee up into his crotch as hard as she could. He wasn't totally unprepared, though. She felt the hard surface of a protective cup jar her knee with bruising force. Despite the presence of the cup, there was a certain amount of force that still communicated through the protective gear.

The man froze, not certain how badly he was hurt. Annja knotted her right hand in his coat and pulled him close. She head-butted him in the nose and heard it break with a loud pop. As he stumbled back, his coat fell open and revealed the pistol holstered on his hip.

Okay, Annja thought, that's good to know. It was better to have the bad news up front. She stuck her foot between Agent Smith's legs to hook a foot behind his, then put her shoulder in the middle of his chest. Agent Smith smashed backward into his partner.

"Help!" Nikolai shouted, going to cover behind the counter. "Help! Police!"

"Try using the phone," Annja urged as she turned back to the door.

Nikolai's hand came up and began feeling around for the phone handset while she bolted through the door. Agent Smith and his partner were already getting to their feet and grabbing for their weapons.

Outside, Annja turned right and ran. She knew the area well. Not only did she frequently walk to Mailboxes & Stuff, but she also jogged in the neighborhood and did most of her shopping there.

She took a firmer hold on the ersatz package as she lengthened her stride. "Excuse me. Out of the way. Coming through." She pushed herself down the crowded sidewalk, jostling the pedestrians.

Most of the men and women shot her looks of indignation. A few of them cursed at her as only a native New Yorker could, and it would have taken a master linguist to sort out all the variations of the single-syllable word they used most.

Then they saw the pistols in the hands of the men pursuing her. Trained by the post-9/11 world, the pedestrians hit the sidewalk and wrapped their hands over their heads.

They also shouted, and the shouts caught up to Annja and passed her. In seconds, the pedestrians in front of Annja had hit the ground, as well. The sidewalk became treacherous with bodies, and there was no way she could lose herself in a crowd.

A gypsy cab with a Buddha swinging from the mirror and blaring Eminem braked to a halt at the curb. The driver hit his horn repeatedly, cursing at the traffic congestion that had gridlocked him.

Annja threw herself across the cab's hood, sliding on her hip in a move made famous on *The Dukes of Hazard* television show. She hit the street on the other side of the cab and managed one step before she leaped again.

This time she sprinted across the next car. Horns blared behind her. The gypsy cabdriver shrilled curses at her, but shut up when he saw the men with guns. Annja used that sudden silence to mark the progress of the two men following her.

The other two men were across the street and tried to set themselves up on an interception course, running along the sidewalk.

By that time Annja was dealing with the oncoming traffic. It wasn't as congested. The flow wasn't moving quickly, but it was moving. Tires shrieked as the drivers in the inside lane tried to halt, but a New York City transit bus advertising the *Late Show with David Letterman* blocked her path.

Annja got her free arm up and used it to cushion her impact against the bus, slamming up against the Letterman photo. The bus never even slowed.

Whirling, Annja ran to the left. She figured the two men trying to intercept her would expect her to run to the rear of the bus and try to get around. Instead, she trusted herself to outrun the bus and the other two pursers.

She ran, breathing quickly, hoping she didn't get a muscle cramp from the cold weather. A quick glance at Agent Smith and his partner showed them trying to negotiate the first lane of traffic that wasn't stalled. Horns blared all around them.

Smith, his nose streaming blood, stopped long enough to yell to the other two men. He waved them back in the direction Annja had gone.

Annja's thoughts ran rampant. Cold air hit her lungs like a fist. She'd gotten acclimated to Florida over the past few weeks, and the weather there hadn't been anything like Brooklyn's.

Going back to the loft is a bad idea, she told herself. She kept running. Then the side mirror of a flower-delivery van in front of her shattered. Pieces of glass scattered across the street. The sound of the gunshot followed immediately.

Panic spread over the street as some of the motorists tried to lock down their vehicles while others searched for a gap to make their getaway.

A limousine ahead of Annja plowed into the back of an older sedan. Immediately a man in a black business suit and wraparound sunglasses got out of the limo and dropped into a crouch. His hand snaked under his jacket.

Annja was pretty sure he was going for a shoulder holster. A shoot-out in the middle of the street was the last thing that needed to happen.

She jumped up in a flying kick just as the man's hand cleared his jacket. The large pistol had a shiny nickel finish.

Swinging her left foot out, Annja caught the man in the forehead. His head snapped back and bounced off the car. He went boneless and dropped, out cold.

Thankfully, the impact didn't throw Annja off much. She caught herself on her hands, prone on her stomach on the street.

Two car lengths behind her, Agent Smith and his friend had gone to cover, ducking behind the florist van. Seeing the unconscious bodyguard sprawled in the street beside Annja, they grew brave enough to shove their pistols around the van.

Annja vaulted to her feet and ran across the back end of the limousine. At least two rounds smashed the vehicle's bulletproof rear window, leaving spiderwebbed cracks in the reinforced glass. The front glass of a coffee shop shattered. Patrons inside screamed and threw themselves to the floor.

Okay, Annja thought as she leaped for the curb. Now we know these guys aren't afraid to use those guns.

She hit the pavement with both feet and stumbled forward. Knowing she had to get off the street and out of the sights of the two men, she raced for a nearby theater.

THE THEATER WAS small, with an upper and lower screen. Decked out in yellow and red, the theater looked as if it were still in the 1950s when it had shown first-run movies instead of hand-me-downs that came out on DVD the same week.

The marquee advertised a couple of movies—one a horror picture and the other a new fantasy picture about a dragon. A line had formed at the ticket window.

Annja ran past them, slamming through one of the front doors. The box she carried absorbed some of the impact.

She was inside the building. A crew of early-twenty-somethings and a few teens worked the counter. The heavy scent of buttered popcorn hung on the air, mixing with the sharp stink of a cherry air freshener. Movie posters of the movies that were currently showing hung on the wall between the two bathrooms.

Barely breaking stride, Annja headed for the theater at the back of building. An usher in a red vest stood at the small podium reading a comic book. He looked up at Annja's approach, then looked as if he was going to say something. By that time she was already past him, and the four armed men came through the door. People began screaming.

Annja ran inside the dark theater, cut around the corner that blocked the light from entering the viewing area and ran down the steps toward the emergency door at the back. She halted, framed by the screen as a band of warriors gathered on a rocky cliff. She looked back at the protective wall.

She knew she hadn't left her pursuers, but she didn't want them to lose her now. The idea of the four men searching through the theater crowd left her chilled. They needed to know where she was.

"Hey, lady!" someone yelled. "Down in front! Some of us are here to see the movie!"

The four men came around the protective wall, briefly backlit by the closing door. Agent Smith pointed his gun and fired. The shot rang out in the enclosed space, but it was quickly drowned out by the dragon's roar on the film. On-screen, the warriors screamed and ran for their lives. Anyone watching would have thought the film was inter-active, because the moviegoers did the same.

Annja turned and ran toward the lighted emergency exit as a line of bullets chopped into the wall behind her. Evidently the emergency factor compelling the men to seize the package was escalating. She couldn't keep up the chase or an innocent bystander was going to get hurt.

# 3

Plunging through the emergency door, Annja ran out into the alley behind the theater. Potholes lined the street. Battered Dumpsters filled to overflowing stood resolute as old soldiers against the wall. She spotted some fire escape stairs to her right and headed for them.

Under the retractable ladder leading up to the fire escape, she leaped up and caught the chain, pulling the ladder down. The ladder clanked through the gears, then halted with a clang that echoed through the alley.

The noise drew the attention of the four men exiting the theater. As they turned toward her, Annja dropped the package she'd been carrying and climbed the ladder. She crunched her body from side to side, taking the rungs three and four at a time, one side pulling and pushing while the other reached for new hand- and footholds. Her backpack thumped against her back.

Agent Smith fired at her, and his aim had improved. One of the bullets hit the rung in front of Annja's face. The round ricocheted with a shrill screech. Two more bullets jackhammered brick splinters that pelted her face and coat.

Annja didn't look down. She looked up, focusing on where she wanted to go. Looking back or anywhere else would have divided her attention and slowed her.

Reaching the rooftop, Annja heaved herself over as a new salvo of shots chopped into the side of the building. She dropped to a squatting position, keeping her head below the edge of the roof.

The gunfire stopped.

Annja forced herself to wait. She reached into the otherwhere for her sword and felt the familiar hilt against her palm. All she had to do was pull and it would be there with her.

But she didn't do that. The sword was only an option when she was out of all other options. Even Joan of Arc, who had first carried the sword into battle, hadn't relied on the sword as anything more than a last resort. Joan's words and actions had brought countries, kings and churches to heel at different times in her young life. Now that the sword belonged to Annja, she knew it carried with it a heavy responsibility.

Not hearing any sounds on the fire escape, Annja relaxed her hand and the sword faded away. Duckwalking farther down the roof, she cautiously peered over the edge into the alley.

Agent Smith had the package. He used a small knife to slit it open. Reaching inside, he brought out a *Star Wars* collector plate that featured Yoda.

"Yoda?" Agent Smith held up his captured prize in surprise.

Nikolai had once coerced Annja into accompanying him to a local sci-fi event. As it turned out, Annja had discovered she had a fan base among the convention goers. She was surprised that Nikolai had shoved his prized plate into the package.

One of the other men spoke rapidly in a guttural language that Annja thought was German. She spoke the five Romance languages fluently, a little Russian and even less German, but she could make her wants known in those languages. The man below spoke too quickly and quietly for her to understand what was said, but she gathered that he wasn't a happy guy.

Agent Smith argued with the man, evidently protective of the plate. That made Annja wonder if they even knew what they had been sent after.

Abruptly, a cell phone chirped for attention. Annja realized it was her phone in the side pocket of the backpack. She pulled her head back just as the men looked up and one of them pointed his weapon at her. The bullet cut through the air where her head had been.

She fished out the phone, hoping it was Bart returning her earlier call. But she didn't recognize the phone number on Caller ID. The string of digits logged there were too long to be domestic, and she knew it was an international number.

The country prefix was 371. She didn't recognize that, either. Curious, not hearing anyone running up the fire escape and thinking that the call might be from Mario Fellini, Annja answered the phone.

"Hello."

"Ms. Creed?" a woman's voice asked in a professional manner. There was an accent, too, but Annja couldn't place it.

"Speaking." Annja crept across the rooftop and took up

another position. A siren screamed in the distance. She hoped that Nikolai had gotten hold of the police.

"You don't know me, Ms. Creed," the woman said, "and I'm sorry to trouble you. Am I calling at a bad time?"

"If you're trying to sell me something, yes." Annja peered over the roof. The four men, satisfied with their ill-gotten gain or not, had elected to leave.

They know who I am, Annja realized. It's not like they're going to have trouble finding me again if they want to.

That wasn't exactly a happy thought. In fact, it made her angry to think she couldn't go back to her loft. Her work was there. Her life.

I am not going to be afraid of going home, she told herself as she watched the men flag a cab. She took her small digital camera from her backpack, focused on the men and snapped off captures in rapid succession.

"I'm not trying to sell you anything, Ms. Creed," the woman said. "I'm looking for Mario Fellini."

"You didn't say who you were."

"I'm Erene Skujans."

Annja tried to place the surname as she watched two of the men climb into the cab. One of the other two crossed the street and flagged down another cab headed in the opposite direction.

A feint at misdirection? Annja wondered. Are they going to separate places, or are they going to meet up somewhere?

She memorized the cab companies and identification numbers on both cabs. Both were medallion cabs fully licensed by the state of New York.

"I'm afraid I haven't seen Mario," Annja said.

"It's important that I speak to him, Ms. Creed."

Annja felt irritated. The woman acted as if Annja was being deliberately evasive about Mario Fellini.

"You did hear the part about me not seeing him, right?" Annja abandoned her post and jogged across the rooftop to the fire escape.

She started down, taking the steps quickly.

"I'm afraid Mario may be in trouble," Erene Skujans said.

Me, too, Annja thought. Especially since a package he sent me has got guys shooting at me.

"What kind of trouble?" Annja asked.

"I don't know the extent of it."

Lie or truth? Annja wondered. She had no way of knowing.

In the alley, Annja sprinted for the street. She ran toward a line of cabs in front of the theater. Evidently the cab companies had heard about the shooting and had massed in an effort to pick up extra fares desperate to get out of the area.

"Again," Annja said, running down the line of cabs, "I haven't seen Mario. I just got back into New York. I've been out of state."

"Mario said he was going to contact you."

"Did he say why?" Annja found a cab that belonged to the same company that two of the men had taken. She shoved two twenty-dollar bills up against the window, fanning them so the driver could see them both.

He was young enough that her looks probably captured more of his attention than the money. He waved her in.

"No."

That, Annja thought as she opened the rear passenger door and slid across the seat, is probably a lie.

The driver peered at her through the security glass and smiled. "Where to?"

"Why didn't Mario try to call me?" Annja asked.

"He left the country suddenly. He didn't want anyone to know where he'd gone."

What country? Annja wanted to ask.

"Hold on," Annja told the woman. She covered the cell phone's mouthpiece and looked at the driver. "Another one of your cabs just picked up a fare on this street. Just a couple minutes ago. I got the number of the cab. I missed a meeting and I'm trying to catch up to a client. If I don't at least try to close this deal, I'm going to be looking for a new job." She tried to look desperate.

Some of the smile left the driver's face and he didn't look so friendly. "Hey, lady—"

Oh, great! Now I'm "Hey, lady," Annja thought. So long sex appeal.

"I got this thing about hauling around psychotic ex-girlfriends," the driver said. "No offense."

"If I was a psychotic girlfriend," Annja said evenly, "I'd wait for him at his apartment." She took another sixty dollars from her jeans with her free hand and held the full hundred against the safety glass. "Now the question is, do you want a big tip or should I find another cab?"

The driver eyed the money and shrugged. "You know, psychotic or not, it's really none of my business. What was the number of the cab?"

Annja gave it and they got under way. The driver called for dispatch and asked about the other cab's fare destination.

"Okay," Annja said into the phone, "I'm back."

The woman was gone.

Thinking the signal had been dropped, Annja called the number back and listened to the double ring tones.

No one answered.

Annja closed her phone, wondering what Mario Fellini could possibly have gotten into that would have involved men with guns and no hesitation about killing. And why would he have brought that to her?

She sat back quietly in the seat and watched the congested traffic around her. They rolled through the Brooklyn-Battery Tunnel and into Manhattan without stopping because the cab was equipped with an E-ZPass that automatically paid the toll.

"I gotta charge you for the toll," the driver said, shrugging.

A hundred-dollar tip and you want to be chintzy? Annja bit back the retort and said, "Fine."

The radio DJ interrupted the music to relay the news about the shooting in Brooklyn at a local theater. The driver eyed Annja suspiciously in the rearview mirror.

Don't look psychotic, Annja told herself.

"So what kind of business are you in?" the driver asked.

Annja put her smile and conversation on autopilot. The driver wanted reassurance that he wasn't making a mistake. "What kind of business would you expect?"

The driver eyed her a little more deliberately. "You're fit. Young. Obviously aggressive or you wouldn't have me chasing after your client right now. But you're not dressed like a stockbroker."

"I'm not a stockbroker. That's close, though."

"How close?"

"I work for a guy who's in business putting talent together."

"Like rock bands?"

"Not that kind of talent. He's a corporate headhunter. Raids other companies of their employees. If they're good enough."

"So the guy you're after…"

"Wrote some kind of computer application my boss thinks is mind-blowing. Now he's not going to rest until I manage to put the two of them together in the same room and he has a chance to pitch him." The story sounded good to Annja. She'd watched something like it on the Discovery Channel while she'd been in Florida. "If we land him, I get a vacation."

"Cool." The driver smiled and nodded.

By the time they'd finished the discussion, the cab rolled to a stop in front of the Sentry Continental Hotel.

"This is it," the driver said.

Annja peered up at the eight-story structure as a uniformed bellman advanced on the cab.

"You're sure?" Annja asked.

"Yeah."

Annja paid him and allowed the bellman to help her out. Settling her backpack straps onto her shoulders, she walked into the hotel, wondering how she was going to find the two men she'd come there looking for. While her mind was occupied with that, her phone rang.

Caller ID showed a number that she was all too familiar with. The number belonged to Doug Morrell.

Annja chose to ignore the call as she entered the hotel's lobby. The decor was marble the color of old bone and had brass ornamentation. Brass planters held arboricola trees, triangle palms and philodendron plants.

The guest registry was tucked away to the right, quietly

blending into the wall. A young woman stood at the desk and watched the action at the bar area a little farther back into the hotel.

Annja's phone rang again, but this time it was a text message.

Hey Annja.
Some guy named Marty Fenelli keeps calling. If you ask me, the guy sounds desperate. Maybe he's just a rabid fan?
Anyway, give me a call when you get this.
Doug

# 4

Crossing over to the hotel bar, Annja slid the backpack off and sat at a table obscured by a palm tree. The bartender's attention was focused more on the television in the corner than on his clientele. It was almost spring and baseball was starting up again.

Annja gazed at the screen wistfully and wished she was home instead of in a hotel she had no business being in. A cup of hot chocolate, made from real chocolate and scalded in a pan, sounded like heaven.

Her stomach rumbled at the thought. Some kind of lunch wouldn't be a bad idea, either. Breakfast had been consumed on the run, a biscuit in the Miami airport that she hadn't bothered to finish.

She read the text message again, then settled back behind the big plant and called Doug Morrell.

"Annja!" Morrell greeted on the first ring. "What a pleasant surprise!"

Annja shook her head. Morrell was in his early-twenties, working at the first job he'd gotten after graduating college. He'd told her on several occasions that all he'd ever dreamed of was working in television. Annja had asked him once how he felt about producing a syndicated show devoted to legends and lore that were often misrepresented. He'd claimed it was the greatest job in the world, and she hadn't been able to doubt his sincerity.

The false representation wasn't done by Annja. She kept her stories concrete, rooted in the bedrock of history and the facts as she found them. Thankfully, the audience for *Chasing History's Monsters* seemed devoted as much to real archaeological work as they were to the fantastic.

The fact that Kristie Chatham wore skimpy and tight clothes, then climbed out of them at every opportunity, probably bought a lot of indulgence on the part of the viewer. Although Doug had told Annja on more than one occasion that if she didn't look the way she did the audience wouldn't have fallen in love with her, either.

"You're not surprised," Annja accused. "You sent that text message knowing I'd call you back."

*"Hoping,"* Doug admitted. "I didn't know. What I do know is that when you choose to ignore your phone, it gets ignored big-time. But I am curious about what Marty Fenelli has that I don't."

"Mario Fellini," Annja said.

"Marty has Mario? Now I'm not so sure I want to hear about this."

"His name is Mario. Mario Fellini."

"Great. So what's he to you?"

"Someone I knew a long time ago." Annja dug out her camera and notebook computer, placing both on the table. "Did you talk to him?"

"A couple of times, yeah. Seems like a nice guy."

"He is." *Was,* Annja reminded herself. Whatever Mario was, he now had dangerous men after him. "What did he want?"

"To talk to you."

"Did he offer any hints about what?"

"Not a word."

Annja connected the camera to the computer by USB cable and uploaded the pictures to the hard drive. "And you didn't press him for answers? That's not like you."

Doug, like Annja, had an insatiable curiosity, but he had no desire to go out into the world beyond New York in general and Manhattan in particular. He claimed that everything he needed was there in the city.

"This guy is good, Annja," Doug said. "I questioned. He avoided. It's like he had some fantastic mutant ability."

Great. The Mario Annja had known hadn't been secretive. Archaeology was all about getting information and spreading it around. Mario loved sharing theories. "Did he leave a message?"

"Yep."

Annja flipped through the photos until she found the best shot of the two men she was following.

"I need to talk to you about your last story," Doug said. "The phantom shark."

"We can do the postmortem on that one tomorrow morning like we have scheduled."

Doug hesitated, then cleared his throat. "We're going to need more than a postmortem on that one. There are some problems."

That temporarily took Annja's mind off Mario Fellini

and the gun-toting goons. The mystery she was currently tracking could take time to solve, but the piece submitted was going to be put into production in a couple of days. Once it was, she couldn't touch it.

She was proud of the work she'd done on the Calusa Indians segment. Their history had been relatively new to her and she'd enjoyed exploring it.

"That was a good piece," she said.

"Sure," Doug agreed. "The Indian stuff was great. Really interesting. And your presentation was awesome."

"Then what's wrong?"

"The phantom shark looks fake."

Annja sighed in exasperation. "The phantom shark *was* fake. That was mentioned in the piece."

"I feel like maybe we need to fix the shark."

"Fix the shark?"

"Yeah. You know. Make it look better. More—I don't know—sharky?"

"That's how the shark looked, Doug." Annja couldn't believe it. "The shark looked fake. It looked fake because it *was* fake," she repeated.

"Fake's not gonna cut it in the ratings."

"Like I said in the piece, the phantom shark is a local legend. A lot of people treat it like a joke. It's there to draw the tourists. The guy who built the shark told me he started pulling the shark around as a prank, and to give the tourists a little excitement. He said not even kids are scared. They know it's fake, but it's all done in fun."

"Our show isn't about fun," Doug said. "It's about creepy. The creepier the better. Marketing *loves* creepy. And scary is even better."

"There's nothing creepy or scary about a phantom shark

carved out of driftwood and painted with airplane paint," Annja said.

"You're telling me." Doug sighed. "Look, we can fix this."

"It doesn't need to be fixed."

Doug ignored her and went on. "I talked to a friend of mine who does special effects for music videos and direct-to-DVD horror movies."

"Terrific." Annja sighed. "Just what I wanted to hear."

"He tells me he can fix the shark. He says when he gets done with it, you'll be afraid to go into the water all over again. According to him, Spielberg would love the shark he's gonna do for us. Postproduction, it'll look sixty or eighty feet long."

"This was a dumb story, Doug." Annja dug her heels in. "You gave me this story."

"Marketing gave you this story. I just went along for the ride. They thought they were getting *Jaws*."

"What did they think? That I was going to go down there and find a sixty- or eighty-foot shark no one has ever seen before?" Annja asked.

"I think maybe they were hoping. You have to admit, you've found some pretty weird stuff before. While you were looking for other weird stuff." Doug tried to sound upbeat. "Everybody here knows that when it comes to finding weird stuff, nobody delivers like you do. You just naturally attract weirdness."

Annja didn't say anything.

"Okay," Doug said. "Maybe that didn't come out like I'd intended."

"The story was stupid. The only reason I went was because of the work being done with the Calusa Indians."

"I know. That stuff is awesome. We're not going to

touch it." Doug paused. "Well, except we may have to edit it a little to add the extra shark footage."

Annja imagined her piece shot through with sightings of the monstrous shark. She fought to keep her voice under control. She was tired from the flight and from being around too many people in the airports and the plane, from being herded through security like an especially stupid bovine.

Getting jumped by Agent Smith and his buddies might have been a lark on any other day. Maybe I am weird, Annja thought. Then she concentrated on defending her work.

"I already edited the piece," Annja said. "We don't need any more footage of the shark. It was just one little piece of the whole story I was telling."

"Marketing thinks the shark *is* the story."

"They're wrong," Annja said.

"Annja, look, without people buying commercial time on *Chasing History's Monsters,* there is no *Chasing History's Monsters.* You and I will be chasing unemployment checks."

"Not me," Annja said stubbornly. "I've had a few other offers."

"I'm sure you have," Doug said good-naturedly. "But we both know that if you had someone else who would give you the budget this show does you'd have departed with a smile on your face that day."

Annja sighed. It was true.

"Look, I know this stinks. I'll be the first to agree with you. But, like it or not, we're stuck with the shark."

"But we're not stuck with the wooden shark carved out of driftwood and painted with airplane paint," Annja said.

"Right. We're not stuck with that one. Annja, I'm asking you to come in tomorrow so we can recut the segment. I need some voice-overs for the new shark segments."

"Oohs and aahs and a bloodcurdling scream or two?"

"I thought that was too much to ask for, but if you're willing to—"

"Doug," Annja interrupted.

"Yeah?"

"It's not going to happen."

"I figured you were just leading me on. That's okay. You've got a few shots coming. I don't hold it against you." Doug cleared his throat. "We're gonna have to deal with the computer-generated shark. It's going to happen. But I'd like to save as much as we can of what you want to show."

"This really stinks."

"It's a fact of life. Gigantic killer sharks are a lot more interesting than Caboosa Indians."

"Calusa."

"That proves my point. People will remember the shark. *I* remember the shark more than I remember the Indians."

"You know," Annja said sarcastically, "maybe you should tell the marketing guys the shark was really an alien robot that disguised itself as a shark."

"And it can take other forms? Like a Transformer?" Doug perked up and Annja knew she'd made a mistake. "That's totally cool. Man, they'd go crazy over that."

"Doug?"

"Yeah?"

"No Transformers."

"I'm telling you, you should rethink that."

"No."

"All right. Are you coming in tomorrow?"

"I don't know."

"If you don't, Editing will do the cuts without you."

Annja didn't want to deal with that. It would just be an exercise in frustration. She focused on Mario Fellini. "Did Mario leave a number where he could be reached?"

"I don't know."

"What do you mean you don't know?"

"I couldn't understand his message."

"He sent you a message? I thought you talked to him."

"I did talk to him. He spoke English when he talked to me. When he left a message on your answering service here at the—"

Annja broke the connection and dialed the studio number, quickly going through the electronic filters to get to her voice mail. She should have remembered it, but she never used it.

Only occasionally did she even go through the messages. Usually they were spam. Most of the people she had contact with, including fans of the show, used her e-mail addresses.

A few exchanges later, she had the message and triggered the playback.

# 5

"Hey, Annja. This is Mario Fellini. Don't know if you remember me, but we worked Hadrian's Wall together a few years ago." Fellini spoke his native Italian.

Despite the tension of the situation, Annja couldn't help smiling as she thought of him. Mario had always carried boyish charm with him and he wasn't forgettable.

Then Annja remembered the woman who had called. She wondered who Erene Skujans was to Mario.

"I got your number from a professional list," Mario went on. "Seems you aren't listed in the White Pages anymore." He laughed at that.

There was a reason for that, Annja thought. Her life had been crazy dealing with the television show even before she'd inherited Joan of Arc's sword.

"You've gone off and gotten famous."

Despite the good-natured and relaxed tone Mario had in his voice, Annja also detected tension. It sounded as if he was calling from a street pay phone. She heard traffic in the background.

That meant that even if the studio had Caller ID on her line or kept track of the incoming calls, the number she got wouldn't help.

But calling from a public pay phone didn't make sense unless Mario was trying to hide.

From Agent Smith and his fun boys? Annja wondered. Or was someone else involved? Maybe a woman with a sexy voice?

"I see you all the time," Mario said. "I ordered the *Chasing History's Monsters* DVDs and I've started recording the show. It's good stuff. I don't know how you work under those conditions, though. And I have to admit, that other woman gets on my nerves."

But do you have one of her posters? Annja wondered. She'd met professors of archaeology who had Kristie Chatham posters on their office walls. A few museum curators in Florida had them as screen savers on their computers.

"You're probably surprised to hear from me," Mario continued. "Or maybe now that you're famous, you're getting calls all the time from old associates."

The traffic noise in the background shifted, and Annja imagined Mario looking around for anyone who might be watching him.

"I hate to bother you with this, but I think I've gotten myself in a bit of trouble." Mario's voice took on a more somber tone. "In this business of digging up the past, sometimes you find things other people would do anything to possess. But sometimes you find things that you aren't supposed to find, and there are people who don't want that, either." He paused. "I'm afraid that's what I've done."

Remembering the men with the guns, Annja knew whatever it was had turned deadly. But where was Mario?

"Anyway, I mailed you something that I'd like you to take a look at. It got here a few days ago, ahead of me. I've been here two days, but I haven't heard from you. I can't give you a phone number, I'm afraid. I'm changing hotels every night. And I don't have a cell phone with me. I've been told people can track you through those if they get hold of your records." Mario took a breath. "The people involved in this, they can do things like that."

Annja looked around the bar, feeling momentarily vulnerable. Following the two men to the hotel probably wasn't the brightest thing she could have done. But it had felt right. If she'd called the police, she'd have been stuck answering questions for hours.

Call me, Bart, she thought. Bart McGilley could cut through the red tape. She hoped.

"Thinking back on this," Mario went on, "maybe I shouldn't have come. Erene didn't want me to come. She felt it was too dangerous."

Who is Erene? Annja wondered.

"Anyway, when you get the package, hold on to it until I call you. I'll keep trying. In the meantime, take care of yourself. These are dangerous men." The traffic noise in the background shifted again. "There's one other thing. When you get the package and see what's in there, just remember what happened to us at Hadrian's Wall."

Several things had happened to them at Hadrian's Wall. A lot of them had been good.

"Goodbye, Annja. I hope to see you soon."

ANNJA SAT BACK and stared at the television, watching the New York Yankees working out at spring training. They threw and batted and ran bases like they didn't have a problem in the world. The sports reporters traded quips with them.

Real life wasn't like that, Annja knew. People struggled every day. Some of them, like Mario now, struggled against deadly and dangerous forces.

In a way, it made sense that Mario had come to her. Annja didn't think it was just because of the past friendship. She felt certain part of the reason Mario had come was because of the sword she carried.

Roux had told her that dealing with trouble was part of the legacy of the sword. The old man had been with her when she'd found the last broken piece of the sword and there again when she'd touched the sword and it reassembled itself—somehow.

Annja didn't like thinking in terms that included magic, but she had no explanation for how the sword worked or how Roux and Garin Braden had existed since before Joan of Arc's execution.

Somehow the sword resided in the otherwhere until Annja needed it.

Thinking about Agent Smith and his friends, Annja took a deep breath and let it out. Okay, she thought. Bring it on. This is part of why I'm here.

All she had to do was find Mario.


ANNJA CALLED Doug back.

"You know," he said sullenly, "I'm not here just so you can hang up on me every time you get—"

"Doug," Annja said.

Doug quieted. "Is something wrong?"

When it came down to it, no matter what their difference of opinion, he was a friend. A good one.

"Possibly," Annja answered.

"Can I help?"

"Could you have my answering service there at the studio switched over so any phone calls coming in there will ring on my cell phone?"

"Sure, but I don't think you really want that."

"I'm sure I do."

"You're going to listen to a lot of trash."

"What do you mean?"

"You get phone calls here every day," Doug said. "People who love the show. People who hate the show. People who want to marry you or just leave obscene suggestions. I gotta warn you, those people can get really creative. It's hard to listen to sometimes."

"Why don't I ever hear any of that?"

"You hear the good stuff. The rest I have wiped off by my assistant."

"Why do you have an assistant and I don't?" Annja blocked the thought. "Never mind. We'll talk about that some other time."

"She's not much of an assistant," Doug said in a low voice.

"I heard that," a female voice said.

"Hey," Doug protested, "I meant that in the kindest possible way."

"Look, you little jerk!" the woman said. "I've put up with the menial little tasks you've had me doing for almost two weeks! I've had it! I'm not going to stand here and be—"

"You creeping into my office and standing behind me

is one of the problems," Doug said. "Eavesdropping on my conversations wasn't in your job description."

"I *quit!*" the woman shouted.

A door slammed.

"There," Doug groused. "I no longer have an assistant. We're even. Are you happy?"

"Switch the phone over for me," Annja said.

THE HOTEL DESK CLERK'S name was Sandy. She was blond-haired, blue-eyed and very understanding about Annja's "problem."

"Guys can be absolute jerks," Sandy said. "Especially ex-boyfriends. They just never seem to get out of your life."

Annja could tell immediately that she'd touched a nerve in the other woman. Usually Annja wasn't up on all the girl-talk issues. She didn't like telling someone else about her private life, which was a direct product of being raised by nuns in a New Orleans orphanage, and she didn't hang out with women who did.

Thankfully, DVD sets of *Sex and the City* and *Gilmore Girls* had given her the tools she needed to discuss her "situation" with the desk clerk.

"I know," Annja said. "This guy isn't the first."

The clerk shook her head. "And the sad part is he probably won't be the last." She looked at the picture of the man on Annja's computer screen. "He's not bad looking."

"Thanks." Like I'm supposed to take some kind of pride in that? Annja tried not to let her disbelief show on her face.

"You said he took a necklace from you?" the clerk asked.

"My grandmother gave it to me," Annja said, touching her neck theatrically. "It's worth a little bit of money, but I want it back more for sentimental reasons. That was the last thing my grandmother gave me before she died."

"What a louse." The clerk looked back at the image, then around the desk. "You know I'm not supposed to do this. It could cost me my job."

"I just want to know if he's here," Annja said. "You don't even have to tell me the room number. If I can confirm he's here, I'm going to file a complaint with the police. They can come talk to him."

"That would be the best." The clerk looked at Annja and nodded. "You need a break, girlfriend. I can hook you up."

"Have you met him?"

The clerk shrugged. "If he hadn't been hitting on me yesterday, I might not have remembered him. He definitely doesn't have a confidence problem." She frowned. "Sorry. That's probably more than you wanted to know."

"He's nothing but trouble," Annja insisted. She wasn't exactly happy with her method of getting the information, but it was working. Don't mess with success, she told herself.

"I hear you." The clerk sighed. "But he is good-looking." Then she turned her attention to the computer in front of her. "If anybody asks, I didn't do this."

Annja mimed turning a key to her lips and throwing it away.

"Dieter is staying in room 616," the clerk said.

"Dieter?" Annja repeated as if confused.

The clerk nodded. "It says here his name is Dieter Humbrecht."

"That isn't the name he gave me," Annja said.

"What a creep." The clerk looked back at the computer. "Let me check something." She typed for a moment, then waited. "Your ex checked in at the same time another guy did. His name is Klaus Kaufmann. Does that sound familiar?"

"No." Annja added the name to her mental list.

"I thought maybe he was using his buddy's name," the clerk said. "Sometimes guys like him do."

"I appreciate your help." Annja closed her computer and shoved it back into her backpack.

"I hope it helps," the clerk said sympathetically.

"Me, too."

# 6

Outside, Annja had one of the bellmen flag down a cab for her. She gave her destination as Fulton Mall, at a small bistro near the corner of Flatbush, then settled in the back of the cab to think.

She could have staked out the hotel, but since the men looking for her already knew who she was, she figured that wasn't a good idea. She needed to know more.

Or she needed Bart to call. Bart could get a lot of answers that she couldn't. She wouldn't have had a policeman's life. As long as she'd known Bart, she'd also known that. Policemen saw too much of the harshness in life.

Then she thought about everything that had happened to her since she'd found the sword.

You're not exactly leading a sheltered life, she told herself.

She made note of the two men's names. At least there was a trail to follow. What she needed was the real package that Nikolai had hidden away.

SINCE SHE DIDN'T WANT to leave her phone number or allow someone to track her calls by getting a court order and looking at her records, Annja used the public phone in the bistro. She watched the street, wondering if anyone had followed her.

The bistro was small. A dozen tables were scattered across the black-and-white-tiled floor. Long-bladed ceiling fans stirred the air slowly overhead. Heat from the kitchen fogged the front window against the lingering winter chill.

Annja dialed the number for Mailboxes & Stuff. A woman answered, sounding a little tense.

"Could I speak to Nikolai?" Annja asked.

"Could I tell him who's calling?"

The strange question pinged Annja's radar immediately. "This is Nicole."

"Oh. Well, Nikolai isn't in right now."

"I see." Annja watched the television as a news reporter delivered an update on the violence that had broken out in Brooklyn. Police were still in the area. "I was just calling to make certain Nikolai was all right. I saw there was some trouble in his store a little while ago."

*Not even two hours ago.* The short amount of time was unbelievable.

"He's fine," the woman said. "He's with the police now. They're hoping he can identify the men who came in here. This is really bizarre, isn't it?"

Annja continued the conversation for a moment longer, then managed a graceful exit. She felt frustrated. But since she was hungry and there was no sign of anyone following her, there was only one place to go—Tito's, her favorite restaurant.

There was no sense in going to her loft. Agent Smith,

or Dieter and Klaus or their buddies might be there by now. She was certain someone would be.

She used the pay phone again, this time calling Wally, her building super. Wally was sixty-seven years old, a retired semipro baseball player who had bought the building with his wife while he'd still been playing ball. Tough and intelligent, Wally was a crusty guy who tended to follow his own line of thinking.

The answering machine picked up.

Annja debated leaving a message, and decided to because she wanted to know about her loft. "Wally, it's Annja. If it's not too much trouble—"

The phone clattered as it was lifted from the cradle.

"Hiya, little lady," Wally said boisterously.

Annja smiled. It was nice hearing a genuinely friendly voice. "Hi, Wally."

Wally's voice quieted, but since he normally talked like Foghorn Leghorn, he was still loud. "Got yourself in some trouble again, do you?"

"I didn't do this," Annja said.

"You shoulda stayed down in Florida with the rest of the snowbirds."

"I can always go back."

"Getting out of the city could be tricky," Wally said. "First of all, you got these unidentified types that have been watching your loft for the last three days."

"Unidentified?"

"I don't know them."

"Okay." Annja smiled a little at the man's protective nature.

"And now you got cops," Wally said.

"The police are there?"

"Oh, yeah. I spotted a couple of plainclothes guys in the neighborhood. After I rousted one and he identified himself, he asked me to let him into your place. I didn't, of course. He had no legal right there, and I told him that. You ask me, he needs to watch a few more *Law & Order* episodes so he knows more about what he can and can't do."

"What are the police doing there?"

"Said they want to make sure you're all right."

"Did you tell them about the unidentified types?"

"I did, but after the police arrived, those guys were gone."

"How did the police find out I might be in trouble?"

"Beats me. The only person giving out less information than the cops was me."

Annja smiled at that.

"You called for a reason, little lady?"

"I'm worried about my home." The loft was the first true home Annja had ever had.

Growing up in the orphanage always meant sharing space, bathrooms, everything. College and her early years in the field had been more of the same. She'd dreamed of having a place of her own ever since she was little. A place with plenty of space.

When she'd locked the deal with *Chasing History's Monsters,* she'd signed a lease agreement with the option to buy with Wally. She hadn't regretted a minute of it.

"Your home's gonna be fine, little lady," Wally replied. "Don't you fret none about that. I'll see to it."

"Thanks," Annja said. She hung up the phone, then walked over to the counter to get a cup of coffee to go.

Her cell phone rang.

Excited, Annja took the phone from her pocket and

checked the Caller ID, hoping it was Nikolai or Bart or Mario. The number was blocked.

Annja answered anyway.

"Hello," an excited male voice said. "Is this Annja Creed?"

"Yes." Annja paid for the coffee and left the bistro, heading for Tito's.

"Cool! I never thought I'd ever get to speak to you! I've been calling and calling!"

"Is there something I can do for you?" Annja asked.

"Oh, no," the man said. "But there is something I can do for you."

When the man proceeded to tell her what it was, Annja closed the phone and put it away. Creep! She suddenly felt unclean. More than anything, she wanted a bath in her own apartment.

The phone rang again. It was another blocked number.

Annja cringed. The possibility existed that the call was from someone she was waiting for. She opened the phone.

"We got cut off," the man said. "I didn't get to finish telling you—"

Annja closed the phone and kept walking.

THE LUNCH RUSH WAS over at Tito's, but there were several regulars who deliberately waited until those people had left so they could have a more leisurely lunch. The fare was Cuban, served fresh and hot, with all the love Maria Ruiz could put on the platter.

She stood at the counter that served as her throne, ruling over her kingdom with a benevolent eye. Everyone who came through the door was taken care of, and those who tried to take advantage of the staff or act in a rude manner were tossed.

Maria was plump and gray haired, dressed in black slacks and a lime-green top under an apron. In her sixties, Maria had transplanted from Cuba as a young woman, then raised a family in Brooklyn. Her oldest son ran the kitchen.

The booths and tables were a festive green and yellow. Strings of glowing red jalapeño-shaped lights framed the windows. Servers wore black slacks, white shirts and smiles. Most of them greeted Annja by name.

As soon as the scent of spices, fajita meat and beer filled her nose, the ball of tension in Annja's stomach relaxed somewhat. Inside the walls of Tito's, she was home.

Maria spotted her. "Señorita Annja!" She held her arms open wide and came toward her.

Annja met the woman halfway, accepting the offered hug and giving one in return. There was nothing like one of Maria's hugs. It was almost as substantial as one of the meals that Tito's served.

"Hello, Maria," Annja said, grinning. After all the confusion and worry of the morning, it was nice to be welcomed.

Stepping back quickly and looking concerned, Maria placed her hands on Annja's jawline. "You're freezing."

"It's cold outside," Annja agreed.

"We've got to get you warm again. Have you eaten?"

"Not since Miami this morning."

"Foolishness. You must eat to keep your strength up. I have told you this many times."

"I know."

"You should listen."

"I know."

Only a few minutes later in a private booth, Annja

nursed a large hot chocolate and a huge platter of food Maria had assembled.

Annja watched the television mounted on the wall. The story about the shooting in Brooklyn had lost out to an apartment fire that had gutted a building. The scenes on the television were grim, and Annja's heart went out to the people who'd lost their homes.

She didn't know what she'd do if something like that occurred to her loft. It worried her even more that the men who'd tried to kill her wouldn't hesitate about setting fire to her home. The unpleasant thoughts took some of the enjoyment from the meal.

She wanted to know what was going on, and she wanted to know what she had to do to get her life back in order. She wished Bart would call.

Maria bustled about her, keeping Annja company only briefly because she was keeping watch over the restaurant and training two new servers. The restaurant opened six days a week, closed on Sundays because that was God's day, and Maria worked every one of them.

The other television was set to ESPN, covering the baseball spring-training camps. Maria wasn't a baseball fan, but she knew Annja was.

"So how come you're eating alone?" Maria asked. "You should have a nice man for lunch."

At that announcement, Annja nearly choked and had to get a sip of hot chocolate, which had just been refilled and was too hot for drinking. She burned her tongue.

Maria looked at her with concern. She was always trying to play matchmaker for Annja.

"All the nice men I know are busy," Annja replied. There weren't many of them. She took another bite of beef enchilada covered in sour cream sauce. The portion melted in her mouth.

"Hmph," Maria said. "You waited too long. A woman who wants a man, she has to move quickly to take what she wants."

Annja just smiled. Her line of work didn't lend itself to long-lasting relationships. There was too much separation while she was out on dig sites for a long-term relationship. Unless she found someone who had the same interests she had. So far, that hadn't happened.

"I'm doing too many things in my life right now," Annja replied. "I don't want a man I'll be tripping over, or one that I'm going to feel guilty about leaving every time I have work to do."

Still, it would be nice to have someone to share her successes and the things she learned. That kind of thinking led her to think about Bart McGilley again. Bart wanted someone in his life who would be there. That was why he was engaged to someone else.

But he was her friend, as he'd always been. She wished he would call.

As she ate, Annja divided her time between the television sets and the magazines she'd picked up at the newsstand earlier. She wanted to be home working on some of the material she'd gathered about the Calusa Indians. Maybe *Chasing History's Monsters* intended to insert a digital shark in her segment, but there were other publications that had already responded favorably to her queries about doing articles. And she was supposed to write three chapters for a book on the Calusa Indians.

The phone rang several times during her meal. Most of the calls were congratulatory in nature, thanking her for one episode or another on the television show. It was almost enough to take the sting out of thinking about the phantom shark.

Then Nikolai called.

# 7

"Annja," Nikolai said dramatically, "you would not believe the day I've been having. First, these hoodlums started stalking the shop. Then they are shooting in the streets. My God, it is almost too much."

"I know," Annja said. "I was the one they were shooting at."

That brought Nikolai up short. "Oh. That's right. Are you all right?"

"I'm fine. Where have you been?"

"At the police station. Looking at mug shots. You know, in the detective shows, the police bring a man in, give him a coffee and sit him in a chair, then give him this enormous book to go through and—voilà!—he puts his finger on the face of the man the police are looking for."

Annja couldn't help herself. She liked Nikolai, but his fake Russian accent got on her nerves when he got it wrong. "That's the wrong word," she pointed out.

"What word?"

"Voilà. That's French, not Russian."

"Ah, borscht." Nikolai gave up the pretense. "I used it with the cops."

"Maybe they'll think you're a Russian who spent some time in France."

"Probably not. They called my mom. She doesn't speak like a Russian. I swear, Annja, people just don't realize how much fun an accent can be. I love getting away with saying inappropriate things. You wouldn't believe the looks, or the help, that I get."

"I take it you're not at the police station anymore?"

"No. I was getting bored. I told them I'd come back tomorrow and look some more. I don't think they really cared. I got the impression they think these guys have left town."

"They haven't," Annja said.

"How do you know?"

"I found two of them."

"Jeez, Annja, you need to tell the cops."

"I'm waiting for Bart McGilley to call me."

"He's your cop friend?"

"Yes. If I try to talk to anyone else, things are going to get too confusing." Given her past history with situations involving police agencies, Annja didn't want to deal with anyone else. After being raised by nuns, Annja didn't like dealing with authority figures if she could help it.

"The police are looking for you," Nikolai said in a quiet voice.

"Why?"

"Because I had to tell them about you. Someone got a picture of you when you ran into the bus with the Letterman ad. This detective—a real jerk, I tell you—told me if I didn't tell him the truth he was going to put me in jail."

"He couldn't do that."

"He sounded like he could."

"You didn't do anything wrong, Nikolai. The police can only arrest you if you've done something wrong. The only way they can get you to offer testimony about something is to get you in court and have a judge order you to answer questions."

"I didn't know that."

"Most people don't. So you told them about me?" Now Annja knew why the police were at her loft. At least it wasn't anything that had to do with Mario.

"They already knew about you," Nikolai said. "Someone identified you from the television show."

Annja took a deep breath and let it out. "Did you tell them about the package?"

"No."

"Do you still have it?"

"I can get it."

"*We'll* get it. I need you to meet me. Do you know where Digital Paradise is?"

"Of course I do."

"Meet me there."

"When?"

"Now. I'll be there before you are. Be careful."

"Why?" Nikolai sounded nervous. "Do you think I'm still in danger?"

"Those guys haven't got what they came for," Annja said. "Right now it's better to be a little paranoid." She shoved the magazines into her backpack. "I'll see you there."

DIGITAL PARADISE WAS located in the middle of the block. Neon tubes glowed in the windows, announcing the presence of Internet, Games, Sandwiches, Beer and Fun.

Annja purchased time on a card, then retreated to the back of the large room where she could keep an eye on the door. She took a seat in the ergonomic chair, flexed her fingers and started typing.

All around her, players sat at banks of computers, playing video games around the world. Most of them were guys in their teens and early twenties, but there were a few women and older people, as well.

Negotiating the Digital Paradise interface, Annja opened her e-mail in one window and let it start cycling through, thinking there was a chance Mario had sent her an e-mail after everything that had happened.

She also accessed her e-mail at *Chasing History's Monsters,* thinking that if Mario had tried contacting her through her answering service there he might also have used the show's e-mail address.

Normally she didn't get the mail from the television show. She'd discovered early on that it was as bad as the phone calls were proving to be. The cell phone vibrated from time to time, diverting her attention and causing no end of frustration.

A quick check through alt.archaeology and alt.archaeology.esoterica sites showed a few promising developments on stories she was planning to do, but nothing that pertained to Mario Fellini.

She Googled a page that dealt with international phone numbers and searched for the 371 listing. She learned 371 belonged to Latvia, one of the Eastern European Baltic countries that had broken away from Russia in the 1990s.

A quick, cursory search on Latvia revealed a history replete with Vikings, amber, German crusaders and world trade. The Hanseatic League, the first trade union made up of merchantmen instead of nobility, included Latvia. From beginning to end, the Latvian people had been subjected to a long string of invasions. World War I had left permanent scars on the country, then the Russians had crushed continued efforts for the country to become independent.

It was all interesting. Annja had read into the history somewhat, particularly fascinated by the formation of the Hanseatic League in the fourteenth century, which had opened the floodgates on international commerce.

In its own way, the Hanseatic League had been as world changing as the Internet. For the first time, the middle class was free to trade, invest and speculate in goods that would be imported and exported.

Before that, royalty had controlled those shipments, only allowing what they saw fit to be bought or sold. Vikings had taken ships with ease. By banding together, the merchants spread their shipments over more than one vessel and provided adequate protection in the form of mercenaries.

But whom did Mario know in Latvia? That was the question.

Annja pursued it.

MARIO KEPT a home page.

Annja found it easily enough after a quick search. She stared at Mario's picture. If it was recent, he hadn't changed much.

He was a handsome man, lean and fit. His coloration was Mediterranean, and his hair was black and crept down past his neckline. The scar he'd gotten over his left eye while they'd worked at the Hadrian's Wall dig was still visible.

Annja smiled at that, remembering how they'd been involved in a bar fight in Haltwhistle.

A local had been selling "genuine" Roman artifacts he'd claimed to have found at Hadrian's Wall. Mario, with maybe a beer or two too many, had taken umbrage with the man and challenged the authenticity of the artifacts.

The man had come up swinging. Mario wasn't trained in self-defense, though, and had gotten the worst of it. Annja had stepped in and made short work of the guy and two of his friends with her martial-arts skills.

At the time, it had been scary, but even then something had seemed to come alive in Annja. Okay, so even before you got the sword you sometimes walked on the wild side, she reminded herself.

Annja read through information, learning that Mario had left his position in Vatican City fourteen months earlier. She hadn't even known he'd worked there.

It made her sad to think that such a prestigious thing had happened to someone she considered a friend and she hadn't even known about it. You're not much on friends, she chided herself.

She knew it was her own fault. Most people she met tended to slip through her fingers. She let them. Friends were hard to manage because they often wanted more time than she had to give.

In truth, most of the time she didn't notice the lack of friends because she was busy pursuing new interests that took her out of Brooklyn and away from her home. She loved being able to come and go as she pleased, and liked that she didn't have many regrets about being gone for weeks and months at a time.

The page didn't say why Mario had left Vatican City,

but Annja suspected it was because he hadn't been given free rein to choose his own subjects to research. Mario had always been extremely independent.

He was currently employed as a curator at a small museum in Riga, Latvia. Annja couldn't read the Latvian language. According to Mario's Web site, the language was also called Lettish. The name of the museum roughly translated into Peering Through Time and was funded by an independent financial source.

None of that explained what Mario was doing in New York, what he'd sent to her or why someone would be chasing after it.

Nor was there any mention of Erene Skujans.

Annja felt frustrated. Deciding to let that line of inquiry rest for a moment, she turned her attention to the two names she'd gotten from the desk clerk at the Sentry Continental Hotel.

She had more luck finding out who Dieter Humbrecht and Klaus Kaufmann were. But that led to even more questions and confusion.

Her research had turned up three articles with Humbrecht's name in them, and two of them mentioned Kaufmann. The first was a news article out of South Africa a few years earlier that listed the men as mercenaries. The second was on the Web site of a man whose personal museum collection had been stolen. The third mention was of an arrest of Humbrecht for attempting to break into an archive in Vatican City. He'd received jail time for his efforts.

Annja looked at the notes she'd taken. The break-in attempt had occurred while Mario was employed at Vatican City. Shortly after that, Mario had left.

The timing bothered Annja and made her suspicious. She'd always liked Mario and would never have thought badly of him. But Mario always did like going after the story, she reminded herself. His curiosity drove him. That, and the desire to become famous for a find that would be recognized throughout the world.

Would a find that promised something that big be enough temptation to make Mario cross the line? Annja didn't know.

At that moment, Nikolai entered the café. The problem was, he hadn't come alone.

**8**

Dieter Humbrecht and one of the other men flanked Nikolai. Looking despondent and afraid, Nikolai glanced around the cybercafe, then locked eyes with Annja.

The two men spotted her, too. Humbrecht shoved Nikolai forward, causing him to stumble. A few of the gamers noticed the action and swapped anxious looks. One of them reached for a cell phone.

Okay, Annja told herself, this is going to have to happen fast because the police are going to be involved soon.

She pushed her things into the backpack and zipped it closed. Then she stood and walked toward the men.

Up close, Annja had to admit that Dieter was a handsome man. Unfortunately, according to the newspaper reports out of South Africa, he was also a killer. He'd been acting to save an employer's life at the time, though.

"Ah, Ms. Creed," Humbrecht greeted with an English accent. "We meet at last."

"I have to admit that this wasn't something I was looking forward to, Dieter." Annja enjoyed the momentary glint of caution that showed on the man's handsome face.

"You know who I am," he said.

"It wasn't hard," Annja replied, hoping it would shake some of the man's arrogant confidence.

"I suppose Fellini told you."

Annja didn't say anything. At this point, the best thing she could do was keep them guessing.

"Actually, that doesn't matter," Dieter said. "Our business here is about finished."

"It is," Annja promised him. She reached for the sword, feeling it grow more solid against her palm.

"I'm sorry, Annja," Nikolai said. "They followed me from the police station. I didn't know."

That explains where the other two went, Annja thought. You should have thought of that.

But she was an archaeologist, not a master sleuth. However, she was also quite capable of taking care of herself.

"It's okay, Nikolai," Annja said.

Nikolai's hands trembled and his pinched expression showed that he might be sick. "They want the package, but they wanted you, too."

Annja looked at Dieter. "Why?"

"Because there are things my employer would like to know."

"What things?"

Dieter shrugged. "This matter is a bit of a puzzle, Ms. Creed. My employer feels that your expertise could be useful."

"Hasn't Mario told you what you need to know?"

Grinning, Dieter said, "Mario was reluctant to tell us much of anything."

No honor among thieves? Annja wondered.

Dieter slid a pistol from a shoulder holster, showing her just enough to let her know he had it. "We need to be going. My men are picking up the package Mario sent you."

Annja looked at Nikolai. "You told them where the package was?"

"Sort of." Nikolai shrugged helplessly.

Dieter looked at Nikolai and grabbed him by his coat collar. "If you've lied to me—"

Taking advantage of the distraction, Annja pulled the sword to her, holding it beside her leg. It was three feet of razor-sharp, double-bladed steel. Whatever beauty the sword had was savage, but there was no denying its presence. The blade gleamed as it splintered the light.

She spoke to Nikolai in Klingon and ordered him to get down. Since the artificial language was severely limited, as was her knowledge of it, she'd ordered him to "put shields up."

Nikolai dived to the ground at once.

Dieter pulled the pistol from inside his coat and brought it around toward Annja. Sidestepping, dropping her right foot behind her left, Annja swung the sword in a blinding arc. The sword connected with the pistol and sent the weapon flying from Dieter's hand.

Shock spread across the man's face, then he kicked at Annja's head before she could bring the sword back. Dropping back a step, Annja let her opponent's kick sail past her head. Spinning, she launched a back-fist at Dieter's head.

He dropped and slid backward. Holding his hands out and twisting them, he freed two ASP batons and caught them. He triggered them and they elongated with metallic snaps.

"Well," Dieter said, smiling, "I don't know how you

managed that trick. Maybe I'll beat it out of you later."
Armed with nearly two feet of gleaming reinforced steel,
he stepped to the attack.

He swung the batons rapidly, aiming for her head, then
her knees, then her head again in a convoluted figure-
eight pattern. Annja was certain if any of the blows had
landed they would have crushed bone.

The computer users abandoned their posts, heading for
the back of the café. The attention of most of them was
riveted on the fight.

They've been playing way too many video games,
Annja thought as she parried Dieter's attacks and gave
more ground. The mercenary was incredible with the
batons. She'd definitely figured him to favor guns.

"Irwin," Dieter growled, blocking Annja's attack with
crossed batons. He held the sword only inches from the
crown of his head. His arms shook with the strain. "Shoot
her."

Okay, he does favor guns, Annja told herself grimly.

Irwin leveled his pistol and fired.

Twisting and throwing herself back, Annja barely
avoided the bullet. It cut through her coat over her midsection. She dropped and rolled toward Irwin, coming up
on her left hand as she drove both of her feet up.

Her left foot knocked the pistol from Irwin's hand, and
her right foot caught him under the chin, lifting him from
his feet and sending him sailing backward. He crashed into
a computer terminal and sank down.

By that time, Dieter was nearly on top of her. A baton
streaked for her head. She blocked it with the sword, then
she rolled to the side and got to her feet. Irwin was out
cold, slumped on top of the wrecked computer terminal.

Dieter didn't offer any more taunts. His face was cold and deadly. She could see he intended to kill her as fast as he could.

Annja parried and blocked, then thrust the sword at Dieter's face. As expected, Dieter dodged back, pushing the sword away with his left-hand baton. Reaching forward, Annja plucked the other baton from Dieter's right hand.

"You're good," Annja told him as she backed away with her captured prize. "Just not good enough."

Dieter launched himself at her, swinging his remaining baton. Annja countered with the sword, then swung the baton into Dieter's forehead. The man collapsed.

Annja glanced around. Everyone had run out of the café. She willed the sword to disappear, then reached down for Nikolai.

"That was incredible!" Nikolai crowed. He was shaking so much he could barely stand. "I didn't know you were Xena quality."

"I'm not Xena," Annja assured him. "Are you all right?" she asked Nikolai.

"You have a sword!" Nikolai said. "I didn't know you had a sword!" Then he looked at her and frowned. "What did you do with it?"

"There was no sword."

"I saw a sword."

"Do you see a sword now?"

"No." Nikolai looked confused. "Where did it go?"

"Nikolai."

He looked at her.

"Focus," Annja said. "They came after the package. I need the package. Where is the package?"

Nikolai blinked at her. For a minute she didn't think her words had penetrated. Then he said, "The package."

"That's right. What did you do with it?"

Shrugging, Nikolai said, "I work in a shipping business. I shipped it."

Annja shook her head. She hadn't been thinking. No wonder Nikolai had gotten the package out from under the men's noses so easily. The easiest answers were always the best ones.

"Where?" she asked.

"To a mail place over on Flatbush Avenue. I take classes at the college and it's near my mom's house."

"I'm going to go get it," Annja said. "You need to get somewhere safe."

"You can't get it," Nikolai said.

"Why?"

"The guy who works there? Tom? He's only going to give it to me."

"You do realize that they could shoot Tom if he doesn't give it to them, don't you? He might change his mind about protecting your package. Unless you're really good friends."

"Oh," Nikolai said. "Well, we're part of the same Starbase."

"I'm sure that means a lot." Annja got him moving up to a run and they flagged a cab.


"MAN, I HATE YOU right now, Nikolai." Tom Gibson sat on the floor of Your Mail Is Here with his head tilted back. He held a fistful of wet paper towels to his bleeding nose. He was a little overweight, about Nikolai's age, and had kinky sandy hair.

Looking around the store, Annja saw that the accessories spinners had been overturned and papers had been scattered across the desk. There was no way of knowing how long ago Dieter's men had left.

"You didn't tell me somebody was going to be looking for that package," Tom accused.

"They were looking for it at my store," Nikolai said.

"Well, when they didn't find it there, didn't you think they would look somewhere else?"

"I didn't think that far ahead." Nikolai looked sheepish.

"And you're our science officer?" Tom rolled his eyes. "Boy are we in trouble."

"Guys," Annja suggested, "maybe we could keep this from being a Starfleet problem."

Tom glared at her. "Who's she?"

"A friend."

"You've never had a friend who looked like this." Tom smiled. "Anybody ever tell you that you're hot?"

"Don't tilt your head back," Annja said.

"It's supposed to stop the bleeding," Tom said.

"It doesn't. It just makes you swallow the blood. Swallow enough and you're going to get sick."

"Great." Tom leaned forward and blood streamed over his shirt. "I'm going to bleed to death."

"Pinch the bridge of your nose." Annja demonstrated. "That will close the capillaries and stop the bleeding faster. Then put some ice on it to keep the swelling down."

"Okay. Thanks. Are you a nurse?"

"No. I'm trying to find that package those men came here for."

"They took it," Tom said.

"Oh, man," Nikolai said. "I can't believe you gave it to them."

Tom pointed to his face. "They broke my nose, dude. Chill. I'm probably gonna look like Cyrano de Bergerac after this."

"How long ago?" Annja asked.

"Couple minutes."

"Do you know where they were going?"

Tom rolled his eyes. "Like they were gonna leave me an itinerary after committing a felony? And it is a felony screwing with the mail, you know."

"Yeah," Nikolai said. "The FBI's going to be all over this."

"I called the police," Tom said.

Annja stood and started for the door. A couple minutes' head start wasn't much. It was probably enough, though, but she had to try to find them. If that didn't work out, there was always the Sentry Continental Hotel.

Unless the local police had found Dieter unconscious at Digital Paradise and taken him into custody.

"Wait," Tom said. "There is something."

"What?"

"Almost forgot. When they first came in, they were looking at the map on the wall by the counter. I asked them what they were looking for. They said the subway. I told them the Flatbush station was a couple blocks over."

Annja went through the doors and broke into a run. The race wasn't over yet.

# 9

Annja ran through crowds of pedestrians, straining her eyes to see the Flatbush Avenue subway station. Footsteps gained on her from the rear. When she glanced back, she spotted Nikolai catching up to her. He was faster than he looked. It helped that he was following in the wake Annja had cut through the people.

"What are you doing?" Annja asked.

"I can't let you go alone."

"This isn't something you should be involved with."

"I know. I keep telling myself that."

"Then go back."

"Can't."

Before Annja could say anything else, her phone rang. She plucked it from her coat pocket and checked Caller ID. The country code was 371.

Latvia.

Pulling the phone to her ear, she said hello at the same time she spotted the subway sign on the next block. She didn't see anyone she recognized as Dieter's men or anyone carrying a suspicious package.

"Ms. Creed," Erene Skujans greeted. "Some time has passed since our last conversation."

"I know," Annja said, breathing a little rapidly. "I tried to call you back."

"I've been busy."

"So have I." Annja tried to keep the anger out of her voice, but she didn't think she was successful.

"Is something wrong?" Erene asked. "You sound out of breath."

"I'm trying to catch a train. Have you heard from Mario?"

"No. I was hoping you had."

"Not yet. I'm looking for him."

"Where?"

"Wherever I can think of."

"Try the Clark Hotel in Manhattan."

Annja hadn't ever heard of the hotel.

"It's a small hotel," Erene said. "It's one of Mario's favorites when he goes to Manhattan."

You know about his favorite hotels? Annja thought, and barely kept from asking that. "Haven't you tried calling him there?"

"I have, but he might be registered under another name."

Why would he be registered under another name? Annja answered her own question before she asked it. Of course he'd be under another name. Dieter and his people were hunting him.

"What name?" Annja asked.

"If I knew," Erene said irritably, "I'd have already called and checked."

That stirred the anger within Annja. She felt protective toward Mario because of the time they'd spent together at the Hadrian's Wall dig and because he'd come asking for her help. Although she hadn't known about it until that morning.

"I need to know what this is about." Annja reached the steps leading into the subway terminal. She hurried down the crowded stairs, eliciting several unkind comments.

"Find Mario," Erene said. "He'll tell you what you need to know." The phone connection clicked dead.

Frustrated, Annja shoved the phone back into her coat pocket and kept running. She reached the landing and peered over the crowd as she cut in line, drawing curses, and thumbed a token into the turnstile.

A large crowd gathered in front of the yellow warning track. The lights flashed and the loudspeaker sounded to announce the arrival of the train. Rumbling filled the cavernous terminal.

Anxious, feeling as if everything was about to slip away, Annja moved through the crowd. The problem was that a lot of people shopped on their way home and carried their packages on the subway.

Then she spotted a familiar face. The man was one of the four she'd seen that morning. He stared straight ahead as the train came to a stop. The air brakes hissed like ferocious beasts.

The crowd moved back, making room for the passengers to get off. Dieter's man shifted in the crowd and Annja thought she'd lost him a couple times.

"There!" Nikolai shouted, and his voice carried in the subway. He also pointed, drawing attention.

"Don't," Annja said. But it was too late.

The man turned and saw them. He nudged his partner, who was standing next to him. Then the crowd surged ahead to board. By that time several of the passengers were staring at Annja and Nikolai.

Trying not to lose the man, forced to wait to see if the two men would only pretend to board and later duck out, Annja ended up getting pushed back a car and barely got on. If Nikolai hadn't made room for her, she wouldn't have been able to board.

The train got under way with a jerk, then settled into familiar swaying as it rattled along the tracks. The car was crowded with the early-evening traffic. Annja made her way forward with difficulty, drawing hostile glares and a few choice words.

She let herself into the next car and saw the two men going forward into the next car.

"They're trying to get away," Nikolai said. "Newkirk Avenue is up next. We'll be there soon."

Annja nodded, knowing that a window of opportunity existed at that point. If the men managed to get out, they could be gone before she could catch them. She went forward faster, unmindful of the invective she incurred. Nikolai made apologies in their wake.

When the door to the next car opened, the two men were nowhere in sight. Instead, everyone in the car was staring at Annja.

Realizing what was happening, Annja put a hand on Nikolai's face and shoved him backward.

"Hey!" he yelped in protest, but he went back and down.

The man on the right shoved a pistol around the door frame. Expecting the move, Annja caught his hand in both of hers and cracked it against the door frame. When the pistol fell, she caught it in her right hand and kept hold of the man's wrist with her left hand.

Stepping into view, the second man pointed his pistol at Annja. She swung her captured weapon above the man's arms and caught him on his jaw with the pistol butt. The meaty impact sounded over the rattling of the car. He sagged and fell.

Annja released the first man in order to grab the other pistol before it hit the ground. Before she could get set, the first man kicked her in the stomach. Doubled over by the blow, feeling nauseous, Annja tried to draw a breath and couldn't. Pain screamed through her.

"You're going to wish you hadn't interfered," her opponent promised, doubling his hands into fists. He punched her in the face, turning her head with the force of the blow.

Black spots swam in Annja's vision. Weakly, she pointed one of the pistols at the man. He took it away from her as if she were a child. Flipping the pistol around, he tried to aim it at her.

She pocketed the other pistol, stepped over the package the other man had dropped and grabbed the pistol, flipping the safety in front of the trigger guard before he could fire. His finger whitened on the trigger, but nothing happened.

"Surprise," she said. Then she threw herself at him and used her knees and elbows in the close quarters.

Annja threw her elbows into the man's face and neck, battering him back against the train car wall. She kneed him in the crotch and thighs, tearing his legs out from under him. He went limp and slid down.

Breathing hard, Annja stepped back. Blood trickled down from her nose and lip.

Someone moved behind her. Instinctively, she lifted her fists and turned to face Nikolai.

"You win," Nikolai said, holding his hands up.

The train slowed and the inertia pulled at Annja as she stood on trembling legs. The adrenaline left her shaky. Getting hit in the face didn't help, she reminded herself.

She reached down and picked up the package. Then she took out a Swiss Army knife and sliced the tape open. Inside, nestled in a bed of foam pellets, was a mosaic tile.

And a note from Mario Fellini.

Dear Annja

It's been a long time since we talked. Doesn't seem so long, though, because I've been busy. I even pulled a stint at the archives in Vatican City. I kept looking for the Da Vinci files, but I didn't find them!

I think they kept them hidden.

But I did find something else that was interesting. I'm on my way to New York City, so I hope to see you soon. I left messages at the television studio, but you haven't called back. I guess you're busy. I hope you're not too busy to talk. I'll even buy dinner!

I've got a lot to talk to you about. If you have time, could you authenticate this mosaic tile? Play fairly with it. The results should remind you of that bar in Haltwhistle. Remember, you can't always be cautious. Omelettes don't get made without breaking eggs.

Take care.

Mario

* * *

"Do you want some more ice?"

Drawn from the letter, which she'd read nearly twenty times, Annja looked at Nikolai and shook her head. She regretted the effort at once.

After leaving the subway, they'd cabbed over to a Starbucks that offered Wi-Fi and television. Annja had immediately set to work on the Internet, trying to find out about the mosaic because it was the only thing she could think to do at the moment.

Going to the Clark Hotel in Manhattan wasn't a good option at the moment. The injury to her face wasn't too severe and already wasn't hurting so much. But, despite Erene Skujans's tip about the hotel, Annja couldn't act on it. Yet. She at least planned to stake out the hotel later that evening to see if Mario went in or out. She couldn't go up to the desk clerk and simply ask for Mario if he was concealed under another name.

Nikolai set another coffee in front of her at the table they shared. "The swelling seems to have gone down."

"It feels better," Annja said. She sipped her coffee. "You could go home, you know."

"I know. I'm going to have to soon. I've got a shift tomorrow and Mom is worried. I've already called her and talked to her, but until I walk through the door, she's not going to believe that I'm all right."

Annja smiled a little and the effort pulled at the swelling. "It must be nice to have a mom like that."

"It is. It gets in the way sometimes, but for the most part I really like having her there," Nikolai said.

"You don't know how lucky you are." Even though Annja had stopped aching over the lack of family in her life, she still felt wistful from time to time.

"Oh, I do. Trust me." Nikolai looked at the tile. "So what's that?"

"A mosaic." Annja picked it up and showed it to him. It was square, each side measuring twelve inches. "It's made up of individual pieces called tessera that are glued to a background. In this instance, the background is glazed ceramic. When early civilizations first started making mosaics thousands of years ago, people just used stones that caught their eye. Later, they began chipping marble and limestone into cube shapes and using them."

"Looks like a lot of work."

"The tessera are laid in twenty-four rows by twenty-four rows."

"So that's like…a lot of tessera."

"Five hundred and seventy-six pieces."

"Is that normal?"

Annja smiled. "I've seen walls two and three stories tall laid with tessera. There isn't a set amount to use. You use what you want to, and what it takes."

Nikolai tapped the mosaic. "This looks like glass."

"It is. That was the next medium artisans started using after they got tired of stones, marble and limestone."

"Is this a dog?" Nikolai pointed to the four-legged creature on the tile.

"It is," Annja told him. The dog stood braced on all fours, frozen in midbark. "These are called *cave canem* images."

"That's Latin?"

"Yes. The loose translation is 'beware of the dog.' Tiles like these were often set into the thresholds of Roman houses."

Nikolai grinned. "People have signs on their houses and yards that say that now. I bet they don't know that the Romans started that."

"Probably not." Annja smiled. Teaching was a sideline of her profession that she'd never expected to embrace. Instead it turned out to be a natural progression.

A lot of curators and archaeologists who loved their work had told her that. Since then, she'd experienced that feeling when she'd explained something to someone who ended up being more interested than they'd thought they would.

"So Mario sent you this tile as a warning?" Nikolai asked.

Annja looked at the handwritten note again. "He says he wanted me to authenticate it." She didn't mention anything about the bar in Haltwhistle.

"Then this could be worth a lot of money? If it's one of those ancient Roman tiles?"

"It's not." Annja looked at the tile. "It's good work, but it's not unique enough to be worth much."

"Maybe it's worth a lot because of the person who did this. Like a famous painter or someone."

"The tile's almost brand-new."

Nikolai slumped back in the chair. "Then I'm confused."

"So am I," Annja admitted.

"What are you going to do?"

"Stake out the Clark Hotel. Hope that Mario shows up. And keep hoping that Bart McGilley returns my call."

"He's the police guy, right?"

"Homicide detective, yes."

Nikolai drank his coffee, and Annja smelled the hazelnut coming off it. "Did you catch the newsbreak earlier? About the guys at the cyber games place?"

"No."

"They got away. So did the guys on the subway train."

Great. They're still out there. Annja took a breath and let it out.

Nikolai's eyes cut back to the tile. "There's gotta be a reason he sent you this."

"I know."

"And there's no clues in the letter?"

Annja pushed it over and let him read it.

"Says he found something hidden at the Vatican," Nikolai pointed out.

Shaking her head, Annja said, "Not everything's about the Roman Catholic Church trying to cover up some dreadful, earth-shattering secret. Usually people in power do things for their own good. To protect or benefit themselves."

"So why are these guys after you and the tile? To protect themselves or for their benefit?"

"I don't have a clue."

"But you do," Nikolai insisted. "That's why Mario sent you this tile."

"He's going to have to explain it to me." Annja's phone rang. She plucked it up from the table and checked the Caller ID.

Smiling, feeling relieved, Annja punched the talk button and said hello.

"Are you doing okay?" Bart asked.

The reserved, professional way Bart spoke brought Annja up short. "I'm fine," she said.

"I heard there were a number of incidents you were

involved in today." Bart's tone was accusatory and Annja didn't care for it at all.

"I tried to call you," Annja stated.

"You could have come in."

"There were things I had to do."

"Like turn Brooklyn into a shooting gallery? Or get involved in the fights at the cybercafe and in the subway?"

"It's been a busy day," Annja said. "Now that I think about it, maybe I don't have time for this phone call." In all the time they'd known each other, she and Bart hadn't always agreed about things, but he'd never tried to go all "cop" on her.

"You need to take this phone call," Bart told her. "Do you know a guy named Mario Fellini?"

"Yes."

"Let me send a car for you."

"No. Just tell me where you are. I can take the subway and it'll be faster."

"There's a hotel. The Clark Hotel. Heard of it?"

A pool of dread opened inside Annja. "Yes."

"Come there. And, Annja?"

"Yes."

"If you don't, I'm going to have you picked up."

"That's not very friendly," Annja said.

"I'm not in a friendly mood, Annja. Get here as quick as you can, okay?"

Annja promised she would. Bart hung up abruptly.

"Problem?" Nikolai asked.

"This is where we part ways," Annja said. "I have to go see the police."

"What about?"

"I'm not sure. Bart wants me to come to the Clark Hotel."

"Where Mario is supposed to be?"

Annja gathered her things, putting everything into her backpack. "Yes."

"And this guy? Bart? He's a homicide detective?"

Annja nodded.

"That can't be good."

# 10

Erene Skujans hid in the darkness outside the castle walls she intended to breach and whose master she planned to kill.

She wore black clothing under a black cloak that absorbed the pale moonlight bleeding through the jagged clouds. The landscape was reduced to almost two-dimensional relief by the absence of the sun. If not for the snow-covered ground, the darkness of the forest and the night would have claimed the grounds leading up to the high walls.

Then she would have been able to approach the castle without fear of being seen.

Leaning against the tree, her long black hair pulled back, only her pale features would have given her away. Her cobalt-blue eyes were widely spaced under arched brows. She carried a crossbow with special-forces blades that were designed to penetrate Kevlar body armor. Over the past few years since she'd left the village where her grandmother had raised her, she'd had occasion to use other crossbows. None had ever failed her.

Besides the crossbow, the quiver of bolts lashed to her left thigh and the combat knife sheathed down her right calf, Erene also carried the weapons her grandmother had trained her to use. If the man she hunted had grown up in her village, he would have feared her wrath. Her warning alone would have sent him away.

Instead, the German—Wolfram Schluter—had chosen to defy her. Worse than that, he'd gone after Mario.

Stop thinking about that, she admonished herself. You're going to get yourself killed. If you're dead, you can't stop this man from hurting Mario.

Erene was still angry over the way that Mario had left without telling her. That had hurt a lot because Erene had thought he trusted her above anyone else.

But he had gone to New York City, pursuing the American woman, Annja Creed. Erene wouldn't have known that if she hadn't checked Mario's computer and discovered that he'd been looking for the woman online. Then she'd remembered how Mario had talked about her, about how he got the small scar above his eye.

What made it even worse was that Mario had tried to hide his Internet searching. Of course, he didn't know much about computers and there had been no way for him to know how much she did.

Getting the woman's cell phone number had been expensive. Erene still had contacts who could provide services that involved hacking into credit reports and finding out the woman's personal information. None of the information Mario had turned up had included that.

Erene knew more about Annja Creed than Mario had when he'd left.

The emotion that Erene felt about the American woman

surprised her. In all her life, she'd never felt jealous. Not once.
There had been many men in her life. Some she had used and
discarded, and others she'd broken in the pursuit of her own
goals. In the end, though, none of them had mattered.

But Mario Fellini did.

He had placed himself in danger, crossing the wishes
of a very dangerous man, and Erene was going to do everything she could to see him through it. That was why
Wolfram Schluter had to die.

She watched the castle for a short time, making sure she
had the guards' pattern down. The castle was an eccen-
tricity of a Russian political figure from back during the
Cold War. For a time the Russian had been assigned to
oversee the military occupation of Latvia.

While in his position, he'd built his castle, all without
the knowledge of his superiors. In those days, it had been
easy for a man so far from Moscow to hide much of what
he did. As long as the fruits of his labors rolled down to
the men who served him, no one would tell his secrets.

The Russian and his soldiers had lived there in the lap
of luxury. Then one day someone had reported him to
Moscow. A KGB strike force had come out and investi-
gated. Then the bloodbath had begun. The Russian and
almost all of his men were killed and carried over to
Rumbula Forest where twenty-five thousand Jews had
been executed during November and December of 1941.

Erene's grandmother had lived through that. She'd been
a grown woman then, and her husband had been one of
those who had been stripped naked, shot in the back of the
head and buried in one of the mass graves.

Sometimes, Erene's grandmother claimed, she could go
to Rumbula Forest and hear the voices of the dead scream-

ing their outrage and crying for their lost lives. Erene believed her. Though she had gone there with her grandmother, and had seen her grandmother talking to the ghosts, she had never heard them herself.

Then again, Erene didn't want to talk to ghosts. In the dark, though, she wondered if the Russian politician still wandered the halls of his castle. She wondered what he would have thought of a man like Wolfram Schluter, whose own past was also tied somehow to Latvia.

The site was less than twenty miles outside of Riga. The location gave relatively quick access to Riga, as well as several other cities in Latvia. Schluter had purchased it for that reason.

The castle was built from native stone and was covered in ivy. One tower stabbed into the air on the north end. Two stories tall, it was an imposing edifice that looked as though it could withstand a siege. The high-peaked roof only held a little snow.

The private road that led to the castle began at the wrought-iron gates manned by Schluter's men. All of them were professional soldiers, hard men who didn't hesitate about taking the lives of others.

They're the same kind of men hunting Mario, Erene couldn't help thinking.

She'd killed one of them days earlier. A car had attempted to run Mario off the road near her grandmother's village. That was the first time she and Mario had known that Schluter had tracked them back there. Before that, Schluter had stationed men in Riga.

Looking back on things now, she believed that her execution of the man had damaged her relationship with Mario. Afterward, he'd been reticent about being with her. Before, since they both had knowledge of antiquities, legends and lore, they'd always found something to talk about.

For the last three days before Mario had gone to New York, there had been almost nothing between them. It had been as if she had died, not the man who had been trying to kill them.

Bright lights flared behind her. Erene leaned in closer to the rough bark of the spruce tree and trusted the shadows under its boughs to keep her hidden.

A luxury car, the kind that took Schluter back and forth to Riga, rolled up the private road. It stopped momentarily at the gates, then the guards opened them. The car continued up the road to the circular drive in front of the house.

Tense, Erene watched, waiting to see if her luck had run out and she could only sit back and watch as Schluter drove away. She knew she should wait, but she couldn't. If there was a chance that she could kill the man, she intended to take it.

Throwing off the black cloak and kicking off her snow boots, clad only in thick socks and the skintight black suit that she'd purchased from a dealer in military surplus, Erene held the crossbow in one hand and sprinted toward the nearest wall. She kept expecting to hear a guard cry out, but no one did.

At the wall, she ran close to it, heading toward the back of the castle. The biting cold helped numb her and drive away the fear that might have otherwise been there.

Schluter had put in guards and an electronic surveillance system, but he hadn't installed motion detectors or dogs. Both of those were hard to beat.

Erene ran with impunity, knowing that the cameras

couldn't see her up against the wall. As long as she wasn't seen by the guards, she would arrive unannounced.

The back wall was fourteen feet high, but the stones were irregularly spaced. A few hundred years ago, when invading armies had marched through Latvia, the wall would have been proof against hostile forces. Defenders would have poured boiling oil on them or simply pierced them with spears when they got close enough.

Erene sought out hand- and footholds and attacked the wall, swarming up it as quickly as a squirrel racing up an oak tree. At the top, she held the crossbow in close to her body, checked to make sure none of the perimeter guards were there and rolled over the edge of the wall.

Effortlessly, Erene landed on her feet without making a sound. She had the crossbow in her hands, ready to fire, but she was in motion at once, sprinting through the fruit trees.

The castle was made of the same stone as the wall, and the same weaknesses existed. She jammed her fingers into the crevices and pulled herself up, finding places for her sock-clad feet. She couldn't feel them at all anymore.

At the second story, she listened for a moment and heard American pop music in the background. Schluter liked his music loud.

Idly, as she broke the window glass with her elbow, Erene wondered what Schluter's society friends would think of his musical tastes. He moved in high circles within Germany. They might not approve of his common tastes.

Of course, they wouldn't approve of his trying to kill Mario to get the Viking treasure, either. Then again, some of the people Schluter spent his time with might have envied him the chance to profit from someone else's death.

Over half of her life, Erene had known men like Schluter.

She reached in and unlocked the window, then opened it and slid inside. The room was a bedroom, but the bed hadn't been slept in. At least, not recently.

Her legs and arms cramped, but she knew it was from the cold and not the exertion. She worked hard to remain physically fit. Her life had depended on that too long to ever forget it.

Breathing deeply, charging her lungs with oxygen so her body would acclimate faster and get warm again, Erene told herself that as long as she heard the music everything was all right. Then she hefted the crossbow and went hunting.

She had the blueprints to the castle memorized. Another acquaintance had provided those for the right price.

Glancing at the bottom of the door, she saw that only a faint stream of light flowed underneath. She guessed that a light was on downstairs.

Carefully, she opened the door and peered out. The crossbow rested naturally against her cheek. She dropped it into position and followed the weapon out of the room.

The passageway outside the bedroom went on for a short distance before turning to the right. Eight more bedrooms occupied the second floor of the castle. No one was in any of the rooms.

That began to bother Erene. Someone should have been there. Schluter's staff included a cook and three domestics. He'd hired them from Riga.

Erene paused at the stairway curving down to the lower floor. Hidden by the marble pillar, she studied the lower floor.

The grand ballroom had been set up to impress guests. Full suits of armor stood on display. All of the armor was Germanic, leading Erene to guess that Schluter had ordered those. Several paintings and vases filled the room.

The centerpiece was the painting above the large fireplace. Flaming logs crackled inside, providing a toasty heat that circulated throughout the room.

In the painting, a fierce-faced knight with curly blond hair and sapphire eyes sat holding a sword thrust up into the air while he was astride a rearing warhorse. The knight and the horse both wore white armor that carried black crosses.

Awfully proud of his ancestors, isn't he? Erene thought. But it suited what she had learned of Wolfram Schluter. The man was still in the Order of Teutonic Knights and took pride in his heritage.

Erene had to resist the impulse to put a crossbow bolt between those arrogant sapphire eyes.

Quietly, her weapon at the ready, she descended the stone steps. The carpet helped muffle whatever sound she might have made.

Too late, she realized that she had walked into a trap.

# 11

By the time Annja arrived at the Clark Hotel, a crowd of media and curious spectators had gathered to find out what had happened. Night had descended on Manhattan, as much as it was able with all the bright lights and neon lighting up the city. The whirling lights of the police cars and the coroner's van stood out.

The Clark Hotel was a gray cracker box fourteen floors high. There were no service frills that came with the lodging, but cable television was offered. The pizza and coffee shops across the street looked as if they were doing great business with the people who had turned out to watch.

Annja headed for the nearest uniformed policeman.

Before coming to the hotel, Annja had stopped back at Tito's. She'd asked Maria to keep the mosaic in a safe place. There was no doubt that if Bart found the mosaic he would confiscate it as evidence.

Annja doubted that anyone at the New York Police Department would know what to make of the mosaic. She still didn't know what she was dealing with, and she was trained to handle investigations of that nature. Not only that, but Mario had sent her a message expecting her to understand it.

The policeman looked up as she approached. "Can I help you, miss?"

Holding out her driver's license, a New York one that she didn't often use except for identification purposes, Annja said, "Detective McGilley sent for me."

The officer waved to an older policeman. "Hey, Sarge. That woman the detectives were waiting on is here."

The sergeant took the proffered ID, consulted it, then grabbed a notebook and made a notation. Then he gave Annja a cord with a temporary ID on it.

"Wear this the whole time you're on the scene," the sergeant said. Then he told the younger officer to take her up to see McGilley.

"ARE YOU SOME KIND of crime-scene specialist?" the young policeman asked when they were in the elevator.

"No." Annja felt tired and worn-out. She wasn't looking forward to what she feared she was about to face.

"I just thought maybe you were some kind of specialist."

"Why?"

"What we're hearing out there is that the body is pretty bad. Whoever killed the guy had a thing for torture."

Annja's mouth dried at that.

"Or maybe it's some kind of ritual. That's what we're hearing."

Steeling herself, Annja watched the floor indicator hit

fourteen. She glanced at the buttons that listed the floors. The numbers ran from one to twelve, then picked up again at fourteen, ending with the fifteenth floor.

That means that the fourteenth floor is actually the thirteenth, Annja thought. She wasn't superstitious, but she knew that some people were.

The officer guided Annja from the elevator to room 1412.

Bart waited in the hallway outside the room. Six feet two inches tall, a square jaw gone blue from too many hours away from a razor, broad shoulders and narrow hips wrapped in a quality dark blue suit that had been tailored to fit well, he was an imposing figure. He wore his dark hair clipped short. He carried a leather coat over one arm and a notebook in the other.

"Hello, Annja," he greeted. There was no trace of friendliness.

"Bart," Annja returned neutrally. She still hadn't made up her mind how she felt about being ordered to show up.

Bart shifted his notebook to his other hand and waggled his fingers. "Let me have the backpack."

"Why?" The request shocked Annja. Bart had never acted so impersonally.

"Because I want to see it."

"No," she replied stubbornly.

Bart sighed. "This is going to go a whole lot quicker and easier if I don't have to arrest you to make this happen."

"You can't just ask to see my computer."

"Sure, I can. I just did."

"You can't."

"I can," Bart insisted.

"Not without a court order."

Frowning, Bart said, "I want you to remember later that I asked first." He reached into his pocket and took out a folded piece of paper. "One court order." He offered it to her.

Annja took the paper, opened it and read through it. The paper *was* a court order authorizing Detective Bart McGilley to search her computer.

Bart waggled his fingers again. "Come on. Neither of us has all night."

Reluctantly, Annja reached into her backpack and handed over her computer.

"I want the backpack, too," Bart said.

Annja slid her backpack over her shoulder again. "Do you have a court order for the backpack?"

Bart sighed.

THE HOTEL STAFF HAD opened up a room for the police to use as a command center for the homicide investigation. It was stocked with coffeepots and doughnuts, but there were some muffins in the mix, as well.

Annja helped herself to a cream-cheese muffin and a cup of coffee, then returned to the easy chair Bart had relegated her to. She did all of that under the stern supervision of an older policeman who looked as if he hadn't smiled in forty years. Bart had told the man, in front of Annja, that if she came anywhere near him she was to be taken into custody.

Noticing the television set in the room, Annja asked, "Can I watch television?"

"No," Bart answered without turning from her computer screen.

"I haven't called my attorney yet," Annja pointed out.

"You don't need an attorney. You're not under arrest."

"My computer is." Annja broke a piece off the muffin and took a bite. Even though she was irritated, she wasn't too irritated to eat. Besides that, she still had the mysterious mosaic Mario had sent her.

Part of the irritability she was feeling was from the certainty that Mario was lying dead in room 1412 and no one would simply tell her that. When she'd asked, Bart had only told her that the coroner's team would be done soon and they could both find out.

Annja hadn't pointed out the obviousness of the coroner's presence. Then she had to admit that even if someone was dead in the room, it didn't necessarily mean it was Mario.

"I can call some of the studio's attorneys," Annja said after Bart ignored her. "They have really good attorneys."

"They're entertainment lawyers." Bart worked slowly at the computer, proving that he wasn't well versed in what he was doing.

"Defending a computer should be entertaining," Annja said. "Not to mention the fact that I'm sure they'll report to a journalist about what's going on up here."

Bart sighed. "All right. You can watch television. Put it on ESPN."

"I've already watched ESPN."

"I haven't."

"Nothing new is breaking on ESPN. Football's over, baseball is just getting started and there's not a basketball game tonight."

Bart shook his head in disgust.

"The Discovery Channel, the Learning Channel or the History Channel," Annja suggested.

"Discovery Channel. There's a special on the tsunamis that have hit India."

"Really?" That intrigued Annja. Tsunamis were an archaeologist's and treasure hunter's dream. The ocean floor shifted and often caused the sea to give up the secrets she'd been hiding for hundreds of years. After storms, shipwrecks sometimes surfaced along coastlines or in shallow waters. Some of the Calusa Indian villages had been uncovered that way.

"Yeah. I had it marked to watch. The DVR back home should be catching it for me."

Annja picked up the remote control, switched the television on and tuned in the Discovery Channel. She knew better than to bother Bart with questions while he was working. He tended to get single-minded when he was working on a problem and wouldn't answer until he was sure what the answer was. She did the same thing so she understood the mind-set.

While she watched the documentary, she worked at the problem presented by the mosaic. Mario had reminded her about the bar fight and Haltwhistle. And then there'd been that comment about omelettes.

There had been a reason Mario had pointed those things out.

"WHO ARE these guys?" Bart pointed at the computer. He'd spread some of the photo images she'd taken across the screen.

Annja muted the television and stepped over to Bart. The uniformed policeman started over at once.

"It's okay, Arnie," Bart said.

The cop nodded and stepped back.

"Bart and Arnie?" Annja asked.

"Don't go there," Bart warned. "You're already in enough trouble. Stay focused on the situation we're dealing with here."

Annja pointed at two of the men, each in turn. "That's Dieter Humbrecht. That's Klaus Kaufmann."

"How do you know that?"

"I looked them up on the Internet. You'll find copies of the newspaper articles I found about them. They've got pictures, too."

"Fantastic. Now you're a detective."

"Actually, there are a lot of skill sets that are interchangeable between your job and mine. We both work with bodies and scenes, and have to have the same respect for what we find there so we can preserve it. We both have to work out theories about what happened based on the physical evidence and knowledge of the social stratification we're dealing with."

Bart shot her a look. "Focus, Annja."

"All right." Annja knew she could go off on tangents when she was forced to sit around. The television documentary had only engaged part of her mind. She always worked, either on an artifact or on her computer or a legal pad, while she watched television. "It was just that, watching you now, thinking about how the crime scene was being handled and the way it's been protected, I suddenly realized that our jobs are very similar."

"Maybe I should be an archaeologist. As least when you dig up a dead guy, you don't have to think about going and notifying his next of kin."

That comment suddenly rushed in on Annja, making her realize that Mario's family would have to be told what had happened to him. She knew they were going to be deeply hurt.

"Sorry," Bart apologized. "I had no right to say that."

"It's okay," Annja said. "You're upset. I can see that."

"This guy was a friend?"

"An acquaintance. But I liked him a lot."

Bart reached for his cup and found it was empty. Annja took it from him, rinsed it out in the sink and poured him a fresh cup. The friendship gesture seemed to ease some of the tension and awkwardness between them.

"Do you know what Mario Fellini was doing here?" Bart asked.

Annja shook her head and sat on the corner of the desk so she could still see the computer monitor. "I was in Florida until this morning."

"I know. I checked."

"And I haven't had any direct contact with Mario."

"I know that, too." Bart sipped his coffee.

"How did you know that?"

"I had your home phone and cell phone records pulled. But you had a phone call from him on your answering machine at the television studio."

"If you pull the phone records for that number, you'll see that I didn't get that message until this afternoon."

"I already did. I know that."

Annja waited for Bart to ask her about the package Mario had sent. But he didn't.

Instead, Bart pointed at the pictures on the computer screen. "Who are they?"

"They're two of the four guys who had the running gun battle in Brooklyn this morning, then showed up at Digital Paradise."

"What about the other two guys?"

"They were the two I fought with on the subway."

Bart leaned back in the chair and massaged his neck. "Who are these guys to you?"

"I've never seen them before in my life."

Bart looked at her. "Why did they come after you?"

"They were after the package that was delivered to me at Mailboxes & Stuff."

"The package that Mario Fellini sent to you."

Annja kept herself calm. Now they were going to get into it, and she knew she was going to have to tread lightly. Bart was good at his job. But Annja had survived years of inquisition by nuns at the orphanage.

"What was in the package?"

"I don't know." That was so close to the truth that Annja didn't mind saying it.

"And you don't know why Mario Fellini sent it to you?"

"No. How did you know Mario Fellini contacted me? You had to have a reason to pull my phone records and get a court order for my computer."

"Doug Morrell called and asked me to run a background check on the guy. Morrell said the guy had been trying to contact you for the last couple of days."

Annja was so shocked she didn't know what to say.

"Don't give Morrell grief about it," Bart said. "He was just looking after your best interests."

"I'll look after my own best interests, thank you very much." Annja blew out a sigh of disgust. "I wasn't aware that you and Doug knew each other."

"Not socially, no. But we've looked into a few things for him."

"Like what?"

"Primarily threats against you or Kristie Chatham."

"I didn't know there were any threats."

"None of them have amounted to anything. But I got to know Morrell."

"Terrific."

"He's a good guy, Annja. Cut him some slack." Bart frowned at her. "Do you have the package?"

"No." That was the truth, too. "Did you ask Doug why he didn't pass the message along?"

"He didn't know you weren't getting the messages until he got another phone call from Fellini this morning. Morrell was under the assumption you checked your messages at the studio."

"I don't."

"The last phone call Mario Fellini made was from this hotel," Bart said. "He called Morrell and asked him to get a message to you. Morrell said he told you about it this afternoon when you called him."

"He should have told me sooner."

"You're a public figure, Annja. You're going to have a lot of people trying to get in touch with you who will do nothing but waste your time while you're trying to get on with your life and your career. Morrell knows that. He was just doing his job and shielding you from what he thought was another one of those people."

"Mario was a friend."

"Friend or acquaintance?"

Annja let out her breath. "I feel like I screwed up, Bart," she said quietly. "I wasn't here when Mario needed me."

Bart looked at her and his eyes softened. He looked like the Bart she shared lunches and dinners with, the one she had attended banquets with—ones that couldn't be avoided because they related to his work or hers—so they'd have someone there to talk to. Those had been good times.

"You didn't screw up, Annja," Bart told her. "Whatever brought Mario here, whatever trouble he was in, was because of something he was involved with. Even if you had been there for him, you might not have been able to help him out with this. These guys you were up against today, they sound like professionals. You were lucky you got away unhurt."

"I know."

"You're out of it now. We'll take care of this. I just need you to do one other thing, then we should be able to cut you loose."

Before Annja could ask what that one thing was, a uniformed policeman knocked on the door and called Bart's name. When Bart swiveled toward him, the policeman went on, "Coroner said he's clear. You can take a look at the body, then he's going to take it downtown."

Bart stood and looked at Annja. "Are you ready to do this?"

"What?" Annja was shocked. "Do you want me to identify the body?"

"Fellini doesn't have any family in New York. I thought maybe it would be better if I made sure he was who I thought he was before I notified them."

Annja took a deep breath, then nodded. She was as ready as she was going to be.

# 12

The men moved too soon to close the jaws of the trap that had been laid for Erene Skujans. Their anticipation betrayed them. Or perhaps it was because she was a woman and they didn't expect her to put up much of a fight. Erene didn't know. But they had come fully equipped to kill her.

They had automatic machine pistols. Bullets chipped the stone balusters supporting the marble handrail. The posts were wide, in the shape of chess pieces. Erene guessed that even if his men succeeded in killing her, Schluter was going to be angry about the damage. She knew from the work Mario had done that the Schluter family fortune wasn't what it had once been.

Flinging herself up the steps instead of down, Erene fired her crossbow through the balusters. The bolt caught a man in the forehead and snapped his head back. He dropped to his knees and then to his face, snapping the bolt's shaft.

Staying low, Erene raced up the steps. Broken pieces

of the tiled wall behind her crumbled. She took a bolt from her quiver and held it in her teeth as she put her foot in the stirrup at the front of the crossbow and yanked the string back. She fitted the bolt into the groove as she heard footsteps coming up the stairs.

Throwing herself prone behind the crossbow, Erene aimed at the man's chest as he ran up the steps. She squeezed the trigger and felt the slight recoil against her shoulder as bullets cut the air above her head. They'd only missed her by inches.

Her own shot hadn't pierced the man's heart as she'd intended, but it had slammed through his neck. The crossbow was so powerful that the bolt had passed completely through. The man halted and held up a hand to the bright blood pouring from his neck. Until that moment, he didn't know how badly he'd been hit.

Taking advantage of the dying man's astonishment, Erene pushed herself up and raced forward. She threw herself at the dying man and seized his machine pistol, then rode him like a sled to the bottom of the stairs.

Machine-gun bullets tracked the wall and splintered the balustrade. At the bottom of the stairs, Erene levered her arm up and opened fire on the man who'd stepped out of hiding. The bullets thumped him in the chest and drove him backward.

Remaining on the floor, Erene checked to see if there were any other men. Nothing moved.

Rolling to her feet, Erene ejected the spent magazine and inserted the spare she'd grabbed from the dead men. She was angry.

Running to the foyer, Erene crept up to the door with the machine pistol in both hands. She peeked around it and saw the ruby taillights of the luxury car and two others streaming through the front gates.

Erene cursed. Schluter had guessed she would be coming. He'd been prepared. And she had no idea where he was going or what had happened to Mario. She felt more frightened and less in control than she had at any time since she was a young girl and had walked out of her grandmother's village.

The man on the floor groaned. Erene ran back inside the room. Covering him with the pistol, she walked over to him and kicked away his machine pistol. She leaned down and tore the man's shirt open, revealing the Kevlar vest that had saved his life. A handful of mushroomed bullets slapped against the floor.

She checked the unconscious man for other weapons and found three knives and a small semiautomatic pistol at the small of his back. She threw them out of his reach, then rolled him onto his stomach while he was still stunned. Cutting the drawstrings from the ornate curtains, she bound his hands behind him, then bound his feet, as well.

When she was satisfied with the job she'd done, she rolled him onto his back again. While she waited for him to recover, she picked up his cell phone and checked through his address book.

She found Schluter's cell phone number and pressed the speed-dial function. The phone rang twice and Schluter answered.

"Is she dead?" he asked in German.

"No," Erene replied in the same language. "She isn't dead. She's alive and she's pissed."

Schluter chuckled. "It appears you're more resourceful

than I'd guessed. The man I had look into your background wasn't as thorough as he should have been. That is going to get him killed."

"It's going to get you killed, too," Erene said in a harsh voice. "If I decide to kill you, you'll be dead. Soon."

"I think we both intended that for each other tonight," Schluter said. "But we're both alive, aren't we?"

Erene didn't say anything for a moment. She gazed at the man lying on the floor. He was conscious, and his eyes were wide with fright.

"You should think about leaving Mario alone," she said. "If you walk away, I won't have a reason to kill you."

Schluter laughed. "Some of the people I've talked to in Riga—the poor, ignorant people you seem to have so much influence over—seem to think you have some kind of powers. That you're something special."

*Witch.* Erene heard the accusation in the back of her mind again.

"You've got three dead men in this castle who know I can be lethal, Herr Schluter."

"Perhaps. And perhaps you merely got lucky."

"Luck had nothing to do with it."

"I'd heard that you were a killer," Schluter said. "I also heard that you were often for sale. Perhaps if you hadn't fallen in love with Mario Fellini we could have been associates."

"I don't think so."

"It's a pity you don't have those powers that so many think you do. Otherwise, you'd know it's already too late to plead for your precious Mario's life. He's been dead hours now."

*No!* Erene wanted to shout her denial, but her voice locked in her throat.

The phone clicked dead in her ear.

She tried calling the number again but was immediately moved to Schluter's voice mail. Furious, hurting, wishing she knew the truth about what Schluter had intimated, she threw the phone at the painting of the Teutonic knight. The phone shattered into pieces and tore the painting.

Taking a deep breath, getting her emotions under control, used to the fact that she had to do such a thing, Erene stared at the man she'd tied up.

"Look," the man said, "you don't have to kill me."

"It's not a matter of having to," Erene said. "It's a matter of wanting to."

The man tried to remain calm. "You don't have to want to."

Erene smiled at him, knowing it was the most terrifying thing she could do under the circumstances. "But I do."

The man didn't say anything.

"Do you know who I am?" Erene opened the bottom of the quiver of bolts she carried. A pouch the size of her fist dropped out.

"Erene Skujans," the man said.

"That's right. Do you know *what* I am?" Erene took a small plastic vial from the pouch. She hadn't forgotten any of her grandmother's teachings even as she'd made her way through Europe learning the other skills she'd needed to survive.

"No."

"Many people around here know me as a witch," Erene said.

"I don't believe in witches," the man replied.

"That's too bad. Because you're about to." Erene

spilled a greenish powder onto her palm and blew it into the man's face.

The man tried to hold his breath, but it was too late. He'd already inhaled some of the powder.

Calmly, Erene waited for it to take effect. The man's eyes turned glassy and sweat beaded on his forehead.

"What's your name?" she asked.

"Wilhelm."

"Good. Now you're going to answer my questions."

"Yes," the man said dully.

Quickly, Erene asked him questions about Wolfram Schluter. She didn't get any information she didn't already know.

Then she asked the question she'd been afraid to ask. "Where is Mario Fellini?"

"He's dead. Dieter killed him in New York."

Anguish tore at Erene's heart. The pain was so acute she didn't think she was going to survive it for a moment. Then she hated herself because she knew she would. She had lived through everything that had happened to her, and there were some bad things.

Since she'd left her grandmother's village, she'd taken her life into her own hands. Most of that time, she'd risked her life to achieve a certain style of living. That risk had made the achievement sweeter. But there had been no one to share her triumphs.

Mario had been the closest she'd come to it, and she hadn't told him everything. That was why he'd left. Because he'd begun to suspect it.

Or maybe Schluter told him, Erene thought. The possibility made her hate Schluter even more, and it allowed her to forgive her own mistakes.

She took another vial from the pouch and poured purple powder onto her hand. Gently, she blew the powder onto the man's face.

Despite his condition, the man held his breath. Some part of him was fighting to be free.

"Breathe," she told him.

He did, drawing the purple powder deep into his lungs. Almost immediately, he started shivering, bucking uncontrollably. Blood leaked from his nostrils, then from the corner of his mouth. He coughed and choked, spitting up scarlet.

"Now," Erene said, "die."

A moment later, the man did. His head rolled to the side, relaxed in death, and his eyes stared off into the distance.

Erene stood and gathered her things. She had to return to the village to figure out what she was going to do next.

And she had to mourn.

# 13

Blood covered the bed, the floor and the walls of the hotel room. Mario Fellini looked small and used up lying crookedly on the bed. Burn marks and knife cuts marred his nude body. Strips of duct tape bound his hands and feet.

It was a hard way to die.

Annja had seen the harshness of death before. At various dig sites she'd uncovered the bodies of people who had withered and died from sickness, from injury and from murder. Those deaths had touched her in their own way, but she'd accepted them more easily than she could accept what she saw before her.

The difficulty wasn't just that she'd known Mario Fellini. That was hard enough. But the fact remained that Mario's family would have to be told and they would grieve, too.

Toughen up, she told herself. You don't want the men who did this to get away with it, do you?

The coroner, a man in his late forties, stood nearby.

There had been brief introductions, but Annja couldn't remember his name now.

Although it had been years since she'd seen him, Mario hadn't changed much. The scar was still above his eye, reminding her again of the fight they'd gotten into over the fake Roman relics in Haltwhistle. He'd grown a goatee.

The Donald Duck tattoo he got when his sisters got him drunk on his twenty-first birthday was a little faded, but remained on his left bicep. His sisters had talked him into that because his English when he was a boy was atrocious. They'd insisted to Annja that Mario had sounded like Donald Duck. They'd picked on him and doted on him at the same time when Annja had gone to Italy with him to celebrate his parents' fortieth anniversary.

All of those memories rushed around Annja's head. The smell of warm bread and laughter. The warmth of the kitchen. The sound of laughter and years-old mischief between loving siblings who showed no shame in front of their spouses and children.

"Hey, Annja." Bart's voice was quiet as he stepped next to her. "Maybe you should do this later."

Annja didn't know why Bart would act so protectively. Then she realized tears were sliding down her cheeks. She closed her eyes and felt them burn. More tears slid down her face.

Brushing the tears away, Annja said, "I'm fine." Her voice sounded strained. She pushed her chin toward the body on the bed. "That's him. That's Mario."

"Let's get you out of here." Bart put an arm around her shoulders and led her from the room.

BACK IN THE HOTEL ROOM Bart was using as a command post, Annja stared out the window. Snow fluttered down, descending on the city again after a brief reprieve.

Standing there with the cold soaking through the glass and into her flesh, Annja wished she was back in Florida where it was warm, and she wished it was three days earlier and that she had checked her answering service at *Chasing History's Monsters*.

"I apologize for that," Bart said.

She glanced at his reflection in the window. "You don't have anything to be sorry about."

"I should have waited. You could have identified the body downtown in a more controlled environment. Something like that is pretty harsh."

Annja folded her arms over her breasts in an effort to warm herself. "I don't know how you do this job."

"It's hard, Annja. I take it day by day."

"But you're always seeing things like..." Annja couldn't continue.

"I am," Bart admitted.

"How can you come back every day? Knowing you're going to have to see so much evil?"

"Don't you see evil things in your career? I seem to recall you've spent some time down in the Yucatán Peninsula. The Mayan people had a bloodthirsty religion."

"They didn't normally provide human sacrifices," Annja said. "That's just a story spread by the tour guides. Human sacrifices were offered only when times were desperate."

"That's generally when murders occur," Bart said. "Somebody gets desperate. Whoever murdered Mario Fellini was desperate."

"They tortured him."

"They did. But it looks like he held out against them for a long time."

"Or they thought he was lying to them."

Bart was quiet for a moment. "You don't have any idea what he was into that would lead someone to do that?"

Annja turned to face him. "No," she replied evenly. "But I intend to find out."

Grimacing, Bart shook his head. "That's a bad idea. Right now you're clear of this thing. You should stay away from it."

"Whoever killed Mario might not see it that way. Mario was changing hotels every night. How long ago was he—?"

Bart frowned and looked troubled. "The M.E. puts the time of death at approximately eight hours ago. Based on the rigor that's set in."

"Then, while Dieter and his friends were hunting me, Mario was already dead."

"Maybe he'd already told them everything they needed to know. Maybe they only wanted the package he'd mailed you."

Annja thought about the mosaic that had been in the box. It hadn't provided any clues that she'd been able to fathom—yet.

"If you're worried about them, get out of town. Go back to Florida and study the phantom shark some more," Bart said.

"I didn't go down there for a phantom shark," Annja replied.

"Morrell said it was a shark."

"I went for the chance to study the Calusa Indians."

"Then go study them some more. You can't be done after a few days."

"I'll think about it."

A policeman knocked on the door. He held up an evidence bag. "The M.E. released the vic's stuff."

"Gimme." Bart shoved a hand out and took the bag.

Annja watched Bart empty the evidence bag on the desktop, then shuffle the items around.

There was a wallet, a watch, change, a key ring, lip balm, a college ring, a gold bracelet and a pen.

"Doesn't say much for what a person leaves behind, does it?" Bart asked dismally.

"If this were a dig site," Annja replied, "these would be artifacts. Clues about the way an individual lived within his society. Do you need to fingerprint these?"

Bart pointed at the grayish powder residue on the wallet. "Crime-scene guys already did it."

Annja pointed to the college ring. "This shows that the individual was intelligent and well-schooled. The ring is from Accademia Britannica di Archaeologia, Storia e Bella Arti."

"Greek to me," Bart said.

"Italian, actually. The British School at Rome. Mario studied archaeology there." Annja moved on to the watch. "At first glance, it tells us that this individual saw a need to keep track of time."

"Or liked jewelry. Watch, ring and bracelet."

"You could read it that way, but look. The ring ties to an accomplishment. A higher education." Annja flipped the watch over to reveal the inscription on the back. It was in Italian. She translated. "For My Son, Mario. Love, Mother."

Her voice broke by the time she finished. Both of them chose to ignore it.

The bracelet had an image of a winged lion on it.

"That's the winged lion of Mark the Evangelist," Annja said. "He's believed to have been the author of the Gospel of Mark."

"The second book of the New Testament?"

"Yes. But the winged lion is also the symbol of Venice. The statue is still there, although it was stolen away for a time before being returned in the fifteenth century." Annja smiled wistfully. "Mario loved Venice."

"The bracelet is a reminder of that?" Bart asked.

"The bracelet is more than that. You have to look below the surface if you're going to understand something fully." Even as Annja stated that, a new thought struck her about the mosaic. Excitement flooded through her. Turning the bracelet over, she revealed the inscription there and translated it. "You'll Always Be The Baby Brother. Love, Your Sisters."

"They were all things that meant something to him."

Annja nodded, then pointed to the wallet. "May I?"

"As long as you keep both hands on the desk where I can see them."

"Are we having trust issues?"

Bart looked at her seriously. "I know you, Annja. You're one of my best friends. One of the first people I'd call if I was in trouble."

But I was one of the last to find out you were engaged, wasn't I? Annja thought.

"I also know that you haven't told me everything you know," Bart said. "Or that you think you know."

"I can deal with that." Annja opened Mario's wallet and

sorted through the contents. She put the cash and credit cards to one side, then looked at the business cards.

"What can you tell me about the credit cards?" Bart asked.

Annja shot him a look.

Bart smiled a little. "See, that's where my cop magic comes in. I can run those through a computer and get a timeline and idea of his activities."

"Archaeologists who study us are going to have a lot more information at their fingertips than we ever did on those we study," Annja said. "If we're studying a culture that kept records, a journal is an amazing find that tells us about everyday life."

She spread the business cards out, noting the addresses.

"A lot of these appear to be in Riga," Bart observed. "Is that in Italy?"

"No. Riga is in Latvia," Annja said.

"Is that where Mario was?"

"I don't know."

Bart regarded her. "Truth?"

"Truth. The last I heard, Mario still lived in Rome. Didn't you track his flight?"

"I did. It originated in Riga, Latvia."

A warning bell sounded in Annja's mind. She'd been played, and now she knew it. "You're devious. I haven't seen this side of you."

"That's because you've never seen me work a homicide investigation."

Annja hoped she never did again.

"You were working me," Annja accused, but she felt no bitterness. The gamut had been well played, and he'd been fair. She hadn't had to insist on seeing Mario's personal effects under the guise of giving him an archaeology lesson.

"No more than you were working me," Bart said.

"So we both get what we want."

"Maybe."

Annja waited, making him play out his ruse.

# 14

"When I checked your phone records," Bart continued, "I noticed there were two calls from Riga. Now that we both agree Mario was in Riga before he got here, I want to know who's been calling you from there."

Taking a moment to weigh her options, Annja decided to go with the truth. Hiding the mosaic was risky enough, and she didn't want to hurt the friendship they had.

"She told me her name is Erene Skujans," Annja said.

"Who is she?"

"I don't know. I've never heard of her before today."

"Mario never mentioned her?"

"Until today," Annja said, "I hadn't heard from Mario in years. If he'd known how to get in touch with me, he wouldn't have had to go through the answering service at the studio."

Bart sighed. He took out his notebook and noted the name. "Since she called you from Riga, it's safe to assume she didn't have anything to do with Mario's death."

Annja returned her attention to Mario's wallet. She felt bad about going through his things, but there was no other way they were going to learn what they might need to know. She realized that was why Bart was allowing her to look freely. She was the best chance he had of getting inside information about Mario without asking painful questions of his family.

Annja found Erene Skujans's picture in with the photos of Mario's family. She'd been telling Bart about Mario's sisters, parents, nieces and nephews. At least, what she could remember of them. There had been new nieces and nephews.

At first glance, Annja had thought the woman might be part of the family. She had black hair that fit, but the rest of the package, the pale skin and deep blue eyes, looked pure Nordic.

"Do you know her?" Bart asked.

"No." Annja turned the picture over and found a note in what looked like the same handwriting that had been on the note in the package.

Erene Skujans. Winter festival. She loves me but she doesn't know it yet.

"That's a lot of confidence on his part," Bart commented.

"Mario has—*had*—six sisters," Annja pointed out. "Growing up in an environment like that, you either have no confidence or all the confidence in the world."

"I guess he had it all."

"His sisters loved him. They wouldn't let anyone hurt him. When he asked me to go to his parents' anniversary, I got the third degree from all of them at one time or another."

"About what?"

"They wanted to know what my intentions were toward Mario." Annja smiled at the memory, then was immediately saddened by it. "Finding out what's happened to him is going to be awful."

"I know," Bart said. "That's why I'm going to handle it myself. It's after 4:00 a.m. over there. I'm going to let them sleep through the night and give them a call in the morning. At least they'll be rested."

The picture showed Erene standing by an ice sculpture of a bear. She was smiling and happy. Annja had to admit the woman was gorgeous. But something haunted her eyes.

"Can I get a copy of this picture?" Annja asked.

Bart said that she could.

Annja used her digital camera to capture the image, then stored the camera in her backpack again.

"Pretty woman," Bart said, looking at the picture.

"Beautiful woman," Annja agreed.

"Still—"

"What?" Annja asked.

"There's something—" Bart shrugged "—*spooky* about her."

"Spooky? Is that a detective term?"

Bart smiled at her. "It is tonight."

Feeling tired and frustrated, Annja checked her watch and found that it was after 10:00 p.m. She asked, "Is my computer released back to my custody? I'd like to get some sleep if there's nothing else."

"Let me get a copy of those pictures you took of the bad guys." Bart pulled out his key ring and slipped the USB flash drive free. "I'll use them on B.O.L.O.s if I can't find a file on them somewhere."

"Interpol will probably have something on one or all of them."

Bart nodded as he ported the flash drive and started downloading the files. "I agree. So whatever you're hiding, Annja, be careful with it."

Annja couldn't lie to him, but she couldn't give up the mosaic, either. However it had happened, the secret it contained had cost her friend his life.

ANNJA WOKE LATER the next morning than she'd intended. She'd spent the night in a hotel not far from the Clark Hotel. She'd also paid in cash so she wouldn't leave an electronic trail.

The wake-up call had come at seven when she'd requested it, flanked by the cell phone and a computer alert. She'd somehow managed to answer the phone and go back to sleep, then ignore the other backup systems. She hadn't awakened until housekeeping knocked on the door at almost nine o'clock.

After a quick shower, she put her clothes back on, grimacing but knowing there was nothing to be done at the moment. All her clothes were in her loft, and she wasn't going there.

As tidy as she could make herself, a lot better off than she sometimes was while at a dig, Annja headed out, eager to get another look at the mosaic.

Taking a cab, Annja stopped at a cash machine for more money. Normally she traveled with a few thousand dollars because cash in hand spoke harder and faster than plastic. Archaeologists the world over had learned that early on. Since she was going to be on the move, an electronic trail there didn't matter.

Since she was downtown anyway, she stopped at Bloomingdale's and bought a new pair of jeans, a black turtleneck, a dark red merino wool blend ribbed tunic, three tanks, socks, underwear, toiletries and a pull-behind suitcase to carry them in.

Annja guessed that she was going to be headed to Latvia—since that was where all trails led—sooner rather than later. She didn't expect to get back into her loft before then.

When the cashier rang up her purchases, Annja handed over a debit card and pretended that the money didn't matter. Since the threat of Dieter and his team was still very real, it wasn't too difficult. After being chased and shot at the previous day, spending was practically painless, even after all the lessons in frugality from the nuns.

Gotta do survival shopping more often, Annja told herself as she changed into jeans and turtleneck in a dressing room.

"YOU HAVE COME for your package, yes?" Maria asked.

"I have. I'm afraid I can't stay long."

"Have you eaten?"

Thinking about it, Annja realized she had skipped breakfast. There had been too many things to do. "No," she answered, accepting the inevitable.

In the end, Annja got Maria to put together a take-out meal despite the woman's protests. Back in the cab, Annja had gone to the Park House Hotel by the Brooklyn Bridge. She'd taken a suite, which came with a living room, as well as a bedroom and kitchenette.

Besides hotel security, Manhattan was only thirty minutes away. Less than that for a homicide detective if he was in a hurry.

While she ate, Annja worked on the mosaic at the desk and tuned the television to the Discovery Channel. Background chatter usually helped keep her relaxed and focused.

She also put all of her electronics on chargers despite having done so the previous night. There was never a good time to run out of power.

What she'd told Bart—about looking beneath the surface—had stuck in her mind. The tile with the dog on the front was an obvious knockoff of a genuine Roman mosaic. So what lurked beneath the surface of the tessera?

She took out her Swiss Army knife and opened the flathead screwdriver blade. Gingerly, she started prying at one of the tessera on the top left corner. On a dig, everything was done by grid identification, grid by grid.

The glass piece popped free without breaking, which was encouraging. She placed the tessera on the table, leaving room for the others as she took them off, as well.

Pushing her plate aside, Annja continued taking the glass squares off the glazed ceramic backboard.

Mario's note had told her to remember Haltwhistle. That had to have been a reference to the fight over the faux Roman artifacts.

The mosaic obviously wasn't an artifact, so it was false. But Annja had to wonder how false it was. Mario had also said that an omelette couldn't be made without breaking eggs. That had to be a clue that she was supposed to take the mosaic apart. At least, she hoped it was. But she kept the tessera in order so she could put it back together if she needed to.

Time to see what's beneath the surface, she told herself. Excitement flared within her. It always did when she felt she was about to make a discovery.

# 15

Wolfram Schluter drove the metallic-silver-and-blue Mercedes-Benz SLR McLaren hard through the late-afternoon traffic flooding out of Vienna. The adrenaline rush from the speed, almost too much for the twisting, narrow highway he was on, flowed through him and he relished it because it washed away the feeling of failure he'd carried with him out of Riga the night before.

He'd departed by private jet from Riga and flown to Vienna. The Mercedes, his private car, had been waiting there. He'd driven it rather than take the helicopter that followed him overhead.

Schluter liked to feel in control of his life. Nothing gave him the same kind of pleasure that driving did. Women, drugs and alcohol all paled in comparison to the excitement he felt behind the wheel of a sports car.

He swooped into a turn. For a moment the tires broke loose, skidding across the road. If he wrecked, he was going to spread four hundred thousand dollars of elegant racing machinery across the thick forest at the side of the highway.

Instead, he slowly muscled the car back onto the road, pushing his foot down harder on the accelerator. Then he was leveled out again and running at over 110 miles per hour.

The big man in the passenger seat held on to his seat belt and uttered a combined curse and prayer. He was a professional bodyguard and had fought in a half-dozen wars scattered throughout Africa.

It amused Schluter that the man was obviously afraid. Schluter was small next to him. Standing five feet ten, with a slender build, Schluter knew that an observer would have thought the big man could break him in half.

At thirty-one, Schluter possessed the inherent good looks of his forebears. He was a true Aryan, and his bloodline was pure. His shock of blond hair looked almost white. His eyes were like bright sapphires. He was clean-shaven and looked even younger than his years.

"What's wrong, Gustav?" Schluter taunted the big man over the roar of German industrial metal hammering through the speakers.

"Nothing, Baron Schluter." The bodyguard's voice was a dry whisper.

Schluter burned up the distance between himself and the slow-moving truck in front of him. "You look worried."

"No," the big man said quietly.

Gunning the engine, downshifting to fourth gear for just a moment, Schluter knew that his bodyguards drew straws to see who would have to ride with him when he chose to drive. None of them wanted to be with him the day he lost the road, and they were all sure that day would come.

TWENTY MINUTES LATER, with almost as many near mishaps, Schluter regretfully pulled off the highway and onto the private road that led to his ancestral castle outside Vienna. Tall spruce and pine trees arched over the road, covering it from view from above.

The bodyguards didn't care for that, either, but the woods had always surrounded the castle and his grandmother wouldn't have it any other way.

Thinking of his grandmother took away some of the pleasure Schluter had derived from the overland trip from Vienna. All of his life, he'd lived under her thumb. But she was getting old. She wouldn't be there to interfere with him much longer. He looked forward to that day.

THE CASTLE SAT on a hill only a few miles from Leopoldsberg, the mountainous area that overlooked Vienna. Since the eleventh century, the castle had existed in one form or another and been home to the Schluter barons. It had served King Jan III Sobieski during the Second Siege of Vienna.

A Schluter had commanded in the Polish Austrian army then, and Castle Schluter had served as a supply depot and quartered the troops and the king at times.

Wolfram couldn't remember which one of his ancestors had been there. If his grandmother knew he'd forgotten, she would have taken umbrage with him. For an old woman, she was quick with her hands.

And Schluter knew she wouldn't hesitate to kill him if she wanted to. She was a monster.

She had murdered his father, then poisoned her own daughter for being weak enough to marry such a man. His grandmother had also forced his mother to write out her own suicide note before drinking the barbiturates. His grandmother had made him watch as his mother died horribly.

Wolfram had been seven years old. It was the worst thing he'd ever witnessed. Especially since he'd thought she was going to kill him next.

His grandmother had looked at him with her bright blue eyes. "You're a Schluter," she'd rasped in her smoker's voice. "You carry the seeds of greatness within you. That's why I saw to it you carry our family's name instead of your pitiful excuse for a father. And it's why I named you after my father."

When he had been born, his grandmother had taken over his rearing almost at once. That had been just as well. His father had been a drunkard and a gambler, and his mother had had a drug problem that she'd no longer had to hide after he was born. His grandmother had stopped caring whether his mother lived or not. She had the male heir she'd wanted to carry on the family name.

He could still remember hearing his grandmother calling the police and saying there had been a terrible accident. Then, when the police arrived, they were properly respectful to her. Everything was "Baroness Schluter" this and "Baroness Schluter" that. The whole time, she held on to his hand and told him that everything was going to be all right.

It was then that Schluter started to grasp the power that his grandmother wielded.

As he'd grown, he longed for the time that that power would be his. Now it was almost within his grasp.

Except for that woman, that *witch* Erene Skujans and her lover. Schluter had made no allowances for her cunning ways. Last night had even more sharply delineated his miscalculation of her.

The gates opened as Schluter steered toward them. He missed them by inches as he roared through. He sped through the meticulously landscaped grounds as the helicopter with his other security guards landed at the helipad at the back of the castle.

When winter had passed, his grandmother would have the groundskeepers busy every day until the roses and flowerbeds once more looked immaculate. Then she would sit in one of the five gardens she'd had designed and built for herself, and pretend that she was going to live forever.

She was eighty-two. She'd already lived far longer than Schluter had thought was possible with the way she smoked and drank.

The main house stood three stories tall and had a distinctly Gothic design. The stone was off-white, almost gray, but it held an air of eternal vigilance that Schluter had always recognized. Gargoyles straddled the roof's edge, staring down at visitors like birds of prey.

There was a bright red Ferrari parked in front of the house. Low and sleek, the sports car gave the appearance that some kind of spacecraft had landed at Castle Schluter.

To visit or to conquer? Schluter wondered, and tried to figure out where that thought had come from.

He switched off his car's engine. The gull-wing doors lifted when Schluter hit the release. He unfastened his seat belt and got out, straightening his suit.

Gustav crawled out on his side weakly and sagged against the fender. "Thank God," he said, then threw up.

"Don't get that on the car," Schluter said mechanically.

He, like his eyes, was drawn to the Ferrari. He knew its specifications as well as he knew the back of his own hand. The Ferrari was the dream car he'd never had.

"Do you like the car?" a deep voice asked.

Startled, Schluter turned toward the main house. A man stood where he hadn't been standing a moment ago.

The man was tall, at least four or five inches over six feet. He was built broad and strong, and looked very fit. His face was strongly chiseled, making the goatee he wore stand out even more prominently. His long black hair trailed down to his shoulders. A gold hoop earring glinted in his left ear. He wore an Armani suit.

"I love the car," Schluter said. "It has a twelve-cylinder engine, a carbon-fiber body and an F-1 sequential shift. Only four hundred of this model were manufactured."

"I have three of them," the man said.

*"Three?"* Schluter couldn't believe it. The car cost in excess of six hundred thousand dollars. He knew because he'd priced them. He'd wanted one but his grandmother wouldn't pay for it.

"Three," the man repeated. Then he grinned. "I couldn't decide which was my favorite color. So I bought a red one, a yellow one and had one custom-painted, blending from sea-foam-green at the front to kelly-green at the back."

"It sounds beautiful."

"It is. I should have brought it." He shrugged. "But I drove it last time."

"I don't know you," Schluter said.

"That's because we've never met," the man said. "I'm an old friend of your grandmother's. She invited me. She said there was a problem and I might be able to help."

All the goodwill and envy Schluter had for the man disappeared in a heartbeat. "What problem?"

The man shrugged as if he didn't notice a change in Schluter's demeanor. "I don't know. We only spoke over the telephone. I just got here myself."

"From Vienna?"

"Yes."

"That's impossible. I would have passed you on the road."

The man grinned, too arrogant and cocky for Schluter's taste. "I don't think so," he said with uncompromising self-assurance.

"What is your name?" Schluter demanded.

The man shook his head. "Let's go in and talk to your grandmother. If she wants you to know my name, she'll tell you."

Angry now, noticing that his bodyguards had appeared around the main building, Schluter shook his head. "No. I'll have your name or you won't enter the house."

The man put on a pair of sunglasses he'd been holding in one hand. "You're making a mistake."

"You're the one who's made a mistake." Schluter turned to his bodyguards and raised his voice. "Throw him out."

The bodyguards started forward at once. Most of them reached for weapons, doubtless because of the man's size.

They hadn't counted on his quickness. The way he moved was fluid and graceful. Before Schluter could blink, the man had a pistol in each hand. They were short-barreled but big-bored semiautomatics.

He pointed one of them at Schluter's head and the other one at the group of men. "Big, big mistake," he commented quietly.

Schluter froze, hesitant to move because he didn't doubt the man would open fire.

"Wolfram!"

Recognizing his grandmother's voice, Schluter cursed. He told himself that he would have escaped the man's marksmanship and that his bodyguards would have killed the man.

"Go away, Grandmother," Schluter said. "I can handle this."

The big man laughed.

Schluter's ears burned with rage. No one had ever treated him like that. He started to speak.

"If you do it," the man promised, "I'll put a bullet right between your eyes."

*"Wolfram!"* His grandmother came down off the steps, hobbling on her cane. She was thin and bent with age, but she had her hair taken care of every week. Schluter was accustomed to her appearance, because there had been few days of his life that she hadn't imposed herself.

Today she looked different. She wore makeup for the first time that Schluter could remember. Rouge showed on her pale, withered cheeks and lipstick on her lips. She wore a dress that Schluter had never seen before, a pearl-gray one that hinted at what little figure she had left to her. The light of the early evening revealed her age.

She glared at him with her pale, watery blue eyes. "You will stop this instant!" she ordered.

Schluter ignored her order. His bodyguards kept their weapons leveled at the man, who acted as though he hadn't a care in the world. But the man's pistol never wavered from Schluter's face.

"Who is this man, Grandmother?" Schluter asked.

"A friend of our family," she snapped.

"I don't know him."

"He was a friend before your time."

Schluter took another look at the man. He didn't look any older than Wolfram. Thirty, maybe thirty-five. But Schluter doubted that. He'd only given the man an extra five years because of the way he conducted himself.

"Have your men put their weapons down," his grandmother ordered.

Schluter returned the man's imperturbable gaze. "He can lower his weapons first. In fact, he can turn them over."

The man smirked, then shook his head to say that would never happen.

His grandmother hardened her voice and stood as straight as her bent back would allow. "You will obey me, Wolfram."

For a moment Schluter wanted to dare her to do her worst. But he couldn't. Her worst could leave him bereft of his inheritance. He wasn't prepared for that.

Taking a breath, he gestured to his men.

They put away their weapons immediately.

The big man shoved the tails of his coat back and holstered both pistols behind his back. He was still smiling.

"Wolfram, I want to introduce you to this man. As I said, he's an old friend. And he's here to help you with your problem."

"My problem is well in hand," Schluter said.

"I don't think so. From what I'm told, your men killed Mario Fellini in New York City without getting the information they were sent there to get."

"He wouldn't tell them," Schluter replied. "Not even when he was tortured." He had long suspected his grandmother had a spy among his men. This latest revelation only proved that.

"I was also told that the woman, the witch, also ambushed you in the castle at Riga."

"That didn't happen," Schluter pointed out.

"You were lucky."

Schluter knew better than to argue with his grandmother when she was in the mood she was in.

"Now I want you to come into the house so we can discuss this in a civilized manner," his grandmother said. Then she turned to the big man. "I'm asking you to forgive my grandson."

The man bowed and took her hand in his. He touched his lips to the withered flesh.

A smile curved his grandmother's lips and it looked as if she was embarrassed, blushing. Schluter was astounded. He'd never seen his grandmother behave that way.

"Of course," the man replied in a soft voice and courtly manner. "Anything you wish, Kikka. I always told you that."

In all of his life, Schluter had never heard anyone call his grandmother by her given name.

The man released his grandmother's hand and turned to face Schluter.

"Wolfram," his grandmother said, "this is Garin Braden. He's going to help us with the Riga problem."

# 16

The work disassembling the mosaic was intense. Annja had to get up a few times and stretch her cramped shoulder muscles. Since the living room area was large enough, she brought out her sword for a while and went through some of the kata she'd been taught.

She was sore from the battles she'd fought. As always, focusing and becoming one with the sword left her more energized than exhausted. She returned to work with renewed focus.

Gradually, the tessera were all removed and placed on the table. When she was finished, she was ultimately disappointed.

There was nothing on the glazed marble behind them.

She stared at the picture of the dog she'd assembled on the table next to the glazed-tile background. She'd put each piece next to its mate, re-creating the picture because that was how she'd been trained to handle artifacts. Everything that was found together stayed together, in the same juxtaposition it had been found.

All that work, and she still didn't have anything to show for it.

Okay, you're frustrated, she told herself. Take the relaxing bath you've been missing the past few days and let the thoughts percolate for a while. Maybe a nap.

Retreating to the bathroom, she got a clothing bag out, stripped down, then dumped her clothing into the bag. She added the old clothes she still had. She enjoyed having new jeans, but until she'd had them for a while they didn't feel like her old jeans. She loved the comfort of familiarity, and the new jeans didn't feel lived in.

While the water ran to fill the tub, Annja went through the selection of bath fragrances and found some bayberry that smelled pretty good. She wanted a long soak, so she emptied the bottle in the water.

Her cell phone rang. When she got to it, Caller ID showed the number started with an international code. It was 06 and she knew that one belonged to Italy.

Dreading the call, knowing it was going to be from Mario's family because she'd told Bart to let them know they could call her, Annja answered the call. "Hello."

"Annja."

The man's voice surprised her. She didn't recognize it. "Yes. Who is this?"

"Pietro Silvestri. I'm—" He stopped himself. "I was Mario's brother-in-law."

"I remember you," Annja said, switching to Italian because she could tell English was difficult for him. "The soccer player."

"Yes."

Annja remembered Pietro Silvestri as quiet and shy among the burgeoning and boisterous family. She'd bonded with him because of that. He'd been early in his marriage to Francesca and not used to the family, either.

"I'm surprised that you remember me," Pietro said.

"I've got a good memory," Annja said. "Plus, as I recall, you and I were both uncomfortable in the madhouse."

Pietro chuckled. "Yes. The inmates haven't gotten appreciably better. Only now some of the loudness is caused by the three children Francesca and I have been blessed with."

Annja retreated to the bathroom and turned off the water. She sat on the edge of the tub, feeling the heat soak into her and enjoying the fragrance. It seemed to lift some of the heaviness.

"Are you guys doing all right?" Annja asked.

"Things are crazy around here. I think Dante and I are going to come for Mario's body. It would be too hard for anyone else."

"If there's anything I can do, please don't hesitate."

"I appreciate it, but there's not much to do at this point. This is just a very sad thing."

Annja silently agreed. She'd put off her own sadness by working, but that wouldn't last forever. Even though she and Mario hadn't seen each other in years, knowing he was gone forever hurt.

"How are you doing?" Pietro asked.

"I'm okay. Sad. But it had been a long time since I'd seen Mario."

"That's what he'd said. His sister always teased him about you. They told him he shouldn't have let you get away."

Annja chuckled. "I think we got away from each other. On purpose. Mario and I weren't exactly looking for anything permanent. We had a good time. It was nice to be friends. Simple."

A child screamed in the background.

Pietro sighed. "I think that was one of mine. You don't get simple after you have kids. I think kids were what made Mario finally want to settle down. He'd been around so many nieces and nephews that he started wanting to have kids of his own."

Annja hesitated just a moment, feeling bad about what she was doing, then forgave herself and said, "I'd heard Mario had someone in his life. Erene?"

"That's right. Erene Skujans. It's a strange last name."

"Not in Latvia. I'm assuming that's where Mario met her."

"Yes. He was over there researching something he was very excited about."

"Do you know what it was?"

"No. Mario liked being mysterious. He was always doing those puzzles—showing the kids how to make cipher keys so they could write messages to each other that their parents couldn't read."

"Playfair ciphers," Annja said, remembering Mario's instruction to "play fairly" with her authentication. She and Mario had whiled away some of the boring hours out at the dig site playing with the idea of codes. Mario had been fascinated by them, and his favorite had been the Playfair ciphers.

"I think that's what they were called," Pietro agreed. "Whatever he was doing, it consumed him."

"What do you mean?" Annja got up and went back to the living room, back to the mosaic and the pieces she'd pried from the background.

"He worked on this project for two or three years off

and on. It was hard watching him sitting thinking about it, then not telling you about it."

Annja began turning the tessera over one by one, working through the rows.

"Whatever it was," Pietro went on, "Mario found out about it while working in Vatican City. That was one of the reasons he quit there."

"He left me a message and told me he was bored." Annja started on the second row.

"That was part of it. I know he said they were too restrictive there. Too many secrets, I suppose."

"Every culture has them." Coming up empty again, Annja started on the third row.

"After leaving Vatican City, Mario worked in Venice for a while."

"Doing what?" Annja started on the fourth row.

"He was a gondolier, if you can believe it."

"I can't."

"He was. Francesca and I went down there to see it for ourselves."

"Why would he take a job like that?" Annja moved on to the fifth row.

"He couldn't find anything else and he wanted to stay there. Whatever he was working on, it had him by the throat." Pietro was quiet for a moment. "He always wanted to be famous."

"I remember. So how did he get to Riga?" Annja asked.

"A few months ago, he told everyone he was moving there for a while. To sort some things out, he said. But you could tell he thought he was on to something."

"But no one knew what."

"No. Then he started seeing Erene."

"She lived there?"

"I believe she still does. One of the things that seemed to captivate Mario most about her was that she was a witch."

"A witch?"

"Yes. Mario seemed quite enamored of her because of that. She was supposed to be something like a hedge witch or a midwife. He said Erene knew a lot of things about plants and herbal remedies." Pietro paused. "Now we don't think we'll ever get to meet her."

"No one has a way of getting in touch with her?"

"No. We contacted Mario through his cell phone. If we don't find a way soon, she may miss the funeral. The most upsetting aspect about this is that Mario's killers are still on the loose."

Nearly halfway into the eight row of tessera, Annja turned over a cube and found a letter. Excitement surged within her.

"You never know," she told Pietro. "That could change at any time."

ANNJA SAT LOOKING at the back of the mosaic, at the secret that had been hidden beneath the surface. There was a message on the back of the tessera. The letters were painted on backs of the tiles. If she hadn't taken the tiles off one by one and placed them in the same order, she'd have lost the message.

If anyone else had taken the tiles off, they would have destroyed what Mario had left behind for her to find. There was no doubt that the message had been intended for her.

The message said, "Hi, Annja. I have no secrets from you. Remember, no Selgovae!"

"All right," Annja said quietly. "That's a no-brainer, Mario. What do you want me to see?"

The Selgovae were a Brythonic tribe from Scotland, and one of the main reasons the Romans had built Hadrian's Wall. It made sense that Mario would use that as a linchpin to get a message across.

But what was the message?

The first part consisted of six letters: "ESIREF."

The second part, on a line four rows down from the first, had twelve letters: "JVLPHNJEMXJW."

Annja took her digital camera from her backpack, then stood on a chair over the table to focus on the tiles. After adjusting the flash and the lens, she took three close-up shots. Then she put the camera away and tried to wrap her mind around what the letters meant.

At first glance the coded message didn't tell her much. Then she remembered what Pietro had said about the ciphers Mario had taught his nieces and nephews.

The Fairplay cipher had been Mario's favorite. Without the key and by keeping the message simple, without a lot of text, the cipher was incredibly hard to break.

Mario hadn't included the key.

Hadrian's Wall is the key, Annja told herself. She got a graph-paper pad and a pen from her backpack. Paper and pencils were still an archaeologist's best mechanical tools. But it was the mind that did the brunt of the work.

Annja checked her memory and discovered that she'd been right about the Playfair cipher. It consisted of five rows of letters by five columns of letters.

Usually a code word or phrase was written across the top, without a break and without repeating letters. *X* was used for the first time double letters—like *EE* or *SS*—were used. The rest of the letters were put in order from left to right, from top to bottom.

Annja wrote "HADRIAN'S WALL" down, then took out the apostrophe and the repeated letters. She was left with "HADRINSWL."

Since "WALL" had double *L*s, she added an *X*. Her final tally was ten unique letters: "HADRINSWLX."

Once she had those, she worked swiftly, slipping the letters into the five-by-five grid. Traditionally *Q* wasn't used, or *I* and *J* were used in the same space. The cipher key took shape quickly.

```
HADRI
NSWLX
BCEFG
JKMOP
TUVYZ
```

Then she started substituting letters. The rules were simple.

Whenever letters were on the same row they were substituted for the ones immediately to their right, wrapping back around to the front of the row as needed.

If letters were in the same column, they were substituted with letters just below them, wrapping back to the top of the column if necessary.

Letters that were in different rows and columns were used as anchors to form rectangles. Then the letters in the opposite corners of the rectangles were substituted out, staying within the same row, not the same column.

The first coded message—"ESIREF"—became "CWHIFG."

Since that didn't look like any answer she recognized, Annja knew something had gone wrong. Her frustration came rushing back. The cipher idea had sounded so much like Mario, she was certain that had been the answer.

Okay, Annja thought, the answer can't be wrong. Therefore the cipher key had to be. She'd missed something. Another clue Mario had to have left.

She stood up from the table and stepped back from the mosaic. What else had been hidden? She knew it had to be on the back of the mosaic.

Or on the front.

She was just about to give up and flip the tiles back over when she noticed a faded line made up of discolored stones. Taking the mini-Maglite she habitually carried from the backpack, she shone the light on the tiles, exploring the discoloration more closely.

Upon dedicated inspection, she saw that the stones had been intentionally discolored. A gentle wash of some kind of stain had lent them a faint yellowish tinge.

At first she'd thought there were only ten discolored tessera. The correlation between the number of tiles and the number of unique letters in the code word didn't escape her.

In the end, she saw that there were twenty-five discolored tiles. The discoloration on fifteen others was less, but it was still there. Not only that, but they were laid out in a five-by-five square.

The center nine tiles were discolored the same shade. That shade matched the fourth tile down in the last column.

Pulse quickening, Annja knew she was close to the answer. The letters in the code word had to be in sequential order. The only orders could be two rows of three followed by a row of four.

Or Mario had begun on the outside and worked his way into a spiral.

"Yes," Annja whispered as she put pen to paper on a clean page.

# 17

"Wolfram, go to your room and clean up. I've had a clean suit laid out for you."

Temples throbbing, Schluter stared at his grandmother and started to argue there in the grand ballroom with the portraits of family members looking down from the high walls. For all of his life, those faces had looked down on him, painted with his grandmother's disdain.

He knew arguing with her wouldn't do any good. His grandmother would have her way. Only the price for his defiance would go up.

As gracefully as he could, he made his exit, then ascended the winding staircase to his rooms. Because his grandmother could no longer go up and down the stairs due to her increasing infirmity, all the rooms on the upper two stories were his to do with as he pleased. He didn't need the space, but he enjoyed having it all the same.

His footsteps echoed in the empty hallway as he entered his bedchamber. A huge round bed was flanked by two wide wardrobes and chests of drawers that had been in the family for generations. All of the decor was antique, and Schluter cared for none of it.

No one had ever seen the room. There was no one he would bring back to the castle. Instead, he spent time with his friends and his women in Vienna, crashing through the nightclubs where he conducted his business.

He looked at the suit his grandmother had chosen for him, then went to his wardrobe and selected a pair of tailored khakis, a silver pullover that hugged the trim and athletic body he'd built in the gym he'd had installed on the third floor and a pair of running shoes.

As a further insult, he added a Heckler & Koch Mk 23 in an expensive Italian shoulder holster. He knew how much his grandmother hated it when he wore a weapon inside the castle.

Maybe she was afraid of him these days. It made Schluter feel good to think like that. The fear in a family shouldn't go only one way.

He took out a pale gray and blue leather jacket he'd had specially made as an accessory to his car.

Stepping into the large bathroom, he walked past the sauna and hot tub to take a shower. His grandmother wouldn't like it that he was making them wait, but he didn't care about that, either.

She wouldn't always run things, he reminded himself.

"DID YOUR FATHER TALK fondly of me, Herr Braden?" Kikka Schluter asked.

Garin stood in the well-appointed study and looked at the old woman. Her age had been the biggest shock for him. Even though it had been sixty years since he'd seen her, and he'd known she'd age, the change in her appearance had astounded him.

When he'd first met Baroness Kikka Schluter, she had been a vibrant young woman willing to explore her own passions away from her cuckolded husband. She'd been blond and beautiful, full figured and filled with energy. A single look from her blue eyes could break a man's heart.

She'd broken his.

And, maybe, he'd broken hers.

Now she was a dried-up old prune of a woman who had turned mean and hard over the years.

Perhaps coming here was a mistake, he thought. But you couldn't stay away, could you? He hadn't needed to see her—he'd wanted to. His wants had always outweighed his needs. If they hadn't, he'd have been able to live a much calmer, quieter life these past five hundred years.

"Please," Garin said, putting on a smile he didn't feel, "call me Garin."

Kikka sat in a tall-backed French chair that might have come from Louis XIV's court.

"That was your father's name," she said.

He'd told her that the Garin Braden she'd known had been his father.

"My mother named me for him."

"It's a good name. A strong name."

Garin nodded. He stood near the fireplace. A dozen ships of various designs occupied bottles on the mantle. A portrait of her grandfather hung above the bottles. He stood regal and erect in full army uniform, sword at his side. He'd been a general in the First World War but had been killed in the Second. The general rank had been added posthumously because Kikka Schluter had insisted.

"Thank you," Garin said. "Father did speak fondly of you. Of course, he never talked fondly of you when Mother was around." He smiled again, and this time he let her see a little of the devil that was in him.

Kikka put her head back and brayed, a full-throated roar of amusement that almost took Garin back sixty years.

"You have a sense of humor about you," she said. "That must have been a gift from your father."

"To my mother's everlasting horror," Garin agreed. He was surprised at how good it felt to talk to her like this. Over the centuries, it seemed as if he was constantly meeting new acquaintances. Precious few of them had left lasting impressions.

Back then records hadn't been kept as  atly as they were today. Garin had had no problem disappearing and reappearing as someone else every few years.

But now, it was harder keeping the fact that he hadn't aged from people he came in contact with.

These days he managed his business through corporate executive boards, rarely meeting any of the people who worked for him. Having to transfer over all his estate, while showing a legal reason for it, wasn't easy. More layers had to be added to invent himself over and over again. Law firms actually allowed him to disappear and reappear more readily.

But the attorneys he hired kept their distance. It was hard to get to know anyone anymore. He missed the human touch.

Sometimes he wondered how Roux, his one-time mentor, dealt with the isolation and loneliness. Then he remembered how it had been during those days when they'd been on the road, before Joan of Arc had lost her life, and after they'd been cursed to find the sword's fragments.

Roux had always been content to be by himself, lost in the study of things in which Garin had never found an understanding or an interest.

"How did your father die?" Kikka asked.

Garin grinned broadly. "In the arms of the new maid. She was barely twenty years old."

Kikka laughed so hard she had to wipe tears from her eyes. Her honest amusement had an effect on Garin, and he found himself laughing with her. Just like the old days when a stolen kiss had set fire to his blood. It was always strange talking about his death. He feared it but at the same time had come to expect it would never happen. Whenever he did talk about it, he always made it interesting.

"That sounds like the man I knew," Kikka said when she'd regained control of herself. "There was a fierceness, a hunger for life I saw in him that I've never seen in any man since."

Garin took pride in that.

"What about your mother?" Kikka asked.

"Gone soon after, I'm afraid. I think Father would like to have thought she died of embarrassment over the way he had been found."

"Didn't your father love her?"

After a brief consideration, Garin said, "He did. But it was in his own way. He wasn't made to be faithful, I'm afraid."

"Then it's a good thing I didn't leave my husband for him."

"Probably," he said. But Garin could remember how much he'd missed her when she'd told him she could no longer see him.

"I have to admit, I was very tempted to leave my husband for your father," she said.

That caught Garin's attention and caused an old ache to flare unexpectedly. "Life would have been very different if you had," he said.

"I know. But in the end I couldn't leave because of my father. He had no male children to carry on the Schluter name, but he could at least leave the title to me. If I had left, there would have been no one. That was very important to him."

"Was it important to you?"

"Not as much then, but in time it came to be." Kikka looked at him. "A man—a *person*—must leave a legacy. Something to mark the fact that he or she once existed. Your father had you. I have my grandson." She paused and nodded to herself as if confirming something she doubted. "Wretch and wastrel though he can be, I have hopes that he will harden and become a man one day."

Garin waited, not knowing what to say. His thoughts roamed from the study to those nights sixty years ago. He could still feel the touch of her skin. Even though there had been hundreds of women since then.

"Do you think your father would have had me?" she asked without warning.

"Yes," Garin answered instantly.

Kikka smiled. "It's nice to think so, but I think eventually we would have done each other in. We were both too exacting. We had our fun, but it was always that. Our time together never became a hardship."

Garin breathed out slowly, trying to ease that ache. He hated weakness in others, though he relished using it to exploit them. But he especially despised weakness in himself.

"But what about you?" she asked. "Enough talk of the past and things better left forgotten. You look as though you've accomplished a lot in your life. Don't tell me you're just living off your father's estate."

"No. I've done quite well with my own investments." Even though it shouldn't have made a difference, Garin didn't want her thinking he was living off anyone's accomplishments but his own. Pride was his strength and his weakness. "What he started has grown into multinational corporations."

"Good. He must have been very proud of you." Kikka sighed and shook her head. "My grandson has yet to learn how to do more than spend the money he thinks grows on trees." She held her hands out to the fire to warm them. "I think the winter months must be getting harsher every year."

Picking up the poker, Garin shifted the logs in the fireplace to create a larger blaze for a little while. He was almost getting too hot himself, so he knew the chill Kikka was experiencing came from her age and frailty. Realizing that made him feel sad. It was an unfamiliar feeling that hadn't touched his life in years.

When he'd received the call from her after all these years, part of him had been vindictive. He'd wanted to come to her and glory in his youth while she was trapped in a sagging bag of skin. He'd even planned to tell her that he was the same Garin Braden, not some fictional son, and prove it by revealing the intimate knowledge of the time they'd spent together.

He'd wanted to see the hurt in her eyes when she recognized he was telling the truth. The same pain she'd delivered to him sixty years ago was going to come back at her a hundredfold.

The only thing that had stayed his hand from killing her in a jealous rage back then had been his love for her. He'd never had a love so passionate or so consuming. In the end, he'd left Vienna, had even left Germany for a time and journeyed to the United States.

Garin watched the old woman as she tried to warm herself. He took a blanket from the couch and brought it over to her.

"Thank you." She seemed embarrassed at accepting the blanket. She'd always hated admitting vulnerability. "There must be a draft in the room," she said.

Garin stood and looked down at her. He'd come to Castle Schluter prepared to ridicule and hurt her. He was surprised at how protective he felt.

"I supposed you're wondering why I asked you to come," Kikka said.

"When you're ready," he told her. But he was curious.

"Let's have dinner," she said. "Let me at least play the proper hostess before we get into why I called you here."

# 18

When she finished blocking in the other letters, Annja examined her handiwork. She'd manipulated the letters, bringing them into the center of the five-by-five grid in a coil.

It looked right. More than that, it *felt* right.

But there was only one way to find out.

She started with the first line of letters, reminding herself to reverse the direction of the progression of letters in the rows and columns. The substitution rules on the corners of rectangles were still in effect.

"Venice."

Annja's excitement soared. According to Pietro, Mario's investigation into whatever prize he'd been chasing had begun in Venice.

Not exactly true, Annja reminded herself. It had started in Vatican City. But she knew she was on the right track. Mario had left a trail for her to follow. She worked the translations on the other lines quickly.

She divided the letters one more time to get the answer: "St. Mark's Books."

A bookstore? she wondered. It would make sense. A bookstore in Venice, given all the history that had passed through that city, could offer a treasure trove.

Or a friend.

Annja turned her attention to the final line of code. "Mjolnir."

There was only one Mjolnir that Annja could think of. Mjolnir was the name of the enchanted hammer carried by Thor, the god of thunder in Norse mythology.

Annja sat back to think about what the message meant. There were still too many questions, too many interpretations.

The Vikings had impacted many countries during their travels. Most people remembered them for carnage and destruction, but mostly the Vikings were explorers and traders. They carried their culture to many places, and brought home culture from other places, which they integrated into their own society, reinterpreted and took back out into the world again.

What had Mario found?

Opening her computer, Annja hooked up the mini-satellite receiver and got online. She googled St. Mark's Books in Venice and immediately got a hit.

Going to the Web page, she discovered that it was a small bookstore specializing in history, maps and walking tours of Venice. The Web page was attractive, looking like sepia-toned parchment. Business hours were from 10:00 a.m. to 7:00 p.m.

The time in the corner of Annja's computer screen showed it was currently 1:18 p.m. Italy was six hours ahead of New York, making it after seven there. There was a possibility that the shopkeeper hadn't gotten out of his shop yet.

Annja scooped up her cell phone and dialed the number shown on the Web page. An answering machine picked up after the third ring and informed her that the bookstore was closed and would reopen in the morning. She decided she'd call again when the store reopened.

Frustrated, but pleased to at least have a lead, Annja exited the page and logged on to alt.archaeology and posted a message.

I'm looking for information regarding Thor's hammer, Mjolnir and any specific ties it might have had to Riga, Latvia.
Anything would be helpful at this point.

She signed it "Hammer Hunter" and left another posting at alt.archaeology.esoterica. Then she pulled up the Google search engine in hopes of scoring something to leverage Doug Morrell. *Chasing History's Monsters* had deeper pockets than she did. Running for her life was expensive.

Plus, if the trail led from Venice to Riga as she thought it might, searching for Mario's killers was going to be even more costly.

She typed in "Vampires Venice" and hit Search. Doug was a sucker for vampire stories. He masqueraded as one from time to time.

WHY ISN'T THERE a vampire around when you need one? Annja asked herself irritably. A few minutes spent searching through various Web pages had shown that vampires in Venice existed only in movies and books.

Then she sighed and reminded herself that vampires in general were nonexistent.

If it hadn't been for Doug Morrell's continuing interest in the subject, as well as most of the audience of *Chasing History's Monsters,* Annja wouldn't have known as much about vampires as she did.

Vampires weren't on required-reading lists for archaeology majors. As for her personal tastes, she happened to like occasional vampire novels. But she didn't understand the fad about vampires that had existed since Bram Stoker first penned *Dracula.*

She couldn't believe she hadn't been able to find even one legend about vampires in Venice. Sultan Mehmet, known as "the Conqueror," had taken Venice back after it had fallen. One of Mehmet's primary opponents had been Vlad Tepes III, also known as Dracula.

That had been as close to a vampire-in-Venice story as she got. Annja had searched as quickly and efficiently as she could but there was no mention of vampires there except on film.

There weren't any serial killers or mass murderers, either. When she wanted to get to a dig site to pursue her own interests, she could usually count on finding serial killers or mass murderers in the vicinity.

Ghosts, she told herself grimly, knowing she was reaching. Gotta be ghosts. She turned back to the computer screen, regretting the cooling bathwater that she couldn't get to.

"YOU MISSED the meeting this morning," Doug said coolly.

Sitting cross-legged on the hotel bed, Annja gazed out

at the gray afternoon sky. The weather had worsened and snow flurries rode the wind.

"Sorry," she apologized. "I forgot."

"You forget a lot."

Ah, we are in a snarky mood, aren't we? Annja thought but she chose not to rise to the bait. "Did the phantom shark turn out okay?"

Doug hesitated, as if afraid of stepping into a trap. "It turned out okay. He's got some tweaking to do to finalize it, but the concept has been approved."

"That's good."

"That's good?"

"Yeah."

"Yeah?"

Annja frowned. "This isn't going to be much of a conversation if you keep repeating everything I say."

"You'll have to forgive me," Doug told her. "I'm not sure which conversation we're having."

"The shark," Annja reminded.

"You hate the shark."

"Did I say that?"

"Yes. Yesterday."

"I must have been having a bad day."

"Or maybe you were suffering a concussion after running into the side of a bus," Doug said.

Annja frowned again. This was going to take more finesse than she'd anticipated. "You saw that?"

"Someone filmed it and sent it in to Letterman. It was featured on his show last night."

Terrific, Annja thought.

"Who were the guys you were running from?" Doug asked.

"Muggers."

"Muggers don't usually shoot up the city chasing a victim."

"Really determined muggers. I thought maybe we could have a drink."

"A drink?"

"Yes. A drink and some conversation."

"We're having a conversation now," Doug pointed out.

"The phone's impersonal."

"It's also easier to say no over the phone."

"You could say yes."

"No is safer."

"You haven't even heard me out yet."

"I don't want to. I find it very hard to tell you no in person."

Annja smiled. That was true. "You're going to love this."

"Then give me a preview now."

"I'll see you at Sherlock's in an hour."

"I'll still be at work."

"I'm getting you out of the office. You should thank me."

"No, because if you were sure about this story, you'd e-mail me and we'd set it up."

"We don't always do the stories I want to do," Annja said.

"We don't always get the stories we expect," Doug parried. "Like the phantom-shark thing. I had to dig into the budget to make that happen."

"Meet me," Annja urged. "Three o'clock. Sherlock's." She broke the connection before he could disagree.

Walking into the bathroom, she let the scented water out of the bath with true regret. Even only settling for a shower, she was going to be cutting it close to get there in time.

# 19

"You're not talking much, Wolfram."

Schluter gazed at his grandmother at the other end of the long dining table. She'd placed Garin Braden at the head, which was Schluter's traditional spot when they entertained on infrequent occasions. And it was always her friends who were invited. Thankfully, there were fewer and fewer of those friends around these days.

His grandmother sat at the man's left and fawned over him so much that Schluter thought he was going to be sick.

Dinner had been an elegant affair that Schluter hadn't seen the like of in months. There hadn't been much cause for celebration for a long time. The fact that the dregs of the family fortune were now dwindling had preyed on them and made their already-strained relationship even worse.

"I was just listening, Grandmother," Schluter responded politely. Actually, he wouldn't have been able to get a word in edgewise if he'd tried. Several times during the meal he'd fantasized pulling out his pistol and shooting Garin Braden between the eyes.

His grandmother smiled as if she were embarrassed, and maybe she was. But it was because she thought she might have come off badly in front of their guest more than the fact she might have done Schluter any wrong. "I'm sorry. We've been wrapped up so much in our conversation that I wasn't paying attention," she said.

As if she ever paid attention to him, he thought bitterly. The only time she acknowledged him was to give him an assignment or take him to task. The resentment Schluter felt was an old and powerful thing. He no longer felt guilty over it. He embraced it because it made him stronger.

He didn't know how much his grandmother had told the man about "the Riga problem," but he was angry over that, too. He'd told her he would take care of it. He would. It was just going to take longer than he'd expected.

"That's all right," Schluter said. "I can see that you've got a lot of catching up to do. If you don't need me, I think I'll go into town."

For a moment he thought his grandmother was going to object and command him to stay home. But he knew his absence would allow her to talk more privately with Garin Braden.

"If you wish," his grandmother said.

"Then I'll see you in the morning." Schluter stood.

"In fact," his grandmother said, "I think we'll retire to the study and continue our conversation there."

Garin was on his feet at once and helped the old woman from her chair. "I'll meet you there in a moment," he told her. "I just want to get a breath of fresh air."

IN HIS ROOM, Schluter opened the safe in the floor. He removed a stack of money and used a disposable cell phone to call Dieter Humbrecht.

"Hello?" Dieter's response was guarded.

"It's me," Schluter said. "Have you found the woman or the package?"

"We know where she's going to be in the next hour or so. Klaus managed to get a listening device into the office of the woman's boss."

"He's not her boss. He's her producer."

"He's also meeting her for a drink. We'll be there, as well."

Schluter closed the safe and tucked the money into his jacket pocket. "Will she have the package?"

"We hope so. She told him over the phone that she wants to discuss something with him. What else could it be?" Dieter paused. "The police are looking for us."

"They've identified you?" That surprised Schluter.

"Yes."

"How?"

"We don't know yet. But we are taking a chance by staying here."

"Don't get caught, Dieter. It's as simple as that. And keep me apprised of the situation." Schluter closed the phone and headed downstairs. Things were heating up on several fronts.

GARIN BRADEN STOOD outside the main house when Schluter arrived there. Schluter had the immediate feeling that the man had been waiting for him. Ignoring him, Schluter started down the steps to his car.

"Wolfram."

The cold menace so naked in the man's voice brought Schluter up short. It sparked a sense of fear inside him. But the fear was instantly replaced by anger as adrenaline flooded his body. He turned to face Braden. Fear had a strength of its own, and he'd learned how to use it.

"What do you want?" Schluter didn't bother hiding his dislike.

"A moment of your time, if I may," the big man said. Shadows draped him where he stood. He looked threatening, primeval within them. Like a beast in its lair.

Schluter flicked a deliberate look at his Rolex. "Only just."

Braden grinned, obviously neither insulted nor challenged. Too late, Schluter realized that by agreeing to stop at all he'd already capitulated.

"I like your grandmother," Braden said. "I've known her for a long time."

"She said the two of you had only just met." The claim confused Schluter.

"I just wanted you to know that," Braden stated easily.

"All right." Schluter turned away.

"If anyone hurts her," Braden said, "I'll kill that person."

It took all of Schluter's willpower not to draw his pistol and shoot the man where he stood. Instead, he stepped up to the man, giving away at least three inches and thirty pounds.

"Well, I've got a news flash for you," Schluter said. "I don't know why my grandmother felt it necessary to call you here, but if you try to take over my operation, I'll bury you."

Bright lights gleamed in Braden's eyes. He didn't back away. "Ever notice the way a little dog makes a lot of noise?" he asked. "But when you get right down to it, it's still just a little dog."

Schluter made himself turn away and walk to his car. He was going to deal with his first problem first, but the matter of Garin Braden had just moved up onto Schluter's top-ten list.

GARIN WATCHED Schluter roar through the outer gates, only missing a collision with the wrought iron because the security guards had been expecting his actions. Probably through dealing with him for years.

Schluter might have been thirty years old, but Garin was willing to bet he'd been acting the same way for the past twenty years. He was willful and spiteful, truly an arrogant ass, and he didn't care about anything but his own skin.

In fact, Garin had to admit there were things about Schluter that reminded him of himself. He wouldn't care to admit that to anyone else, though. He would never admit it to Roux.

Ah, Kikka, you've certainly birthed your own punishment in this life, haven't you? he thought.

Before coming to Schluter Castle, Garin had researched Kikka Schluter over the Internet. There hadn't been any pictures of her in forty years, and the stories suggested she hadn't left her house in all that time. Garin suspected it was because of the tragic murder-suicide of her daughter and son-in-law twenty years earlier.

He took a final breath, then returned to the house.

"DID YOUR FATHER TELL YOU about the promise he made to me on the night we separated?" Kikka asked.

"That he would help you if you ever needed it?"

Kikka looked at him, and Garin knew she was remembering how it had been all those years ago. That knowledge made him feel good and sad at the same time. The experience was confusing.

"Yes." Kikka smoothed her dress over her knees. "You came because of the promise your father made?"

"I came because of curiosity," Garin said truthfully. That was only part of it, though.

"That's another trait you share with your father."

"People tell me I'm very like him."

"You are." Kikka studied him and her intense scrutiny made him feel more vulnerable and exposed than he had in centuries. "I never expected to have to call," she said.

Garin waited.

"But I did," the old woman went on.

"Anything," Garin said. "My father made me promise. If it's money, simply tell me how much."

Pride stiffened Kikka's bent and withered spine.

Garin knew at once he'd made a mistake.

"I didn't call for charity," Kikka said with a hint of the old fire that had burned within her during the time Garin had known her. "I would never do that."

"I apologize," Garin said, dropping his head in deference. "I didn't mean to offend."

For a moment the old woman said nothing. Garin thought she wouldn't allow herself to ask him for anything and that she would tell him to leave.

Evidently her desperation was great.

"You've heard that I've fallen on hard times," she said.

Garin looked her in the eye and didn't lie. "Yes."

"It wasn't all my own doing," Kikka said. "The businesses the Schluter money has been in, businesses that we've had for years—factories and real estate—have struggled recently."

"It's the shifting labor pool," Garin said. "Global trade and the ability to outsource so much labor-intensive business has affected everyone."

"That's what my investment counselor told me," Kikka admitted. "Unfortunately, I tried to manage my investments for myself for a time and what's left of our fortune is leveraged." She paused. "If something doesn't happen soon…"

Garin waited, knowing Kikka would only tell the story when she was ready. He stood quietly and shared his attention between the old woman and tending the fire.

"I've read about you, you know," Kikka announced. "It appears you've inherited your talent for business and no-nonsense approach from your father."

"Thank you."

"I also saw an article on you in *Forbes*. You're something of a treasure hunter and collector."

Garin shrugged. "That greatly depends on the treasure." Curiosity tugged at him. Kikka Schluter had never been one to go chasing after treasure. She'd always remained firmly fixed on her family's standing and fortune.

"Your father loved the idea of hidden treasure," Kikka said. "He told me about some of the finds he'd made."

Garin hadn't told her all of the stories, though. He'd only embellished a few of the more entertaining ones. In too many others he'd arguably played the villain, though that was never a role he would assign to himself.

A servant came to the doors with a serving tray and two brandy snifters.

"Your father was a brandy connoisseur." Kikka waved the servant in.

"I've developed a taste for it," Garin replied.

The servant placed the tray on the table and departed. Garin picked up the snifters and offered one to Kikka. She took it and swirled it around, gazing through the glass against the light to check the quality.

"I called you here to offer you a business proposition," Kikka said. "For hundreds of years," the old woman said in a soft voice that barely reached Garin's ears, "there has existed within the barony the legend of a fabulous treasure in Latvia. Early in the thirteenth century, one of my ancestors went to Riga in search of it."

Garin wasn't impressed. There were many myths and legends about buried treasures and lost fortunes in the world. Even back in France, when he'd first been apprenticed to Roux, they had tracked down several legends. Some of them, a very few, had turned out to have a grain of truth in them. On occasion they'd found amazing things. Garin owned a few of them now, though he didn't completely understand them. An image flashed in his mind of Annja Creed and her sword.

"Are you familiar with the history of the Baltic states?" Kikka asked.

"I am." Garin knew he wasn't as studied as Roux, but he knew a lot about history because he had lived through so much of it. "Latvia has constantly been a country in turmoil. It was, and remains, a major trade hub in the Baltic Sea. But trade brings wars and conquerors. They've seen more than their share of both. Russia has wanted control of that area because of the deep-sea ports."

Kikka nodded. "Your father was a very intelligent man, too. I always appreciated that about him, though I don't think I ever told him."

Never, Garin thought. But he appreciated the comment even if it was sixty years too late.

"The Vikings went there often," Kikka said. "To trade and to loot. There is a story that was handed down to us through Baron Frederick of Schluter. He was a Teutonic knight. A devoutly religious man who worked to carry out the mission of the order."

Garin took that information with a grain of salt. Kikka had always overemphasized her ancestors' successes and altruism. Garin had known her father. Baron Erich Schluter had been a fierce military man, a warrior on the battlefield who in the end had been forced to turn from Hitler.

"While he was there, establishing churches and spreading Christianity—"

At the end of a sword, Garin thought, and struggled to keep a straight face.

"—he found, in one of the pagan churches, the journal of a German trader who recorded a legend from Courland." Kikka sipped her drink. "According to the German trader, Vikings attacked a village in Courland in 1104, somewhere west of Riga along the coastline. To a man, the Vikings were killed."

"That's unusual," Garin admitted. There had been no fiercer warriors than the Vikings during their day.

"The villagers had help. There was a warrior among them they had rescued from the sea. He was a fierce man— of Viking birth, perhaps—who carried a magical war hammer that could call down the lightning itself."

That caught Garin's attention. He wasn't sure, but he believed he'd seen references to such a relic in Roux's books.

"He called the hammer Mjolnir," Kikka said.

Garin looked at her and smiled. "You do realize you're

saying that Thor, the Norse god of thunder, lived with those people."

Kikka's eyes turned flat and hard. "I do not wish to be mocked."

No, but you do wish to believe in anything that will help you save your castle and title, Garin thought.

"Baroness," Garin said, "you must at least allow me the courtesy of being caught off guard. We are talking about one of the most powerful entities in Norse mythology."

"That's exactly who we're talking about," she insisted. "Not only that, but Thor left a treasure with those people."

"What makes you think the treasure is still there?"

"Thor hid it. He left it there for his wife and children. Unfortunately, his wife died in childbirth and he left the village."

"He didn't take his fortune with him?"

"They say that losing his wife drove him mad for a time. Perhaps he still is."

Garin was silent for a moment. He didn't believe that a god had taken up residence with a barbaric tribe along the Baltic coast. He knew that something existed beyond the mortal realm; otherwise he wouldn't have lived over five hundred years. But the idea of a god living a hand-to-mouth existence among barely literate people was ridiculous.

Still, legends were generally based on some small truth.

"Wolfram has gone to Riga in an effort to track down the fortune, but there have been problems."

"What kind of problems?" Garin was thinking about hearing her out, then getting in his car and avoiding all the foolishness. This was desperation, pure and simple.

"There is a woman who is believed descended from the Curonians. She's supposed to be a witch, as was her grandmother before her."

"A *witch?*" Garin was amused.

"She's more than a witch. She's very skilled at killing. She managed to murder three of the mercenaries Wolfram employed to help him seek the truth over there."

That was much more intriguing. "What's her interest?"

"We think she's seeking the treasure, as well. She had taken up with an Italian archaeologist named Mario Fellini."

The name meant nothing to Garin.

"Wolfram arranged to have the man killed—"

The casual way Kikka said that surprised Garin. He'd known she was selfish and vain, but he'd never known her to be so cold-blooded.

"—but not before he involved another archaeologist. He sent her a package, but we don't know what the contents were." Kikka grimaced. "That woman has proved even more irksome. And it appears now she's hunting the treasure, as well."

"Who is she?" Garin asked.

"Her name is Annja Creed."

Garin took a breath. His pulse quickened in anticipation. Annja's participation in the hunt put things in a whole new perspective.

# 20

Sherlock's was a small club on the second floor of the building where *Chasing History's Monsters* was housed. The clientele were dedicated mystery enthusiasts. Book covers and movie posters decorated the walls.

Lights at the booths ranged from mock Victorian lamps that conjured images of the great detective and his faithful Watson to green shaded desk lamps that would have looked at home on Philip Marlowe's desk to stained glass ones bearing beer slogans that would have made Mike Hammer proud.

Annja got there before the afternoon rush and managed to get the Thin Man table. Beneath the poster of William Powell and Myrna Loy, she opened her notebook computer. Taking the mini-satellite receiver from her backpack, she logged on and checked the Web sites where she'd left messages.

The first reply was from NorseGoddess@hallsofvalhalla.net.

Hey, Hammer Hunter, Good luck with your project! Sounds interesting. I've been a fan of Norse mythology since third grade. Seems like everybody likes it. Comic books. Movies. *Star Gate*. Jim Carrey's movie, *The Mask*, even said the mask he wore was made for Loki, Thor's evil half brother. There was even a *Lost in Space* episode where Billy Mumy found Thor's hammer and gloves. I'll look around and see what I can find.

MiredInMidgard@asgardbound.com wrote, "Cool quest! Can I play?"

Annja straightened for a moment to work the kinks out of her back. She was a little stiff and sore from the physical confrontations yesterday.

Sherlock's began to fill up around her as office workers stopped in to get a drink before heading to the subways to go home. Spirited conversations over books and movies began, and Annja found them slightly distracting. Book people were passionate about what they read, and she loved the conversations.

It sounded a lot like when archaeologists got together to compare, argue and recommend. She took a look around for Doug, glanced at her watch and realized that not much time had passed, and resolved to return her attention to the message boards.

Before she did, though, she noticed that a nerdy guy in glasses sitting across the bar was watching her. Fortyish and lean, he had a notebook computer open in front of him. He wore an ill-fitting suit and had a beanie pulled down to his ears.

When she looked directly at him, he glanced away, obviously embarrassed.

You're paranoid, Annja told herself. He's not a threat.
Loremaster@norsearchives.org sent:

Fascinating subject. Latvia, as you probably know, has
a tumultuous history. Everybody that was anybody has
walked all over that country. The Vikings. The
Germans. The Russians. The people living there must
have felt like they'd lived in the path of a steamroller
for hundreds of years.

I've been doing some research into that subject. I was on
summer break last year and went to Riga with my archaeology prof. He was there doing research on the indigenous tribes that lived in Latvia prior to the twelfth century.
While we were there, we visited a bar in one of the
small, virtually nameless villages outside Riga proper.
That evening we happened on an old man who knew
we were with a university.

I suppose he thought we might be generous enough
to buy him a few beers. We were. And he told us this
fascinating story that he said just wouldn't die.

Apparently Thor washed up on the shores of one of the
Curonian villages—if you can imagine that—and decided
to stay. While Thor was there, he fought off Vikings and
amassed a great fortune that he supposedly hid.

That's all I know. I can't tell you any more. Except there
seem to be a few people interested in the subject. It's
weird how these things keep getting out but you can't
find anything to back them up.

We stayed a few weeks, visited some of the churches
and read the archives left by monks and historians, and
did a little work at one of the Crusader castles to gather

information for the prof's book. But it was really more like one long beer run. The book met the prof's publish-or-perish requirement and he got tenure. But I really don't think anyone ever read it.
Good hunting!

And from valkyriedream@meetyourmate.biz:

If you're looking for tall Nordic women, we have them! They're waiting just to meet you! Hot and ready! Just sign up at www.meetyourmate.biz today!

You gotta love spam, Annja thought. She took a moment to write a reply to loremaster.

Thanks for the info! This sounds promising. If you don't mind, could I ask you to dig a little deeper? Do you have any maps of the area where you were? Narrow down the village where you heard that story?

"I'd be interested in a tall Nordic woman."

Looking up, Annja saw Doug Morrell gazing over her shoulder. "Didn't your mother ever tell you it was impolite to read over someone's shoulder?" Annja asked.

"She was just happy I learned to read." Doug was twenty-two, younger than Annja, but bright and brash. Except for the whole vampire fetish he insisted on clinging to.

Doug sat across the booth from her and flagged down a female server with a smile. As busy as Sherlock's was, anyone else would have had to use a police whistle. Annja had seen Doug use that smile at night in a forlorn part of Manhattan and seemingly pull a cab out of thin air.

"What are you having?" Doug asked.

"Hot chocolate." Annja closed the notebook computer.

Doug gave her a raspberry.

"It's cold outside," Annja protested. "Alcohol thins your blood. You get colder faster."

"You should consider thinning it to the point you go numb," he replied. Then he ordered another hot chocolate for her and one for himself.

Annja raised an eyebrow. "Not drinking?" Doug wasn't a big drinker, but he didn't have to be. One or two drinks usually made him pliable. And she wanted him pliable.

The producer shrugged. "Coming in here makes me want to act like one of those tough-guy detectives. You know, give me a shot in a dirty glass."

"I think that's generally what evil gunslingers say in bad Western movies."

"Whatever. I'm not into detectives or cowboys. I'm all about monsters, serial killers and deviants."

A table of elderly women who'd been comparing the merits of Agatha Christie to some of the crop of cozy writers pinned Doug with their sharp gazes.

But Doug smiled at them and they stopped just short of reaching over to pinch his cheeks. They shifted their looks of disapproval to Annja.

Great. I attract the fallout. Annja ignored them and took her hot chocolate as the server returned. There were, of course, people who had placed orders ahead of Doug, but after Doug smiled at the server, they'd been forgotten.

Annja shook her head.

"What?" Doug asked.

"You."

"What about me?"

"You don't even realize how lucky you are?"

"What? Just because I can get hot chocolate really quick?"

"Everything comes easy to you."

Doug spooned up his whipped cream and sucked down a dollop. He looked pleased. "You don't come easy to me."

Annja looked at him.

"I meant that in a totally non-sexually-threatening way," he said quickly.

Be nice, Annja thought. And normally she was. She often saw Doug for dinner, drinks or a movie. The attraction wasn't there, as it was with Bart, so things were simpler.

Except for the work part.

Doug just couldn't help being Doug.

"Because I don't want you to kick my butt," Doug added.

"I'm not going to."

"Good." Doug looked relieved. "Because that would be *sooooo* embarrassing."

"Business," Annja said.

"Sure."

"Before you say no, I want you to hear me out."

"Okay."

"I want to go to Venice—"

"No."

Annja looked at him. "That was hearing me out?"

"Yep. Everything after the 'I want to go to Venice' part doesn't matter."

"It might matter."

"No, it won't. We don't have the money in the travel budget to get you to Venice."

Annja took a deep breath and decided to play hardball. "Doug—"

He rolled his eyes.

"Don't roll your eyes like that," she admonished.

"I don't know any other way."

"You owe me for that stupid phantom shark in the Calusa Indian piece."

"No. That wasn't the Calusa Indian piece. That was the phantom-shark piece. And now, thanks to my connections, we not only got a price break, but we got a good-looking fake shark, too."

Annja leaned back in the booth and crossed her arms. She noticed that the geeky-looking guy across the room was watching her again. When he saw that she was aware of him, he looked away.

"Don't go all passive-aggressive on me," Doug said. "You know I hate that."

"The annual schmooze-fest is coming up," Annja said. Every year Annja and the network's other show hosts were expected to attend a dog and pony show for the advertisers. Annja detested every second of every event.

"I know."

"I've been invited to a dig that same weekend. There could be a conflict."

"Annja," Doug whined, "don't do this."

"The dig is in El Salvador," Annja went on. "It's warm this time of year."

"The corporate event is only one day. The dig can live without you for one day."

"I'd lose two other days flying back and forth. All of a sudden we're up to three days."

Doug sighed. "Do you realize you're probably the only person in the world who doesn't give in to me?"

Annja didn't say anything.

"Why," he protested, "did I have to end up working with you?"

"Everybody has to have an Achilles heel."

"Don't get all sports medicine on me."

Annja started to explain.

Doug held up a hand. "Hold on, professor. I was just kidding. I know what an Achilles heel is. I saw Brad Pitt in *Troy*."

"I want to go to Venice," Annja said.

A serious expression filled Doug's face. "I'm sorry. There's no budget for this."

"What happened to the budget? I certainly didn't spend it down in Florida. I stayed with the professor at the dig. There wasn't even a hotel bill."

"I know, and I appreciate that." Doug shook his head. "I hate having to explain Kristie's expenses."

"Shouldn't be too hard," Annja said. "All you'd have to do is unfurl one of those posters she's done and flash her—"

The ladies at the Agatha Christie table were staring at her with full disdain.

Annja sighed.

Doug took a notepad out of his jacket pocket and wrote quickly. "I gotta try that poster thing. Could be offensive with the women in the room, but that pretty much sums up what we're selling with her, and why the advertisers pay so much for time during her segments."

That took Annja aback. "There's a difference in the advertising charges?"

Frowning, Doug said, "You weren't supposed to know that."

"I do now."

Doug drummed his fingers on the table. The server thought he wanted attention and came over immediately. He waved her off.

"Okay," he said, "tell me what you have in Venice and let's see if I can sell it. Vampires?"

"No," Annja said.

"Too bad. We can always push vampire material. Serial killer?"

"No."

"Mass murderer?"

"No."

"Mythological monster?"

"No."

Sighing, Doug asked, "What do you have?"

"Ghosts."

Doug shook his head and looked at her in disbelief. "I can't have heard you right. "Did you just say ghosts?"

"Ghosts can be monstrous," Annja said defensively. "Poltergeists are destructive."

"You don't believe in ghosts."

"I don't have to believe in them. Just hunt them. People love a good ghost hunt."

"What if you find a ghost?"

"I won't find a ghost. Ghosts don't exist."

Doug frowned.

"Okay, if I find a ghost I'll interview it or trap it. How does that sound?"

"Annja," Doug said patiently, "*everybody* does ghosts. We try to offer something a little different. You know, more sophisticated."

"More sophisticated?" Annja shot Doug a look of pure disgust. "My Calusa Indian piece now has a phantom shark in it."

"It's a very sophisticated phantom shark."

"Do you want to tell me how a phantom shark is different than a ghost?"

"Sure. It's a phantom, not a ghost. *Phantom* sounds much creepier than *ghost*. And it's a shark. People have a serious fear of sharks. That's why they do shark week on the Discovery Channel. Either a phantom or a shark would be enough to guarantee an audience. We've got both."

"I want to do this story, Doug. It would be easier to do it with the show's backing." Annja knew she could probably put the finances together to make the trip, but there was something magic about telling people that their story was going to be on television that opened a lot of doors. She could lie about it, of course, but once she started doing that and letting people down, word would get around.

"I wish I could help you." Doug looked uncomfortable.

Annja let Doug stew a little. At least she tried to. Doug, so far, appeared to be impervious to guilt. But there had to be a breaking point.

She gazed around the bar, hoping for inspiration. She saw the geeky guy was watching again. Probably listening in on our conversation, she thought.

Four men filed through the bar's front door. They wore long coats and Annja didn't recognize them. By the time that she did, it was too late.

Dieter Humbrecht dropped into the booth beside her and jammed a pistol into her ribs. "Hello again, Miss Creed."

Another man sat next to Doug.

"Wait a minute," Doug protested. "Nobody asked you to—" His face went white. His hands came up as if he were a victim in a bank holdup.

"Put your hands down," Dieter ordered. "You look like a moose."

Doug put his hands down. He looked worriedly at Annja and whispered, "He's got a gun in my ribs."

The man shoved hard, causing Doug to wince and jerk in pain. "Okay, okay," Doug said. "No talking. I get that."

With a quick movement, the man beside Doug lifted a quick elbow into Doug's nose and bashed his head back against the high booth seat. He yelped in surprise and pain.

"Okay," Dieter said. "Now we're going to get out of here. Miss Creed, you and I will go together. My friend will bring your friend. If you decide to be difficult, I'm going to have my friend shoot your friend in the head. Do you understand?"

"Yes," Annja said.

"Good." Dieter showed her a cold smile. "Now, let's go, shall we?"

# 21

The loud ring was shrill to Roux's ears. He groaned and pulled a pillow over his head. For the past six days, he'd competed in a Texas hold 'em tournament in Monaco. Things hadn't gone entirely as planned and he'd been beaten in the end by a young Englishwoman named Mai Lin Po.

The phone rang again.

"Aren't you going to get that?" a young woman asked.

"No," Roux answered.

"Someone calling at this time of night usually means trouble of some kind."

"Yes. And that's further inducement not to answer the thing."

"It could be a friend who needs help."

Roux didn't point out that he didn't keep friends. He had no use for them. He didn't know the woman well enough to tell her that, nor did he want to get to know her that well. They'd had a good time playing cards, and spending time together afterward had been an unexpected windfall.

The phone stopped ringing. Roux breathed a sigh of relief and his mind drifted back toward sleep. He still felt tipsy from the wine they'd had earlier.

Then he heard the woman speaking again.

"Hello?" She paused. "No, he's here." She laughed. "Me? I'm the woman who won two million dollars from him in a poker tournament." She paused again. "No, he didn't cry and this isn't a *mercy* anything. He's got natural charm." She listened. "Yes, I noticed that he was an older guy. I happen to like older guys." She laughed. "No, I'm not disappointed." A moment later, she laughed again. "Yes, I've had other lovers and I'm not easily impressed." She was silent for a moment. "On a scale of one to ten?"

Roux peeled the pillow from his face and gazed irritably at the woman as she chatted amiably on his satellite phone. He knew whom she was speaking to. "Enough already," he said.

Mai Lin Po was exquisite, barely over five feet tall, slender and in her early twenties. Her black hair was cut to her jawline and her almond eyes gleamed with amusement. She wore a tiny red robe with jeweled dragons stitched on it.

She came from a privileged background, and her father had bankrolled her first few poker tournaments until she'd gained enough experience to start winning some big purses. Now she lived on her own and had an agent to handle her appearances in the media.

She laughed again and told the caller to hold on a moment. Covering the mouthpiece, she said, "He says he knows you. His name is Garin."

"I'll talk to him." Roux dragged himself out of bed and pulled on a pair of pajama bottoms while he cradled the phone on his shoulder. "Hello."

"She says she took all your money at poker," Garin taunted.

Quashing the irritation that instantly rose in him, Roux said, "She did. She's quite good. Exceptional actually."

"Does it make you feel better to tell someone you were beaten by an exceptionally good player? I mean, you're still a loser," Garin said.

Looking back at the bed, Roux discovered the young woman was lying on her stomach and watching him, grinning widely.

"Well," Roux said, "I don't feel like a loser at the moment." He crossed to her and kissed her.

Turning away, he walked to the hotel balcony and stared out over the glittering night scape of Monaco. Yachts trolled the harbor and a few cars trailed along the mountain highways.

He studied his reflection, knowing the woman was staring at him. He didn't fool himself into thinking this was anything other than mutual curiosity. They would probably play each other again at some time, and it would help to know more about the psychology of the opponent.

"Why did you call?" Roux asked in Latin, using that language so the woman wouldn't understand his conversation.

"Can't I just call and say hello without having an ulterior motive?"

"You never have. Where are you?"

"Austria."

Roux detected a note of sadness in Garin's voice. That

was definitely unusual. In the hundreds of years that he had known Garin, the boy—and especially the man—had been too selfish and sullen to care about anyone but himself.

You can't say that, Roux told himself. He carried you out of an underground city when he didn't have to. Garin had also extracted a promise from Roux to help him at some point in the future. So far he hadn't asked for that help.

Roux wondered if tonight would be the night and what it would mean.

"What are you doing in Austria?" Roux couldn't help reacting to the melancholy and uncertainty in Garin's voice. Despite over five hundred years of trying to kill each other, there had been a time when Roux had raised Garin and taught him everything he knew.

Roux had never been a father before that time. He'd always managed to avoid such circumstances by design or by luck.

"I'm helping a friend," Garin said.

In all the years that Roux had known him, Roux had never heard Garin claim anyone as his friend. The words were filled with threat.

"Who's your friend?" Roux asked.

"You don't know her."

Her? Ah, the light begins to dawn. Roux smiled grimly. He'd never expected to see Garin capable of loving someone. Not with the horror that had been his childhood.

"If I don't know her," Roux said, "there's a good probability that I won't get to know her. So why call me?"

"My friend is interested in finding Mjolnir."

Roux was surprised. "Thor's hammer is a myth," he said.

"Is it? It seems that I've read something about it in those ancient books of yours."

The television flared to life behind Roux. The reflection looked gray in the window. Mai Lin had muted the voice.

"I doubt very much that whatever you're after is actually Thor's hammer."

"Did Mjolnir exist?"

"Something like it may have. The sword isn't the only powerful weapon that exists. That weapon has had different names."

"So you're not interested in this one?" Garin asked.

"If it were truly Thor's hammer, I would be."

Garin's voice turned harsh. "That would be too bad."

"Does your *friend* want to acquire Thor's hammer?" Roux asked.

"She only believes in the treasure that's supposed to accompany it."

"I would caution you that greedy friends aren't the best friends."

"The days when you could choose my friends are over."

Roux was silent for a moment. "Why did you call me? I hadn't known about your friend's desire before this. Now I have to admit to some curiosity."

"Stay out of this," Garin growled. "I called you because Annja is involved. I want you to keep her out of my way."

"I can't control her any more than I can control you," Roux said.

"Then you'd better find a way to convince her. If you don't, there's every likelihood she's going to get hurt."

The phone clicked dead in Roux's ear.

He returned to the bed and put the satellite phone back on the nightstand.

"Problem?" Mai Lin asked.

"Family squabble."

"Was that your son on the phone?"

Roux lay back on the bed. "Yes." It was as good an answer as any.

"He sounds interesting. Very confident."

"Arrogant."

"Then I'd say he takes after his father." Mai Lin looked at him. "Are you going to see him?"

"I don't know. We haven't been close in a long time."

Mai Lin looked sympathetic. "That's sad."

"Some days," Roux said. "Some days it is."

GARIN CLOSED HIS PHONE and put it on the bar in front of him. Listening to the blues music around him, he regretted his choice of drinking establishments. But if he'd gone to a heavy metal bar he wouldn't have been able to have the conversation with Roux. The calm exterior contained a dark wood interior that had fit his mood.

You could have called from your car, he thought, staring at his reflection in the mirror on the wall that ran the length of the bar.

Behind him, several couples swayed to the whiskey-throated crooning of the lead singer. Other couples sat at the small tables and talked over candlelight.

The city had changed dramatically since Garin had sat at a similar table and enjoyed Kikka Schluter's company. But in his mind it only seemed like yesterday.

"Would you like another?"

Garin looked up at the young bartender. He had a shaved head, a goatee, tattoos up to his chin and several piercings.

"Another drink?" The bartender pointed at Garin's empty glass.

Garin nodded and pushed the glass forward.

Amber liquid sloshed into the glass.

"Bad call?" the bartender asked.

Garin knew the man didn't really care, that he was only making conversation. A small time investment to earn a larger tip.

"Difficult," Garin admitted.

"Girlfriend?"

Garin thought about that. He could have just said yes and been done with the conversation. But he said, "My father."

"Ah, bummer." The bartender leaned on the bar and shook his head. "The relationship with your dad can wear you out. Both of you have these expectations, and both of you—even though you didn't plan on it—end up living in different worlds."

Although he and Roux were not related by blood, Garin found that the assessment fit their relationship more closely than he would have expected.

"But I'll tell you something else, too," the bartender said. "I lost my dad last year. His heart gave out. We fought for years over what we both thought I should do with my life. Never agreed. But the thing is, now that he's gone, I really miss him. Once they're gone, they're gone. You can't bring them back. Might be something you want to consider every now and again." He threw his bar towel over his shoulder and went down the bar to tend to a new customer.

Left alone with his thoughts, Garin wondered what would happen if Roux were gone. He'd tried to kill the old man on more than one occasion. And Roux had returned the favor.

But what would happen if Roux were really gone?

Don't think, he told himself. You're not a philosopher like that old man. Life is to be lived. Get on with living it.

But he knew that seeing Kikka in the condition she was in—old and frail—had him thinking such things. He was going to be better off getting this thing done and getting away from her. Leaving before he accomplished that was out of the question, though. He felt he owed her that.

He asked for his check, then added a generous tip and went back out into the night. He needed to get moving, to shake loose all the thinking and just react.

He didn't believe Roux would be able to dissuade Annja Creed from following whatever trail she was on if she was already involved. During his time with her, he'd come to grudgingly admire her.

Like him, she didn't suit Roux's idea of what she should be, but he knew she came closer to the mark. It was just one more thing to dislike about her.

# 22

"Couldn't we talk now?" Doug asked. "I mean, it couldn't hurt, right? If you play this right, you can get more money than just robbing us. I don't know about Annja, but all you're going to get out of me is plastic. I never carry cash."

Annja felt sorry for Doug. He was entirely out of his element. She didn't know if he'd even been mugged before, much less taken by force at gunpoint, and he definitely wasn't the confrontational type.

"They're not going to rob us." Annja stood out in front of the building. The winter wind swept through the heart of Manhattan and pulled at her calf-length coat. Coming off Long Island Sound by way of the Atlantic Ocean, the wind was bitter and piercing.

"Kidnapping's not very smart," Doug said. "You can get the death penalty or life imprisonment for that."

"Not if you don't leave any witnesses," one of Dieter's men said. "And especially if you don't leave a body in enough pieces to be identified."

"Okay, that is not a happy thought." Doug wasn't smiling anymore. He appeared positively glum. He looked around. "Do we have to stand out in the cold?"

The man standing behind Doug slapped him on the back of the head hard enough to cause him to stumble.

Doug glared at the man. Then he looked at Annja. "Are you sure this isn't some kind of trick to convince me to get you the money to go to Venice? Because if it is, it's not working."

Annja kept looking out into the street where cabs glided through the falling snow. She didn't know whether to hope for a police officer or not.

Having Doug in the middle of everything hampered her. If she fought free, she was certain Dieter would kill Doug as an object lesson. Or out of spite if she got away.

Dieter focused on her. The pistol bulged in his pocket.

"You're planning on going to Venice, Miss Creed?" Dieter asked.

Annja didn't say anything.

"Mr. Morrell, was Miss Creed trying to make arrangements through you to get to Venice?" Dieter asked the question without looking at Doug.

"Uh…" Doug responded.

"Mr. Morrell, if you attempt to lie to me, I'm going to kill you right here."

"Yep." Doug nodded vehemently. "She was all over me about wanting to go to Venice. Couldn't say enough about it. Wheedled. Pressured. Guilted me. I sat down at the table and she started in about Venice."

"Shut up," Dieter commanded.

"Okay." Doug grew quiet, but it was hard on him.

"Why were you going to Venice, Miss Creed?"

"I got this one," Doug volunteered. "She was going to investigate ghosts."

"Ghosts?"

"Yeah. They don't have any vampire stories or serial-killer legends in Venice. And we don't just make stuff up. Okay, maybe we *enhance* things a little, but we do claim creative license in the show. Right before every episode."

Dieter frowned.

"You see," Doug went on, "those are some of the best standby—"

To Annja's left, a cargo van pulled around the corner and slowed behind a cab just starting to pull away from the curb. The van was coming to a stop in front of them. One of Dieter's men stepped up to meet it.

Anxiety filled Annja. If they were placed in the van, their chances of escape would lessen. Now would be the best time to escape.

A muffled sound came from behind her, then a growled oath in German.

Turning, Annja saw the small man she'd noticed earlier in Sherlock's standing with his notebook computer case in both hands. The mercenary standing closest to the man was rubbing his head and looking thoroughly irritated.

"What's going on?" Dieter demanded.

"The little idiot struck me with his computer."

They spoke in German, but Annja understood enough to follow the conversation.

"Uh-oh," the stranger said.

"What do you think you're doing?" the mercenary demanded.

The little man closed his eyes and swatted at the man again. This time his feet shot out from under him on the icy sidewalk and he fell headlong toward the mercenary. Dieter's man grabbed him out of self-preservation.

Taking advantage of the situation, Annja caught Dieter's gun hand, trapped it against his body and kicked his feet out from under him. He went down face-first on the sidewalk. She helped him along. The impact was a meaty smack.

Still bent at the waist, Annja kicked backward, catching the man next to Dieter full in the face. He was dazed by the kick even before he slammed into the side of the van.

Several passersby made sure they kept on passing. No one even asked what was going on.

Annja grabbed Dieter's head with both hands and bounced it off the sidewalk again. If he wasn't out, he was at least too dazed to show any interest in the fight for a moment.

She spun toward the third man, feeling her feet slide treacherously out from under her. Catching the man's arm as he freed his pistol, she slipped her thumb between his and the pistol, then grabbed hold of his little finger with her other hand. She bent both. The pistol dropped free as one of the captured digits broke.

Flailing a hand, she caught the back of the man's foot and yanked. He sat down hard as Annja pushed herself to her knees. Before he could move, she punched him in the temple and he turned limp at once.

Seeing what had happened to his partners, the fourth man tried to free himself from the little man, who was hanging on to his gun hand with all his strength.

The van door opened behind Annja as she got to her feet. Standing, she lurched toward the van. She hit the door with both hands, knocking it into the man's head as he tried to climb out. She managed to grab the door and swing it closed twice more. The man slumped, half in and half out of the vehicle.

Annja's breath came out in rapid clouds. Looking back, she saw the little man still maintained a death grip on the remaining mercenary. The mercenary finally backhanded the man and knocked him to the ground. He swung his pistol toward Annja.

She caught the pistol by the barrel in her left hand, yanked down and squeezed hard. The man fired. The bullet struck the sidewalk and ricocheted into the van's tire, blowing it out and causing the vehicle to sag heavily to one side.

Still holding the pistol barrel after preventing it from blowing back to chamber another round, Annja drew her right leg back and delivered a roundhouse kick that knocked the man senseless. The blow almost knocked her from her feet.

Holding on to the pistol, Annja reversed it, then worked the action and sent the empty brass spinning through the air. She released the slide and stripped the top round from the magazine, chambering it.

Swinging around, she saw that all five men were unconscious or dazed.

"Wow," Doug said, gazing around. "I can't believe you just did that."

Annja pressed the gun barrel into the back of Dieter's neck. "Hands out. Like you're making a snow angel."

Dieter complied.

Taking the man's pistol from his coat pocket, she looked up at Doug, who stood idly by watching in stunned fascination.

"That was terrific!" Doug enthused. "Why can't we

get something like that on *Monsters?* This is like ultimate fighting!"

"What are you doing?" Annja snapped. "This is the part where you call the police."

"Huh? Oh, yeah." Doug reached into his pocket, pulled out his phone and dialed 911.

"YOU WERE LUCKY."

Annja didn't say anything. She disagreed, though. She'd trained for years to handle herself. Of course, she'd never planned on having to do it on a regular basis. But the training was there.

She stood under the building canopy with a cup of hot chocolate in her hands. Bart and Doug stood beside her. Thankfully Bart was blocking some of the wind.

"It wasn't luck," Doug said. "You should have seen her, man. It was a Jet Li moment. She was all over the place. Really fast. Those guys never had a chance."

Bart looked at Doug. "You're not helping."

"Oh." Doug looked chagrined. "Sorry. But it was totally cool."

Dieter and his men were handcuffed and loaded into the backs of police cars. Other officers interviewed a few witnesses.

"Five guys." Bart shook his head. "Do you even know what these guys want from you?"

"They didn't know she wanted to go to Venice," Doug said. "When they found that out, they were really interested."

Annja shot Doug a look. "You're *not* helping."

Doug frowned. "I'm confused. The bad guys weren't supposed to know you wanted to go to Venice. Now you don't want the good guys to know, either?"

"*Not* helping," Annja said.

Pointing back inside the building, Doug said, "I'm just gonna go get a cup of coffee."

Bart looked at Annja. "What's in Venice?"

"I don't know."

Sighing in exasperation, Bart said, "You held something back on me, didn't you?"

"Maybe a little," Annja admitted. She knew that reticence on her part made Bart's job harder, but telling him everything made hers harder.

"What?"

"The part about the treasure."

Bart blew his breath out in a big cloud. "Tell me about the treasure."

"Do you want to know about Thor, too?"

"Is Thor Dieter's connection?"

"Thor. The thunder god."

Frowning, Bart said, "The Marvel Comics superhero? The guy with the long blond hair and the big hammer?"

"That was a different Thor."

"There was a *real* Thor?"

"That depends on your definition of real," Annja said.

"QUIT," BART SAID a few minutes later. "You're making my head hurt. I liked this better when Fellini was maybe killed by a rival archaeologist or someone who was after some kind of priceless object he was carrying. Writing this up is going to be a nightmare because there's nothing concrete about this. It's all guesswork."

Annja hadn't told Bart about the mosaic, only that she'd received an e-mail from Mario that she hadn't known about earlier.

"These guys killed Fellini over a treasure that might or might not exist?" Bart asked.

"I think they believe it exists," Annja said. "Otherwise they wouldn't have killed Mario and come looking for me."

"So they came after Fellini for the map?"

"I don't know."

"Where's the treasure?"

"I don't know."

"If you have to guess," Bart encouraged.

"I don't guess," Annja reminded him. "Not about my work. Not until I'm closer to knowing what's going on."

Bart shook his head. "Do you know when the last time was I had to work a homicide starring a guy that got killed for a treasure map?"

"No."

"*Never* is when. This is something I'd expect in an Edgar Allan Poe story."

Annja was quiet for a moment, but she couldn't hold in the pain, confusion and anger. She faced Bart. "Whether it sounds like a Poe story or not, this is *not* my fault. It wasn't Mario's fault, either. Dieter and his men killed Mario because of what he'd learned. All Mario ever wanted to do was find something important, some hidden piece of history that no one had ever found before. That's all anyone who works in this field wants to do. There's no crime in accomplishing that." She turned and walked away before he could answer.

"Annja," Bart called after her.

"I know, I know. Don't leave town, right?" Annja didn't look back at him. She didn't want him to see the tears. She was tired and she wanted to rest.

One of the policemen working the scene called out to Bart. In the reflection in the window glass facing the street, Annja saw Bart hesitate for a moment, then go to the police officer.

She hunkered in against the window, ducking out of the wind as much as she could. Freezing and unhappy, she was feeling totally frustrated because she was certain the events of the past few minutes hadn't changed Doug's mind about Venice.

Laying her head back against the glass, Annja tried very hard not to think about anything.

"Excuse me. Miss Creed?"

Opening her eyes, Annja saw the little man from Sherlock's standing in front of her. He held his coat collar up to block the wind from his face. A woolen cap covered his head but came to a blunt point that made him look slightly ridiculous.

"Hi," Annja said. "I'm sorry. I never did thank you for saving our lives."

The man looked embarrassed. "It wasn't much. Not compared to what you did."

"If you hadn't done what you did, I wouldn't have had the chance to do anything."

Preening a little, the man smiled. "You're very gracious." He glanced over his shoulder. "I couldn't help hearing you talking to that policeman. You said you had to get to Venice?"

Curious, Annja nodded. "That's right."

"I can make that happen," the man said. "If you'll allow me."

Suspicion clouded Annja's thoughts. "How?"

"My card." The man made it appear with a flourish.

Annja tugged her glove off and took the card, tilting it so she could read it in the light.

Stanley Younts
Author

For a moment, Annja couldn't place the name. Then it clicked into place. She looked at the man. "I know you."

Younts smiled shyly and pushed his glasses up his nose. "I'm surprised. Have you read any of my books?"

"No, I haven't. I'm sorry," Annja said.

Younts shrugged. "It's no big deal. It's just that a lot of people have."

"I don't read much fiction."

Annja realized that over the past seven years, Stanley Younts had been one of the best-selling novelists of all time. All of his books dealt with adventure and intrigue, with an interesting historical background.

"I scheduled a meeting with Doug this afternoon," Stanley said. "That's how I happened to be in Sherlock's. That's also why I was staring at you. I thought I recognized you, but I couldn't be sure. You look different on television. Or maybe after seeing the shows you've done, I just don't expect to see you in ordinary environs."

"Why did you want to meet with Doug?"

"I wanted to know if you would help me out with some research for my new book. I'd heard you helped with research."

"Not that kind of research. I sometimes help museums, auction houses and independent collectors," Annja replied.

"Fiction and nonfiction, we work with the same histories. We just deliver what we learn and what we think in different ways." Stanley smiled. "I just wanted to spend a few days with you. Get to know what you do and how you think. Then I'd reinvent it for the heroine I plan on writing about."

"I don't think what I do is all that interesting."

Stanley looked around at the crime scene. "I wouldn't say that."

"This," Annja stated emphatically, "is *not* normal."

"I'd hope not. I like to research characters I'm going to write about. My next novel is going to feature a female archaeologist who finds an alien artifact."

"Alien? As in otherworldly?"

"Exactly. It opens up a wormhole to another world, and she gets a chance to study the archaeology there, as well."

"Actually," Annja said, "I don't believe in aliens."

"I do," Stanley replied. "A lot of people do. I'm going to write a best seller that deals with genetic manipulation through the ages by an alien caretaker group that died thousands of years ago on a distant world. I've mentioned it to a few people in Hollywood, and there's already talk of a movie."

"Congratulations. But everything you've talked about—the genetic manipulations and aliens—isn't in my job description."

"I just need to see you in action. Maybe ask a few questions."

Annja tried to be polite. Stanley had risked his life in an attempt to help her and Doug. That kind of effort needed to be recognized. "This really isn't the time."

"I was going to suggest we could talk on the jet."

"What jet?"

"My private jet. I flew in from Montana this morning for the meeting. You said you wanted to go to Venice. I heard Doug tell you he couldn't make that happen. Well, I can."

# 23

"Will it hurt?"

Erene Skujans looked into the child's eyes and thought of lying.

The girl was six, tiny and frail. She had big eyes, but they were made even bigger by the fear inside her. She cradled her right forearm, which was swollen and discolored.

Even without X-rays, Erene could see that the arm was broken and badly set. The mother had waited for days before seeking help. By now the bones had attempted healing, but they were healing badly. If they healed the way they were presently set, the girl wouldn't get much use from the arm in years to come.

It needed to be rebroken and reset. There would be considerable pain because of the stressed tissues around it.

Not telling the truth would have been the easiest, but Erene hated thinking of the repercussions. Few in the village trusted her as it was. She shouldn't have cared.

If they didn't trust her, they wouldn't come to her. There would be no more calls in the middle of the night to go birth a baby, no more interruptions during a meal to sew up a man's foot or leg where he'd mishandled an ax, no more infections to look at or warding off curses placed on one member of the village by another.

That would have been easier. And she knew how to lie. She was one of the best many people had ever seen.

But, in the end, that wasn't how her grandmother had trained her. As a hedge witch, the keeper of arcane health and lore, she was supposed to be a good force that the community could trust.

So she told the truth to the little girl lying on the table in the small house that had belonged to Erene's grandmother.

"Yes," Erene said, "it will hurt."

The child cried and tried to get away, rolling into her mother, who sat at the table's side. Tears rolled down the girl's face, and shrieks filled the small living room that doubled as Erene's surgery. The mother wept, too, but she didn't say anything. Nor did she try to take the daughter away.

Erene sat quietly by the table in the chair her grandmother used to occupy. If her grandmother had been here dealing with this, the arm would have already been fixed. But she'd had the complete trust of the village. They had come to her grandmother with everything. Most of the people living there now had been birthed by her.

Being inactive was hard for Erene. Especially knowing that Mario was dead somewhere and that she would never again see him. She felt tears prick the backs of her eyes.

"You can do this, yes?" the mother asked in English.

"I can," Erene said. They spoke English to her as if she

was an outsider even though she'd been born in the village like most of them. But she'd left when she'd been seventeen, making her way first to Riga for a few years, then on into Europe.

Desperation lit the mother's eyes. "You can take away the pain, yes?"

"I can."

The mother's mouth trembled. Erena nodded, more to herself than anyone else. "I can."

"Then…please."

Erene looked into the woman's eyes as the little girl shrieked louder and tried to hold her mother even more tightly.

"Please," the mother repeated.

Erene opened the bag her grandmother had always kept ready. She rummaged inside and found the pouch of leaves she needed. Taking a pestle and mortar from the shelves built into the wall, she crushed the leaves until the sap gathered at the bottom.

Working carefully, she heated the sap over a candle. Like the rest of the village, the cottage had no electricity. When the sap began to bubble and the astringent smoke had started to make her nose burn, then tingle and start to go numb, she put the leaves on a cheesecloth, then poured the sap over them again.

Carrying the cloth by the ends, avoiding the sap and the leaves, Erene returned to the table. She placed the poultice on the child's neck.

"This will take the pain away," Erene said calmly. She made herself smile even though she couldn't stop thinking about killing Wolfram Schluter.

The girl started to reach for the poultice.

Erene captured her young patient's hands. "No. You mustn't touch the medicine. Okay?"

The girl nodded, but already her eyelids were growing heavy as her skin absorbed the narcotic and flushed her carotid arteries with it. Erene knew she didn't have to worry about the air passageways getting swollen. One of the herb's effects was to facilitate breathing.

When she judged the girl was sedated enough, Erene removed the medicine and put it aside. Later she would bury them so no animal would be tempted to eat them. Consuming the leaves could prove lethal.

Glassy-eyed, the girl lay back on the table, suspended between life and death.

"Is she all right?" the mother asked.

"She's asleep," Erene said.

"Those plants are dangerous. We are taught to be careful around them because they can cause death."

"They can. But they can also be used to take pain away. Don't you know what they're called?"

The woman shook her head. Turning her head and catching the candlelight as she did revealed the old bruise under her left eye.

"They're called yellow monkshood." Erene couldn't believe how little the people in the village knew about the natural world around them. Most struggled to save enough money to buy American jeans and music from the Russian and Chinese black marketers in Riga.

"But she's all right?"

"She's going to be fine. I'm going to let her sleep for a little longer, to make sure the herbs do what they're supposed to."

"The hedge witch taught you this?"

"My grandmother taught me this," Erene corrected. She hadn't realized how much her grandmother had taught her until she got out in the world that existed beyond the village. When she'd lived with her grandmother, she just accepted that her grandmother knew so much just because she did.

It wasn't until she was teaching herself her second vocation—the one that had allowed her to live if not in luxury then at least well in many of the cities she'd lived in—that she realized how much training her grandmother had given her. Erene had adapted easily and learned quickly, impressing the people she worked with.

"I meant no disrespect," the woman said.

"She took care of this village all her life."

"I know. We miss her."

But not enough to see that her grave is kept clean, Erene thought. She pushed away her anger. She was in a bad mood, about to do something that wasn't easy, and she wanted to take it out on someone.

"How was your daughter's arm broken?"

The woman hesitated.

Erene knew the woman was choosing her lie and was disgusted.

"She fell," the woman said. "It was most unfortunate."

"Fell?" Erene put as much disbelief into that one word as she could muster.

The woman nodded but wouldn't meet Erene's eyes. "She was caring for the goats. There was ice." She shrugged.

Erene caught the woman's chin in her hand and turned her head to better observe the black eye. "I suppose you slipped, too."

"Please," the woman whispered. Gently, she pulled free of Erene's grip. "I don't want any more trouble. My daughter and I have enough trouble in our lives."

"Your husband did this," Erene stated.

"Please treat my daughter."

Erene took a deep breath. "I don't want to heal her just to have her hurt again. Do you understand?" She spoke in Latvian now, and didn't even notice until she'd asked the question.

"He has a lot of anger in him," the woman said. "Things are not easy for him."

"Things aren't easy for anybody. There's no excuse for this."

The woman stroked her sleeping daughter's head. She wiped the tears from her face with her shirtsleeve.

"Where is your husband?" Erene asked.

Shaking her head, the woman made no reply.

"My grandmother," Erene said, knowing she spoke the truth, "wouldn't tolerate something like this."

"I know," the woman said. "She would threaten to put a curse on my husband. But she isn't here now, and he doesn't believe in things the way most of us do." She paused. "Not everyone believed in the hedge—in your grandmother."

The words cut into Erene. Not just the narrowly avoided slight against her grandmother, but the reminder that she, too, had abandoned her grandmother's ways.

"My husband," the woman went on, "is from Russia. When he first got here, I thought he was just a soldier who had seen too much fighting."

Erene knew that those men still wandered into the countryside. There were fewer now that Russia had adopted Western ways, but it still happened.

"Now I think he is just a criminal who wanted a place to hide." The woman shrugged sadly. "All the pretty words he gave me are gone these days. He works when he wishes to, but my daughter and I never see any of the money. If my friends didn't give us food to eat, we would starve."

Erene cursed, and the harsh words caused the woman to flinch.

When her grandmother had lived in the village, nothing like this would have happened. Her grandmother had involved herself with the lives of the villagers. They had respected and, in part, feared her.

"You can't have one without the other, Erene," the old woman would tell her. "Respect and fear almost always go together."

And the hedge witch's healing powers are nothing without the ability to punish, Erene thought. She focused on the woman again.

"I will heal your daughter, but I don't want her hurt again," she told the woman. "Do you understand?"

The woman nodded.

"Then you will tell me where he is when we are finished here."

Slowly, uncertainly, the woman nodded.

Taking a deep breath, Erene turned back to the child. Then she reached over and calmly rebroke the sleeping girl's arm.

# 24

"I don't think I've ever seen a woman pack faster," Stanley commented at Annja's hotel. He stood looking down at the new suitcase she'd purchased only that morning. "My mother takes at least ten suitcases every time we go somewhere."

"That's because I don't live here. I came here to stay out of harm's way." Annja worked as quickly as she could. She'd gotten permission from Bart to go home to relax for a bit, then he wanted to meet with her and get a written statement. She turned her attention to the mosaic Mario had sent her.

Stanley approached the table and peered over the tops of his glasses at the mosaic lying there. "This is some puzzle."

"Yes. It was." Annja scooped the tessera into a reinforced mailing package she'd picked up at a convenience store on her way to her hotel.

"You solved it?"

"I did."

"Want to explain what it means?"

"Not exactly." Annja sealed the envelope and addressed it to herself care of Mailboxes & Stuff. She planned to leave it with the concierge to have it couriered over. Dieter's men were all in custody, but there might have been a few left.

"This is why you want to go to Venice?"

Feeling a little guilty, Annja turned to him. "Stanley, I have to tell you something."

He looked nervous. "Sure."

"I had a friend named Mario Fellini. Those men who attempted to kidnap us at Sherlock's were probably the ones that killed him."

"Wow."

"There's more," Annja said. "This *puzzle* is part of the reason Mario was killed and why they were looking for me."

Stanley nodded.

"Mario left a message for me in the puzzle. I'm going to Venice to find out how all this started."

"You're looking for whatever he thought he found."

"I am. But what you need to know is that these people are dangerous. Dieter and his buddies are mercenaries. Professional killers for hire."

"I know what mercenaries are. I wrote a book about corporate mercenaries just last year."

Terrific, Annja thought. "I appreciate you flying me to Venice. I really do. But you need to know that if you go with me, your life is going to be in danger."

Stanley smiled. "Cool."

Annja shook her head. "Not cool. You'd be better off dropping me at Venice."

"That wouldn't be very gallant."

"Gallantry has killed a lot of people," Annja said. "But I'm truly sincere when I tell you that if someone shoots you between the eyes, you're going to be dead."

Stanley paled a little at that. "It'll be okay. I've done missions with the CIA, the Army Rangers, and SWAT teams in Philadelphia. Those carried a lot of danger, too."

"There's a difference between me and those units," Annja said. "When they got into trouble, they had people they could call. I don't."

"It'll be okay. I can handle myself. I've had self-defense and gun classes."

And that's why you attacked an armed man with your notebook computer?

"If you want the jet," Stanley said, "I'm the only game in town."

Annja sighed, then grabbed her suitcase and headed out with Stanley Younts, intrepid writer, at her heels.

STANLEY'S PRIVATE LIMOUSINE waited in front of the hotel. The driver took Annja's suitcase and stowed it in the trunk. She kept her backpack with her as she crawled into the backseat. She slid over to the other side of the car.

Snow followed Stanley in as he took his seat. He took out a BlackBerry and attached a small keyboard. "Do you need anything for the trip?"

"Like what?"

"Supplies. Weapons."

"You can have them delivered to the jet before we take off?"

"I think so. We can ask and see."

"How can you get weapons here in Manhattan?"

"I did a book involving the arms industry and the private-security sector. You wouldn't believe how much firepower those guys can move when the price is right."

"No," Annja replied. "But thanks anyway." She slipped her computer out of her backpack and opened it up to rest on her knees.

Stanley reached out and pressed a section on the seat. The seat cushion flopped out and revealed a table with Internet hookups.

"It's all wired into the limo's onboard satellite system," Stanley explained.

In disbelief, Annja tugged on the Ethernet cable and it spooled out easily. She plugged it into the back of her computer and saw the Internet accessibility icon come up at once.

"Writing books got you all of this?" Annja asked.

"When you get lucky or do it right, being an author is quite lucrative. My agent and publishers tell me I've done both."

ANNJA CHECKED the message boards, then started cruising the Internet. She referenced Mjolnir and followed the web of information that spun out of that. Even though she didn't know what she was looking for, she'd always found research to be a good investment. It was better to search wider and deeper than a topic suggested. Connections were made up of what she knew, so in order to better connect, she had to know more.

Her cell phone buzzed for attention while the limo driver slid quietly and quickly through the Manhattan night. The number was listed. Annja recognized it as coming from France. Although she knew a few people in Paris through her archaeological connections, she only knew of one person who would call this late at night without a prior arrangement.

"Hello," Annja answered.

"Hello, Annja. This is Roux. How are you?" He sounded upbeat and jovial, which wasn't normal.

"This is unusual," she said.

"What?" Some of the snide snarkiness she knew him capable of returned.

"You calling me. Usually I have to initiate contact, then you point out—subtly, of course—that all I'm offering is an unwanted interruption."

"That's not what—"

"And I'll go ahead and take this time to point out that your subtlety rivals that of an agitated porcupine."

"I didn't call to be subjected to insults," Roux said.

Annja sighed. She was upset and she knew it. Viewing Mario's savaged body yesterday had been hard. The last thing she needed was Roux calling her to tell her that there was something he needed help with.

"I'm sorry," she said. "I'm in a bad mood."

"Well, I certainly didn't have anything to do with it."

Not this time, Annja thought. "Why did you call?"

"I was just thinking about you."

"You'll have to excuse me. I was unprepared. I'm going to need to roll my pant legs up if we're going to get deep in horse manure that quickly." Annja was aware that Stanley was watching her but she ignored it.

"I could be thinking about you."

Annja glanced at the time in the lower right corner of her computer screen. She did the time conversion, adding six hours. "It's almost three o'clock in the morning there. Want to try again?"

Roux sighed. "Dealings with you are fraught with disenchantment, do you know that?"

"Thank you. The feeling is mostly mutual." Annja scanned the available Web pages and knew that if she couldn't narrow down her search it was going to be like searching for a needle in an incredibly huge haystack.

"What are you currently working on?"

Annja sat up a little straighter. Roux wasn't just snooping around for casual information. He was deliberately searching for something.

"The Calusa Indians," she replied. "The indigenous tribes that lived along Florida's western coast and inland waterways."

"I know who they are," Roux snapped irritably. "I was there with Ponce de León when he was looking for the Fountain of Youth."

The announcement stunned Annja. Although she hadn't known him for long, and only as intimately as he would allow because he was a very private person and didn't intend to be turned into a history lesson for her, it was easy to forget that he had lived through so much history.

More than five hundred years, she reminded herself. Roux had never given any clue as to how long he'd actually lived.

"You never mentioned that before," she said.

"It's not something that's likely to come up in casual conversation, now, is it?"

Growing a little angry at his abrupt treatment of her, Annja said, "I'm busy. Either get to the point or I'm getting off the phone. I've got things I'm doing."

Roux grumbled. "What do you know about Mjolnir?"

Startled again, Annja looked down at the computer screen. The Web page was all about Norse legends, featuring Thor.

"Mjolnir who?" Annja stalled. Even as she said it, she realized how weak her response was.

Roux cursed. "I've talked to asses that weren't as dense as you pretend to be. If you persist—"

Annja broke the connection, took a deep breath and placed the phone on the seat beside her. Outside the tinted windows, Manhattan was cloaked in unnatural whiteness that battled the night. Fat flakes swirled through the air in front of the lighted signs that marked the way to LaGuardia. The windshield wipers moved like metronomes, but she couldn't hear them in the soundproofed compartment.

"IS EVERYTHING all right?" Stanley asked after a few minutes had passed.

"Everything's fine." Annja took a deep breath and let it out.

Stanley hesitated, then obviously couldn't let the situation go. "I don't mean to pry, but it sounds like you're a little stressed."

"Maybe a little," Annja said.

"Is it the detective? Because if it is, I have a very good attorney who could—"

"No, it's not the detective. It's just someone I know."

"Oh."

The phone rang again.

Annja glanced at Caller ID and saw that it was from Roux again. She let the phone ring twice more, tempted to let the answering service deal with it, before she punched the Talk button. The last thing she needed to do was deal with the riddle wrapped in a conundrum and covered by guile that Roux represented.

"What?" she demanded.

"We got disconnected," Roux said warily. "I've never trusted these electronic inconveniences. They drop signals at all the wrong—"

"It wasn't a dropped signal," Annja interrupted. "I hung up on you."

*"What?"* Roux thundered.

Annja hung up on him again and focused on the computer screen.

DESPITE HER BEST ATTEMPTS, Annja couldn't focus on the computer or the Web pages she accessed and downloaded as image documents for later review.

Stanley looked at her sympathetically. "It's not going well, is it?"

Exasperated, Annja wanted to tell Stanley that the problem wasn't anything to worry about. Instead, all the tension of the past two days, the anger and sadness over Mario's death and the unknown nature of what might be waiting for her in Venice made her emotions come boiling to the surface.

There was something about Stanley Younts's calm demeanor and honest brown eyes behind his glasses that drew her frustration out.

She said, "He never listens to me. He always thinks he knows best, and that he knows more than I do. He's unwilling to give me credit for being able to think for myself." She let out a long breath. "What he doesn't get is that I would like to just sit down and talk to him. I'm well aware that he knows more than I do. About a lot of things. Instead, he's got to be all mysterious about things. Like not telling me why he's calling tonight."

"Maybe," Stanley suggested, "he just cares about you."

"I'm not even sure about that," Annja said. "I mean, sometimes I think he does, but other times I'm just as sure that the only reason he even acknowledges that I'm alive is because he feels like he owes me something."

Stanley nodded. "I know the feeling. Fathers are tough."

"Fathers?" Annja looked at him.

"That's who you were talking to, right?"

Annja tried to answer but Stanley cut her off.

"Take my dad, for instance," Stanley said. "He was a corporate guy. One of the youngest CEOs ever in the entertainment community. A real mover and shaker in Hollywood. He was a guy that got things done."

"But I'm not—"

Stanley seemed lost in thought. "It was hard growing up and meeting his expectations. I sucked at baseball. I mean, look at me. I was too short and small. But did that keep him from hiring personal trainers who worked me every day till I thought I was going to die? No. He just kept on—"

"Stanley," Annja said loud enough to get his attention. He blinked at her.

"I haven't been talking to my father."

"Oh, a significant other. That can be bad, too, even though I've never—"

"Not a significant other, either. He's my—" Annja tried to think how best to describe Roux "—mentor."

"Mentor—got it." Stanley looked sheepish. "Look, that stuff about fathers? The media doesn't really know how I got along with my dad before he died. I'd rather not see that in print anywhere."

"I won't tell a soul." Annja glanced at the cell phone, fully expecting it to have rung again before now. Instead, it lay there quietly.

"The really weird part?" Stanley said. "I didn't realize how much I loved him and needed him until he was gone. My first book hadn't even been published."

"I'm sorry," Annja said.

Stanley swallowed hard. "Maybe I'm a little naïve. People tell me that all the time. They don't expect that in me after they read my books. But I am." He sighed. "I guess what I'm trying to say is that maybe if I hadn't over-reacted to my dad trying to help me—and I have to admit neither one of us were really skilled at being parent or child—then maybe I wouldn't have lost all that time with him." He paused. "It's just something to think about."

Annja glanced at the cell phone, which continued not to ring.

"If he thought enough to call at this time of night and interrupt whatever he's doing," Stanley suggested, "don't you think it's possible that he does care?"

"You're right." Annja picked up the phone.

Stanley smiled.

Still, Annja struggled with the idea of calling. It was like admitting defeat. She couldn't get around that. Finally, filled with curiosity as to why Roux had called, she pulled up his number and called.

"You'll feel better," Stanley said.

Annja hoped so. She was thinking that maybe she shouldn't have been so short with Roux because it wasn't his fault, but things were piling up too quickly. It was as if the stakes rose with every tick of the clock.

The phone rang again and again. There was no answer.

"C'mon, Roux, pick up," she mumbled.

But he didn't. Instead, Call Waiting signaled an incoming call. Glancing at the information window, Annja saw that it was Bart. She debated picking up, then decided it was better to be informed. They'd almost arrived at La-Guardia. In another few minutes, she'd be out of New York.

"Hello," she said.

# 25

Wolfram Schluter eased his car into the parking spot near the refurbished manufacturing plant in downtown Vienna. The building had originally housed a munitions plant during World War I, then again in World War II. In between it had produced canned goods.

Twelve years ago it had become a club. Three years ago, without his grandmother's knowledge, Schluter had bought a major share in the club and used it to run his designer drug business. He'd renamed it Club Ripper.

Two men immediately stepped out of the security office overlooking the parking area. They were there to keep the riffraff moving along, and to provide security for the club's guests. People who got mugged tended not to come back, and Vienna still had problems with thieves and armed robbers. Some of them were Schluter's best customers.

However, whenever Schluter was parked at the club, their job was to protect his car. He got out and locked the car with the electronic keypad, then set the alarm.

"Good evening, Baron Schluter," one of the men said, echoed almost instantly by the other.

Schluter nodded at them.

The building's exterior was grim and foreboding, covered in soot and grease left there over tumultuous decades filled with anxious workers. Desperation seemed to have eaten into the bricks that made up the building. Schluter felt it every time he went there, but he didn't let it bother him. He kept his own dreams alive by feeding on the misery and addictions of others.

The two doormen stood a little straighter as he walked through the entrance. "Good evening, Baron Schluter."

Schluter nodded and never broke stride. After passing through the foyer, he stepped into the main entertainment area.

The dance floor was huge, packed with Vienna's youth. Industrial music pounded through giant speakers and threatened to turn bones to jelly. Bars on both sides of the room served an endless array of alcoholic beverages.

On the massive stage at the far end of the room, six band members played deafening death metal and screamed obscene lyrics. The three women on the stage wore leather and lace, looking provocative under the swirling light.

The bad mood that had settled on him when he met Garin Braden clung to Schluter as he made his way around the perimeter of the dance floor. Two security men fell into step ahead of him and bulled through the crowd, leaving disgruntled club-goers in their wake.

Schluter ignored them. In the end, they didn't matter. The club turned a profit, but it was modest. What really drove Schluter's finances was the drug trade.

Behind the bar on the right, Schluter went up to the offices on the second floor. A narrow balcony stuck out over the dance floor, offering a splendid view of the operation. The security cameras that constantly swept the dance area stripped away the shadows.

Felix Horst stood at the security system and stared out over the crowd. He was round faced and round shouldered, but Schluter didn't know anyone who was better at picking bands and music.

"Good evening, Baron Schluter," Horst greeted.

"Good evening, Felix. We've got quite a crowd out there." Schluter sat at his desk, which was identical to Horst's, and tapped computer keys to bring up the financial reports.

"We do," Horst agreed. "It's a new band I discovered. They're getting some play in the trades and the local word of mouth is positive."

"How long are they going to be playing here?"

"I signed them for a month, but I'm going to be surprised if they last that long. I've already had other talent scouts in the club."

Schluter scowled. Since the band had been signed, profits had gone up twenty-three percent. That was a significant move.

"If any of the talent scouts get overly aggressive," Schluter said, "let me know."

Horst shot Schluter a pained look. Horst loved music and didn't care for the other aspects of the club. But he also loved the fact that the club provided enough money for him to hire emerging local talent.

"I'm serious," Schluter said.

"I know."

"What about the band?"

"What about them?"

"Can any of them be leveraged?" By that, Schluter meant blackmailed, bribed or physically beaten into submission. It had worked on other bands before.

"The lead singer has a younger sister with an ecstasy habit," Horst said. "She's got a long history of drug abuse. He's been trying to get her into rehab, but the good ones that can actually get the job done are just too expensive."

Schluter thought about the increase in profits. "If we take care of his sister, put her in a rehab center where she can get the help she needs, will that buy us some time with him?"

"I think so."

"Then get it done."

"That's only going to work for a while," Horst said. "In the end, that band is going to get a record deal and go big."

"Then we'll sign him to some exclusive nights here."

"You can't guarantee that."

Schluter grinned. "If we get his sister cleaned up in rehab, we can always threaten to kill her later. I'll bet he comes around then."

A pained look filled Horst's round face.

"Profit is profit, Felix. You're going to have to learn to be hard if you're going to survive in the music industry."

"I know." Horst sounded tired.

"I'll be needing the office tonight," Schluter said.

Horst looked troubled. "Is there a problem?"

Schluter smiled. "Nothing I can't handle." He nodded toward the door. "Why don't you get out of here? Go get something to eat for an hour or so."

"All right." Horst went to the cherrywood armoire in the corner of the room and took out his coat. He left without saying another word.

Schluter settled back to wait, his mind filled with dark thoughts about his grandmother and Garin Braden.

GARIN STOOD in the snow a few blocks from Club Ripper. He ignored the cold, covered from neck to calf in a luxurious coat. His phone rang.

"Hello."

"Mr. Braden?"

"Yes."

"We're coming for you now, sir."

Garin looked down the street. "Do you know where I am?"

"Of course, sir. That's why you pay us. Look to your left."

Garin did and watched as a cargo truck rounded the corner and came toward him.

"Get in the truck, sir."

Folding the phone, Garin shoved it into his pocket and waited as the truck slowed to a crawl. A side door opened, temporarily revealing an interior that looked as if it could launch a NASA shuttle.

"Mr. Braden?" A young man in a black turtleneck and black slacks stood in the center of the cargo space. A half-dozen techs sat at computer workstations around him. The young man had round-lensed glasses and a goatee. "I'm Gunther Zellweiger. Please call me Gunther."

"All right, Gunther."

The young man smiled, but Garin couldn't tell if the effort was an honest one or just for show. Gunther wore a headset with a small mouthpiece at his cheek.

Garin looked at the monitors on the walls. All of them showed exterior and interior shots of Club Ripper.

"You have the whole club wired?" Garin asked.

"We do," Gunther said. "We are the most sophisticated and successful surveillance business in the country, Mr. Braden."

Garin grinned. "I know. That's why I bought the company six years ago."

"Of course, sir."

"Where's Schluter?"

Gunther spoke briefly. Almost immediately the view on the wide-screen monitor in the center of the wall changed perspectives and showed the interior of an office.

Wolfram Schluter sat at the desk, looking bored and restless.

"You've already received the background on the club, sir?" Gunther asked.

Garin knew it was the man's polite way of asking if he'd read the file. "Yes. Have you got any financials on Schluter's drug business?"

"He's deriving extra income from the sideline," Gunther said. "But it's only enough to keep the club operational and make some extra money. It's not enough to support his present lifestyle."

"So he's still largely dependent on his grandmother's money?"

"Yes, sir."

Garin didn't like the sound of that. If Schluter had been making enough to be responsible for himself, things would have been different. But he wasn't.

"Have you got his supply network mapped?" Garin asked.

"Give us another couple of days, sir, and we'll get it all for you."

Garin nodded. He didn't know the time frames or the scope of his involvement there yet. The men had been working on the surveillance job less than twenty-four hours.

"Hold on, sir," Gunther said. "It appears we have something interesting going on." He spoke into the microphone.

Immediately, the main screen changed again. This time it showed two men dragging a canvas bag from the back of a sedan. When the bag hit the ground, something inside it moved.

SCHLUTER'S PHONE RANG. He picked it up from the desk, expecting one phone call but instead getting another.

"Mr. Schluter," the man said, "I'm afraid I have some bad news, sir."

It took Schluter a moment to recognize the man's voice, then remember that he'd sent him to watch the developments that took place regarding the woman, Annja Creed.

"What?" Schluter demanded.

"Dieter Humbrecht and his men have been taken into police custody."

Surprised, Schluter leaned back in the desk chair. "What happened?"

"They tried to apprehend the target, but she was able to overpower them."

"One woman?" Schluter was incredulous. Dieter and his men had fought in several campaigns throughout Africa.

"Yes, sir."

Schluter thought about that. Dieter knew a lot about him. They'd been working together for almost four years. Doubtless the New York Police Department knew that Dieter and his people were responsible for the death of

Mario Fellini. Schluter wasn't certain if the Americans could indict him and have him brought to their country to stand trial, but it would all be extremely embarrassing.

On top of that, there was the Viking treasure to find. He was certain the last time he'd been to Riga that he was getting closer to it.

In spite of their friendship, there was only one thing to do. "Get someone inside the holding cell. Buy someone inside. I want Dieter and his people out of the way."

"Yes, sir."

Schluter closed the phone. He had to get things under control. Nothing was working out as he'd planned.

A moment later, the phone rang again.

"Baron Schluter," the gruff voice said. "We have your package."

Schluter glanced at the monitors displaying the parking area outside the building. He spotted the men dragging the canvas bag and settled down to wait.

At least someone was about to have a worse night than he was.

# 26

"Annja?" Bart sounded short-tempered.

Why, Annja asked herself, am I having that effect on everyone tonight? "Yes," she said.

"Where are you?"

"I'm writing up the statement on what happened tonight."

"No, you're not. I sent an officer to your hotel room to check on you. Imagine my surprise when he discovered you'd checked out."

"Bart, you couldn't have been that surprised if you sent someone to check on me. You could have called me."

"You would have told me you were writing up that statement."

Annja couldn't argue that.

"You've got a history of doing what you think you need to do," Bart said angrily.

That's something to be proud of, Annja thought. She remained silent.

"I was worried about your safety," Bart said.

"If you were worried about my safety, you'd have shown up yourself."

Bart cursed. "I've been kind of busy cleaning up the messes you've been leaving."

"That fight wasn't my choice," Annja said.

"No, but you seem to be at the center of it."

"Is this going to get personal?" Annja asked.

"It doesn't have to be." Bart spoke in a carefully measured tone.

"Good. After the last couple of days of being chased around New York—"

"Which you still don't have a reason for, right?"

Okay, that was sarcasm. Annja grimaced.

"Tell me where you are," Bart said. "I'll come get you."

"I don't want to be gotten."

"Annja," Bart said, "you're in over your head. These guys aren't playing around."

"I kind of got that when they killed Mario," Annja replied coldly.

The silence on the line lasted long enough that Annja thought Bart had hung up on her. It wasn't her night for performing well at phone relationships.

"Bart?" she said. "Look, I'm sorry."

"I know." He sounded tired.

Annja felt guilty because she knew she was partly the reason for that. "Those guys killed Mario. I'm sure that you'll find a way to prove that they did. And maybe you'll even find out who hired them to do it."

"Believe it or not, I'm good at my job," Bart said.

"I know that."

The limousine passed through security and rolled out

onto the tarmac toward the hangars where the private air-craft were kept.

"The guy behind this is out of the country," Bart continued.

"They're German," Annja said. "Mario was Italian."

"But he had recently moved to Riga."

"That's a lot of area to cover."

"Then how do you know who hired Humbrecht and his team?"

Annja answered honestly. "I don't."

"Then why are you going to Venice?"

Gazing through the window as the limousine slowed, Annja saw the small airplanes and jets sitting in front of the hangars. Evidently a few people were taking off for parts unknown.

"Mario wanted to consult with me about something he'd found."

"And he left you a clue where to find it?"

"I think so."

"You could let the police handle this," Bart suggested. "It might take a little time, but I can get some coordination between the NYPD and the Venice police."

"No offense, Bart, but I wouldn't try to tell you how to lift a fingerprint or interrogate a suspect—"

"Person of interest," Bart interjected. "We don't say 'suspect' anymore unless we're certain someone has done something."

"The point being, you've got your specialty and I've got mine. I'm not trailing a murderer. I'm leaving that for you. I want to try to find whatever Mario found."

"You don't owe him that. From what you've said, you hadn't even been in touch much over the last few years."

"We hadn't been."

"Then why—?"

"Because we shared the same dreams, Bart. You live your whole life hoping you'll find something incredible that will add to what we know about the world that went before us. Something that will illuminate some dark little corner of history and culture that we hadn't seen before."

"You've done that."

Annja thought of everything she'd done since she'd entered the field. She'd been fortunate even before she'd found the sword.

"I have," she said, "but Mario hasn't."

Bart was quiet again. "I understand, but I still worry about you."

"I know. I appreciate that."

"I'll see you in a few minutes."

Before Annja could ask what he meant, Bart hung up.

A FEW MINUTES LATER, the limousine glided to a stop in front of a sleek Learjet. An unmarked police car sat on the other side of the aircraft.

Even without the flashing lights, Annja recognized it for what it was. And she knew whom it belonged to. Her heart pounded. She wasn't looking forward to the coming confrontation.

Clad in a black leather jacket, Bart leaned a hip against his car and watched the limousine's approach. No emotion showed on his face.

"Oh, dear," Stanley Younts said.

"Do you have that attorney of yours on speed dial?" Annja asked.

"Yes."

"Good. We may need him just to get out of town." Annja gathered the straps of her backpack and stepped from the limousine.

"You're here." Annja stopped in front of Bart.

Bart shrugged. "I'm a detective, and this was easy. You disappeared. Stanley Younts disappeared. You wanted to go to Venice. Younts is a big-deal author and has a private jet. When I talked to Morrell, he told me that Younts had scheduled a meeting that day to get an interview with you. When I found out you weren't at the hotel, I came here."

"You got here fast," Stanley commented.

"It helps if you have the siren and lights," Bart said.

Tension filled the space between Annja and Bart as the snow continued to fall.

"Uh," Stanley said, "why don't I go wait in the jet?" He looked at Bart. "I can still get on my jet, right?"

"Yes." Bart didn't look at the writer.

Hesitating, Stanley pushed his glasses up his nose and looked at Annja. "Are you going to be all right?"

"I'm going to be fine," Annja replied.

"I thought so." Stanley shoved his hands in the pockets of his coat and walked up the steps into the jet.

Annja stayed just out of Bart's reach. Only a few feet away, the private jet's engines roared. The door was open and lighted stairs led to the aircraft's interior. All around her, the biting wind hammered her and stung her exposed flesh. She'd gotten so cold even in just the short walk that she no longer felt the snow hitting her.

"I'm getting on the jet," Annja said.

Bart sighed. His breath came out in a long gray stream that was torn to pieces in the wind. "I know. I can't stop you. I would if I could. I think you're making a mistake."

Annja didn't say anything. There was no need to. She was leaving in a few minutes and that was all that mattered.

"While you're looking for whatever Mario Fellini thought he found, other people are going to be looking for it, too," Bart said.

"I know."

"Whoever had him killed isn't going to pull any punches."

"I know that, too," Annja said.

Bart made no move to step away from the unmarked car. "I wish you wouldn't do this."

"Bart, I—"

He held a forefinger up to his lips. "I know. I had a partner a few years ago who was ambushed on a follow-up interview. He ended up in a coma for two weeks, then got pensioned off the force with a permanent disability."

Annja didn't know what to say. That was a story Bart had never told her. It surprised her that there were still any of those left.

"I moved heaven and earth trying to find out who did it," Bart went on. "I spent most of my time trying to pin the murder attempt on the guy Ross went to interview that day. Long story short, that guy didn't do it. Ross got popped by a jealous husband whose wife Ross was seeing."

Annja waited.

"I got put on suspension for a month for getting too physical with the guy I thought did it," Bart said. "Then, while I was in the hospital sitting with Ross, his wife came in. She told me she'd thought Ross was having an affair. I could see that she was hurt. I didn't believe it, but she helped me put it together. I went and talked to the husband. He was relieved he was finally caught. Sometimes it works out like that."

A jet took off, screaming overhead and putting an end to the conversation for a time.

"The guy shot Ross because he was scared of him," Bart said. "Ross's wife got hurt because he cheated on her. I got suspended and hurt because I believed Ross couldn't do any wrong." He took a breath. "What I'm trying to say is—"

"Sometimes people you think you know disappoint you," Annja said. "I get that." Then she smiled at Bart. "But sometimes the people you know are everything you think they are. You're here now."

Bart looked a little embarrassed. "Maybe. I came here to give you a heads-up." He reached into the car and took out a packet, then handed it to Annja.

"What's this?"

"Background stuff you shouldn't have," Bart answered. "Stuff you wouldn't have if you didn't have a friend with connections. It's interesting reading material."

"Something that's going to disappoint me?"

"Something that's going to open your eyes. Mario Fellini's girlfriend—"

"Erene Skujans."

Bart nodded. "She's got a record. She was an antiquities dealer in Romania. She got busted for misappropriation of assets. I figured that was fancy museum talk for—"

"Theft," Annja said.

"Exactly. Since then, she's been independently employed, but she's wanted for questioning by several international law-enforcement agencies regarding a lot—and I do mean a *lot*—of burglaries. Does that sound like the kind of woman your friend would have taken up with?"

"No," Annja said.

Bart heaved a sigh. "He met her over there, right?"

"Yes. I confirmed that through the family."

"Then the possibility exists that he didn't know what she was all about."

"He told his family she was a hedge witch at the local village where he was staying."

"Yeah, well, I'm not a big fan of witches, either."

"Witches aren't always bad," Annja said. "It carries a negative connotation here, but there are still women in the Appalachian Mountains who tend to the medical needs of the community. And the role is reprised in several other cultures where medical help isn't available. They're given several titles."

"Maybe so," Bart said, "but this is one witch my spider senses are warning me about. I just want you to know that."

"Okay."

Bart nodded toward the jet. "I'm holding you up. You've got an important discovery to find."

"If it exists."

"Other people believe it does." Bart looked at her. "You believe it does."

"I," Annja said, "believe in my friends."

"So do I. Just make sure you take care of yourself so you can come back and tell me the whole story."

"I will." Annja headed for the jet, then stopped and went back to give him a hug. He held her fiercely for a moment, then let go when she did. "Thanks," she said.

Turning, Annja walked through the snow and boarded the jet. Buckled into her seat, she gazed through the window and waved a final goodbye to Bart as the jet taxied away.

But her thoughts were on Mario and the woman, Erene Skujans. Annja opened the file folder and began to read.

# 27

The village was not far removed from what it had been when Erene Skujans lived there as a little girl. Stone buildings and houses sat too close together to allow more than a single line of cars. Few visitors came through. Mostly they were black marketers who wanted to increase their earnings or off-load items they hadn't been able to sell in Riga.

Dressed for the freezing wind that whipped through the village, Erene walked down the hill to the center of the village. Her grandmother had always lived away from the villagers. Outside of the village, she had more room for her gardens, and it was cleaner.

No one cared about the village. It was an eyesore. Frozen horse and dog dung littered the narrow, snow-covered streets that wound around the small stone houses.

The downtown area consisted of five two-story buildings. A hundred years earlier, merchants had conducted business there. Now they were just squats for those too poor or too lazy to seek out better shelter.

However, there was a bar in the bottom of one of them. Fermented goat's milk was the drink of choice, but there was also black market vodka for those who could afford it. The owner maintained a kitchen there, as well, but the cook was his wife and her efforts weren't much appreciated until the men had started drinking.

Women didn't go there except to sell themselves or steal husbands. When they did and they were found out, the other women of the village ran them out of town. The only thing those who sold themselves hoped for was to get enough money before being ostracized to get a start in Riga.

Erene's grandmother had never gone there. Erene had never gone there, either, until Mario took her there. They'd shared his rented cottage or her grandmother's house.

Thinking about Mario upset Erene again. She felt the ball of pain in her stomach like a heavy stone. She knew it would never leave. She hoped that killing Wolfram Schluter would help. She believed it would.

Despite the man's departure from the area, Erene knew he would return. The lure of treasure was too irresistible. After all, it had kept her there all this time.

She had visited her grandmother on occasion, but those times usually ended in arguments and guilt. The strained silence between them, the annual birthday card, those things had seemed more comfortable.

Of course, that meant she hadn't known of her grandmother's death until eight months after the fact. Erene had stood at the overgrown grave where the villagers had interred the remains of Misha Skujans. Erene, who thought she'd known everything there was to know about her grandmother, hadn't even known her age until she'd read it on the crudely carved headstone.

A group of squatters had taken over her grandmother's house. Erene had come back and let them know the house would remain as it was until she decided what to do with it.

Then she'd found Mario in town. For a week she'd watched him as he'd talked to the villagers and went trekking around through the ruins outside the village. She'd heard about what he'd been looking for, but all of her life she'd never believed it existed.

The tavern was a rectangular room with a low ceiling. Timbers covered the bare stone walls, holding a mix of mud and straw that served as insulation. In many places, scars from bullets—from Russians, as well as Nazis—showed on the timbers.

A hodgepodge of chairs and tables occupied the room. Only three lanterns, one of them on the bar, lit the space. The others had been dimmed and the surviving lanterns had pulled the final few men together near the wood-burning stove against the back wall.

"The witch!" someone growled.

"What's she doing here?"

The bartender, an old man with gray hair and gold-capped teeth, leaned toward Erene. "Can I help you?"

"No," Erene replied.

The six men seated at the two back tables looked away from her.

Erene walked toward the tables and stopped a few feet away. "Viktor Ivanov," she said.

Five men got up from the tables to join the bartender at the bar.

The remaining man looked at her and grinned insolently. He was at least eight inches taller than Erene. At one time his body had been lean and muscular; his wife had a picture of them together in those happier times. But now he'd gone soft and paunchy. He outweighed Erene by at least one hundred pounds. His brown beard and hair were long and shaggy. He wore tattered clothing and a large parka.

Calmly, he took a drag off his cigarette. "I am Viktor Ivanov," he said.

"Your daughter's arm was broken," Erene said.

Ivanov shrugged. "She is careless." He smiled a little. "Like her mother. Both of them are careless."

"I had to rebreak your daughter's arm tonight to reset it," Erene said. It was cold enough in the room that she could see her breath. "I've never had to do it to a child before."

Ivanov grinned. "Breaking a child's arm is very easy. Now, a man? That is much more difficult." He sneered. "Perhaps you're better at curses. They say your grandmother was."

Without a word, Erene planted one of her boots in his face. The impact jarred along her leg. His head snapped back and rebounded from the wall behind him. Before he could move, Erene grabbed a fistful of his hair, turned and slid a hip into him, then yanked him from the chair and flipped him to the ground.

Ivanov landed hard on the floor. The wind whooshed out of him. He flailed at her weakly, still stunned. He tried to catch his breath. His nose, flattened across his face, bled profusely.

Shoving her hand into her pocket, Erene slid out the switchblade knife she carried there and flicked the blade out. Avoiding his attempted blows, she sank to one knee beside his head. When she laid the keen knife edge against his neck, he ceased his struggles.

She leaned close to his ear and whispered, "I curse you, Viktor Ivanov. With your own blood." She nicked the flesh of his neck, and crimson mixed with his beard. "If you are not gone by tomorrow morning, if I find you here, I will bury you and cover your body in lye so that your bones will burn forever."

There, that sounds positively witchy, doesn't it? she asked herself.

He shuddered. Part of her gloried in Ivanov's fear. That was the part of her that was savage, the part that always lurked just below the surface and that her grandmother had never understood. She couldn't bring Mario back, but striking out—even against someone else's monster—made her feel better.

Ivanov said nothing.

"Do you understand?" she asked quietly.

"Yes," he said quietly.

"Good." Erene stood and closed the knife.

Ivanov tried to get up.

Erene placed a boot on his head. "Don't get up," she said. "Not until after I'm gone."

He nodded and snuffled blood.

Erene went to the bar and reached into her pocket for money. "A bottle of vodka."

The bartender reached behind the bar and brought up a stoppered bottle. There was no label.

"It's black market vodka. Locally made. I've nothing better at the moment," he said.

"How much?"

"For you? Nothing. On the house."

Erene left too much money on the bar. If this had been

another town, she would have taken the bottle for nothing. But she didn't want to owe anyone in the village.

She took the bottle and left, hoping the vodka was strong enough to kill the pain she felt over knowing Mario was dead somewhere in New York City.

Outside, she unstoppered the bottle and took a deep swig. The liquid burned the back of her throat and brought tears to her eyes that trickled down her face and felt like icicles. After another drink, she turned and headed back to her grandmother's house.

THE GRAVE WAS in a small cemetery behind the house. Erene's grandmother was the last to have her bones laid there. Few spaces remained. Moonlight shone through the wispy clouds. A crooked picket fence missing a few slats surrounded the graveyard and set it apart from the forest that threatened to encroach and devour it.

Numb from the cold, the adrenaline and the vodka, Erene walked to her grandmother's grave and knelt there. She wiped tears from her cheeks with the back of her arm, but it was wasted effort because the nylon material slid smoothly across her face.

Lifting the bottle to her lips, she tried to take another drink but discovered it was empty. She'd consumed all of it on her way up the hill. It was the most she'd drunk in years. Angrily, she flung the bottle away.

She was confused. She didn't know if she was crying for Mario, her grandmother, the little girl whose arm she'd had to rebreak—

Or herself.

The last thought was the most upsetting. Erene couldn't

remember a time when she'd cried for herself. And she'd rarely cried for others.

"Oh, Misha," she whispered, reaching out to touch the carved headstone, "I wish you were here."

Only silence answered her at first.

Then a deep voice said, "I've always been told that it's all right to talk to the dead, but when you start waiting for them to answer, you've gone too far."

Erene spun around, reaching for the pistol that she'd habitually carried for the past few years before realizing it was still packed away with the other personal belongings she'd kept from Mario's sight.

A tall, thick man stood at the graveyard's entrance. He had a broad face and his skin was ruddy.

"Dalton," Erene whispered.

"Erene," the big man greeted. His name was Dalton Hyde. For years they'd been sometime business associates and lovers, dropping into and out of deals that had benefited both of them.

"Where did you come from?" Erene asked.

Hyde hooked a thumb over his shoulder. "I was down to the tavern when you went in there looking for trouble." His big face split wide in a white grin. His accent was Hungarian, but he'd lived all over Eastern Europe while he plied his trade.

He was one of the most gifted artists Erene had ever seen, but he didn't have an honest bone in his body and had an attraction to easy money. Usually someone else's. Normally he was a confidence man, arranging for investors to buy fake art or antiquities he'd crafted himself or had others create.

But he was also a thief. He knew electronics, hardware and systems, and he was a sophisticated hacker. He'd taught Erene everything she knew about breaking and entering.

"I wasn't looking for trouble," Erene said. She knew she slurred her words but didn't care.

"I guess not," Hyde said. "From where I sat, you delivered more than you got."

"He broke his daughter's arm."

"I gathered that."

Erene frowned. "What are you doing here?"

"I came to see you."

"You're not exactly the type for a casual hello."

Hyde shrugged. "I came to talk to you about a possible job—"

"I'm not interested."

"I don't think this is the appropriate time to talk about it," Hyde said.

"Why?"

"Because, dear girl, you're plotzed."

"I won't be interested later, either."

"You won't be drunk later," Hyde said.

"Go away." Erene walked toward the house.

"Is that how you're going to treat an old friend?"

"I've got an excuse. I'm drunk."

"You're not that drunk."

Erene slipped and nearly fell. Head spinning and feeling sick, she grabbed hold of the picket fence and threw up. She purged so hard and so long she had a headache. She was barely aware of Hyde picking her up in his massive arms and carrying her into the house. Sleep came almost the moment he placed her on the bed.

## 28

Garin watched as the men carried their squirming package through the club's doors, across the dance floor, then up the staircase to the offices.

As he watched, the cameras changed smoothly, rolling through the views until he could see inside the office where Schluter sat looking as if nothing was out of place. The men spoke briefly.

"Can we get audio on this?" Garin asked.

"No," Gunther said. "We didn't have the opportunity to do that. The staff there watches the day-to-day operations pretty closely."

Garin accepted that, watching as the men unzipped the sack and emptied the contents onto the floor. A man, bound hand and foot and his mouth covered with duct tape, spilled out of the bag and onto the floor.

The man was young and wide-eyed with terror.

The computer monitor tightened up on the scared man's

face, then froze. Another window opened up on the screen, and head shots started cycling through.

"Perhaps we'll find out who he is in a moment," Gunther said.

As Garin watched, two of the men in the room grabbed the helpless individual by the elbows. Schluter walked to the rear of the room and pressed a hidden switch to reveal a sliding panel in the wall.

"Hidden passageway," Gunther said. "We found it when we scoped out the blueprints on the building. There's a room under the building."

Schluter stepped into the open doorway. The men, half carrying the prisoner between them, followed.

"Do we have video down there?" Garin asked.

"Yes, but it was tricky. We couldn't go in through the office, so we ended up tapping the room through the ceiling conduits. As it turns out, the hidden room also has electricity. We tapped in through that."

SCHLUTER LED THE WAY down to the basement and turned on the lights. Revealed in the pale white glow, the room was twenty feet square and empty.

When he'd found it, Schluter had instantly seen the dark promise of such a room. There was even a floor drain in the center of the space. He'd had the water supply line added.

Gesturing toward the center of the room, Schluter slid out of his jacket and rolled up his sleeves.

Two of the men put the bound man on his knees. His choking, wailing cries filled the room, cascading in the enclosed space.

Through it all, the incessant gurgling of the sewer below the drain echoed around Schluter. The original design hadn't had a trap and had allowed the stench of the foul water to fill the room. The trap in place now blocked that, but decades of reeking odor had permeated the brick.

"Shut up," Schluter commanded.

The young man tried to control himself, but the effort was doomed to failure. He knew what he'd done, and he knew what was going to happen. This wasn't his first visit to the basement. Schluter ripped the tape from the man's mouth.

"I gave you a chance," Schluter screamed, "and you betrayed me."

"Please!" the man begged. "Please, Wolfram! I needed the money! I swear to you!"

"I paid you," Schluter responded. "You had money. You just wanted more and helped yourself to it."

Tears leaked down the man's quivering cheeks. He shook his head in denial so forcefully he almost fell over. One of the men put a hand on his shoulder to steady him.

Schluter fed on the rage that filled him. He lived in his grandmother's world so much of the time that it was hard to remember that he had control over parts of his world. This was one of those times when he could do anything he wanted.

"My brother is sick," the man cried. "He needed money for medical treatment."

"Liar," Schluter said. "Even if you had a brother in dire straits, you wouldn't help him."

"I can pay you back!" the man promised. "I swear, Wolfram! If you'll just give me a chance, I'll pay you back! I'll work for free!"

"You're vulnerable and weak," Schluter said. "Eventually the police will get to you. Then, instead of losing just what you've taken from me, I'll lose everything."

The man shook his head. "No! I swear!"

Schluter crossed the room to a metal toolbox. He pulled out a small ax. The man's wails and sobs grew louder and more desperate. Schluter ran his thumb along the edge, reveling in the sense of power that he had.

"SIR?" GUNTHER ASKED.

Garin knew the man wanted to know if he wanted the surveillance team to interfere. They had a team on-site, inside the club.

"No," Garin said, watching Schluter step forward with the ax.

"He could be a policeman."

"That's not our problem. We're not here to protect anyone. We're here to learn what we can."

Gunther looked at another screen. "He's not a policeman."

Following the man's line of sight, Garin saw that the window beside the action taking place on the central monitor had frozen on a face. It matched the one worn by the man on his knees in the basement room.

"His name is Bruno Frantz," Gunther said. "Apparently he has a long history of being on the wrong side of the law. Drug possession. Intent to distribute. Armed robbery."

"Not exactly a pillar of the community, then, is he?" Garin asked. It wouldn't have mattered if the man were a police officer, though. Garin had never seen himself as the savior of the world. Not even Roux had thought that way.

Garin watched the screen as Schluter lifted the ax high and brought it down. The men around the unfortunate on his knees quickly stepped away. Blood sprayed everywhere.

Even when he was covered in crimson gore, Schluter

didn't stop raising the ax until his arms were too tired to lift the weapon anymore. The amount of energy Schluter had invested in the effort impressed Garin.

"Well," Garin said, staring at Schluter as he stood there with his chest heaving, "he doesn't mind getting his hands dirty, does he?"

"No, sir," Gunther replied in a calm voice.

Garin knew the man didn't mind the violence. While with the surveillance corporation, he'd seen worse. Garin didn't suffer enemies gladly, either.

"What do you want us to do?" Gunther asked.

"Keep him under surveillance. Let me know what he does, where he goes. Knowing that he has a taste for killing and doesn't mind doing it up close is knowledge I needed." Schluter wasn't just a jackal, then. He was more dangerous than that.

"I wouldn't just say Schluter has a taste for it, Mr. Braden. That's more of an appetite. He enjoys doing what he just did."

Studying the blood-drenched figure, Garin had to agree. But a smile pulled at his lips. "This makes it a little easier, though. I'd thought he was just a cowardly cur living off his grandmother's goodwill. Now I know he's dangerous. In some ways he'll be more predictable."

"I take it you're going to continue your business with Baroness Schluter."

"I am." Garin had made his promise sixty years earlier when he'd loved Kikka Schluter. Part of him still did because he could glimpse flashes of the woman she'd been inside that wrinkled and sagging flesh. He didn't give promises often, but he always carried through on them.

"Then you'll want to be careful, sir. Schluter is more of a threat than we'd thought."

"Perhaps," Garin said. "But he's not as dangerous as I am."

FRESHLY SHOWERED in the bathroom he kept off his office and clad in a new outfit, Schluter left the club and crossed the snow-covered lot to his car. He whistled happily to himself, thinking that maybe he should catch people stealing from him more often.

By now Bruno Frantz's bones were sluicing through the Viennese sewers, broken into slivers. The rats would eat his flesh. Only the bones would remain, and probably not enough of them to make identification an issue. Schluter had been very thorough with the ax, reducing the man to a shattered mess.

His men had dumped Frantz's remains into the sewer, then hosed the room clean. They'd sprayed bleach from a special container, sluicing the liquid over the room to break down the DNA.

Sliding into his car, Schluter keyed the ignition and heard his cell phone trill. "Yes."

"Baron Schluter," a man's calm voice replied, "the problem in New York has been dealt with."

Schluter took in a deep breath and let it out. Dieter Humbrecht and his team were dead. "That's good. I'll see that there is a bonus."

"There is, however, another problem."

Checking the sparse traffic, Schluter pulled out onto the street. "What?"

"The woman has left New York."

"How?"

"By private jet as I understand it."

Schluter grimaced. "Whose?"

"A man named Stanley Younts."

The name didn't mean anything to Schluter and he said so.

"Younts is a very popular American writer," his man said.

"How did he get involved?"

"While we were monitoring Annja Creed's producer's office, Younts showed up to have a conversation regarding a possible interview with the woman about her career."

"Why?"

"He's researching a book."

Schluter thought about that. "So he flew her out of New York?"

"Yes."

"Do you know where they're going?"

"When Dieter intercepted her, she was trying to get her producer to agree to send her to Venice."

Schluter drove through the narrow streets, but he felt the jaws of a trap closing on him. Venice was where Mario Fellini had started his investigation, and that investigation had sent Schluter's grandmother into desperation to find the treasure.

"When will you be able to confirm the destination?" Schluter asked.

"We're working on it now."

"Let me know as soon as you find out."

"Yes, sir."

Schluter punched the phone off and cursed. He drove for a moment, his mind screaming for an answer. Then he called Tomas Piccoli, one of the mercenaries whom he'd sometimes employed to arrange "accidents."

"Yes?" a thick voice answered.

"Are you working?" Schluter asked.

"I could be. I'm not involved in anything that I can't walk away from. A babysitting job that's more show than activity. Low threat level, but it keeps the money coming in."

"I have a high-priority project I need to have handled right now."

"Bonus?"

Schluter hesitated. Paying a bonus on top of Piccoli's usual rates would be expensive. "You haven't even heard about the job yet," Schluter protested.

Piccoli laughed. "If you're not having Humbrecht take care of this for you, that tells me you're either spread thin, this thing is happening faster than you can handle—which means more trouble for me—or Humbrecht's already tried and couldn't do it. If you told me what the case was, I'd better know how much to charge."

Ignoring that, Schluter said, "I want the problem isolated. Failing that, I want the problem removed."

"Only one problem?"

"Yes."

"You may be getting overcharged."

"Bring the problem in isolated and you'll get more. The details will be e-mailed to your drop."

"I'll be waiting."

Schluter punched off the phone and tossed it into the passenger seat. Adrenaline from killing Frantz still coursed through his system, but it warred with the anxiety that filled him. Things were getting more and more complicated. But he had a trump card in place in Latvia that no one knew about.

He took a deep breath and let it out. Perhaps once

Piccoli had finished the task in Venice, he could turn his attentions to Garin Braden. Finally, a smile spread across Schluter's face. No one was immortal. If things went well, maybe he could even arrange for Braden to be brought to the club basement for a private session.

Schluter looked forward to that.

# 29

The jet's sharp descent woke Annja from a nightmare. She started to get to her feet into a martial-arts ready position, but the seat belt restrained her. Anxious, she gazed around the dark cabin.

"Are you awake?" Stanley Younts sat across the aisle. He worked at a specially built table that provided a stable base for his notebook computer, complete with docking and recharging stations. For much of the flight, Annja had worked there.

"We're landing," Annja said.

"Yes."

It was dark outside the jet.

"You'll have to advance your watch to match local time," Stanley said.

Annja did.

"It'll be after nine when we touch down." She wasn't happy about that. It meant they'd have to wait until morning to go to St. Mark's Books, the shop that the Playfair cipher had pointed to.

"I've booked us into a hotel," Stanley said. "Separate rooms."

Annja smiled at him despite the fatigue that still weighed her down. The writer's innate naïveté was refreshing. During the long flight, he'd continued to be hospitable, occasionally asking questions about how and why she conducted her research. Both of them had been pleasantly surprised that their techniques didn't differ that much. They both performed the same basic groundwork, then shaped it into different end products.

"Thank you." Annja was looking forward to a real bath, which she hadn't had since Florida. "I know you haven't gotten much out of the time we spent digging into Latvian history yesterday, so—if you can fit it into your schedule—I'd be happy to take you on a more *relaxed* dig."

"Actually," Stanley said, "I've been quite happy with this one." He pushed his glasses up. "It's going to be different dealing with physical locales instead of written documents, though. I look forward to that."

"Me, too," Annja admitted. "I love books and records. There isn't anything like them. But being on-site, in an area where you can still see the history—or imagine it taking shape—is awesome."

"I know. When I'm able to take research—something historic or scientific or emotional—and present it in a context that involves the reader so much that he or she is compelled to write to me and tell me that I made them feel like they were there, that's when I know I've hit a home run."

THEY LEFT THE JET and made their way into the Marco Polo International Airport terminal. The airport was located on the Italian mainland.

Few people were in the terminal and all the shops were closed. Stanley hired skycaps to handle their baggage, but Annja carried her backpack.

A group of teenagers stood at the doors leading to the pickup area. A girl looked at Annja intently, then approached her. She wore a cropped top and fringed jeans, her red hair pulled back in a severe ponytail.

"Ms. Creed," the girl called out. She waved and smiled.

"I guess you have a fan of the television show," Stanley said.

It wasn't too unusual. *Chasing History's Monsters* did have a solid following and was internationally syndicated. Annja had been approached by fans before.

The girl did indeed have a recent copy of a magazine that included an interview with Annja. She honestly couldn't remember talking to whoever had written the article, but it had been an excuse to plaster her on the cover in a tight shirt and khakis.

"Can you sign my magazine?" The girl spoke in Italian and held out a pen.

The pen was ornate and heavy, and Annja noticed the discrepancy at once. Then she saw a familiar-looking crested *R* on the pen's barrel. It was simple and understated, almost tasteful.

"Wow," Stanley said. "That's some pen."

The girl rolled her eyes. "Maybe you could announce it to the rest of the airport, you doof." Her English was impeccable and carried just the right hint of full-on, acidic snark.

Stanley was startled. "What?"

Annja signed the magazine. "Who gave you the pen?"

"The old man."

He's here? Annja's pulse quickened.

"He gave me a hundred bucks to tell you that some guys are waiting outside for you."

"I speak great Italian," Stanley said in that language.

The girl and Annja looked at him.

"I just thought you should know," Stanley said weakly. "Probably not so important right now."

"He said to go out front and he'd meet you there," the girl said.

"Who's 'he'?" Stanley asked.

"A friend," Annja said, taking the writer by the elbow and pulling him into motion.

"Wait. Where are we going?"

"Out."

Stanley went along reluctantly. "My Italian really is good."

"It is," Annja agreed as she pushed through the first set of doors.

"And I'm sure I distinctly heard that girl say there was someone out here waiting for us."

"We'll be all right." Annja hoped that was true. Despite the situation, she knew they couldn't stay there. If they didn't come out, whoever was hunting them would doubtless come in. And if they wanted them badly enough, the security guards inside the terminal wouldn't be able to stop them. There might have been a chance for them to return to the jet, but the aircraft was an awfully large target.

Outside, Annja stared across the parking area in front

of the terminal. Covered awnings led to the waiting line of cabs, buses and private cars pulled in next to the curb.

Two two-lane streets picked up and dropped off passengers inside three covered structures. Glass awnings connected them. The streets had an upper and lower level, allowing for a large amount of traffic to flow into and out of the terminal. Islands of trees, grass and landscaping separated the streets on the lowest level.

As soon as Annja stepped outside, she saw a group of men start for them. She counted seven, then gave up. Glancing over her shoulder, she saw that they'd been followed from inside, as well.

"You know, I've been under fire before," Stanley said.

"Me, too," Annja told him.

"But I still get nervous."

"Me, too." Annja reached and felt for the sword. It came comfortably to hand but she didn't pull it from hiding yet. She remembered how Mario had looked in the hotel bed, how he hadn't had a chance against the men who had killed him.

Maybe these weren't the people who had killed him, but they were men just like Humbrecht and the others. She squeezed all doubt and mercy from her heart. Tonight she wasn't just fighting for her life—she was going to send a message to the man who had ordered Mario Fellini's death.

ON HIS COMPUTER at home, Wolfram Schluter watched the action at the airport with keen-eyed interest. The thirty-two-inch plasma HD screen rotated through eight different cameras worn by the men Piccoli had contracted to do the job. None of those men knew about Schluter. Piccoli was the only name they knew.

"Are you watching?" Piccoli asked.

"Yes." Schluter sat on the edge of the ergonomic chair, his elbows braced on his knees, his forefingers under his chin. His grandmother was still entertaining Garin Braden in the study, staying up far past her normal bedtime.

"I don't know what the big deal is about this woman," Piccoli said in bored tones. "I don't know why you insisted on all the extra manpower."

"If you don't need it and you feel you've been overpaid, you can always return part of the fee," Schluter replied.

Seeing the action on the screen, he wished he could be there. The woman had cost him the service of Dieter Humbrecht, who was going to be hard to replace. Schluter had trusted Dieter, and that wasn't something that came easily.

Piccoli laughed at the suggestion. "I never turn down easy money."

"Just remember, you get a bonus if you take her alive, and if she escapes you don't get the other half."

"That's not going to be a problem."

"I hope not."

The woman had disappeared for many hours. For all of that time, Schluter had waited anxiously for her to re-appear. He'd fretted constantly. His grandmother had pressured him to get back to Riga and look for the treasure that was supposed to be hidden there. He'd finally forced her to acknowledge that having Annja Creed, with whatever knowledge Mario Fellini had passed on to her, would be desirable.

Through all of that discussion, Garin Braden had never said a word. He'd sat back and taken it all in. Schluter had the feeling that the big man had only been amused by everything they were doing. Schluter had even expected Garin to volunteer to go get the woman himself.

But he hadn't.

"Okay," Piccoli said, "we're going to take her now."

"I HAVE A FAVOR to ask, Garin."

"Anything," Garin told Kikka as he poured her another glass of wine.

Kikka looked at the wine. "I really shouldn't."

"You only live once, I say." And that's what you used to say, too, Garin thought, remembering those nights sixty years ago.

"You're right." Kikka picked up the glass and sipped. "What did you want to ask?"

Kikka blotted her lips. "When you and Wolfram go to Riga, I want to go with you."

Garin sat across from her, enjoying the wine, the warmth of the fireplace and the memory of the sparkle in the woman's eyes sixty years ago.

"Do you really think that's wise?" he asked.

"No, but this could be my last chance at adventure." Kikka smiled and shook her head. "I never saw myself ending my final days wasting away inside these walls."

Neither did I, Garin thought. His phone buzzed for attention. "Arrangements can be made," he said. "Excuse me." He took out his phone and answered it.

"The woman has landed," his contact said.

Garin stifled a curse. He'd hoped that Roux would get Annja clear of the situation, but evidently that hadn't been the case.

"Schluter's people are all around her," Gunther went on.

"We've hacked into his systems. You should be able to view the video feed he's using."

"All right." Garin knew that Gunther was holding back from reminding him they could have had a team in place there. As well as the other airports that serviced Venice.

But there had been no reason to think that Annja was flying there. Her name had never appeared on any passenger manifests at the airports. He'd had those monitored by Gunther's people so there would be no surprises. Garin hated surprises.

"I can hack into his system and stand down the team he has there or send for the police," Gunther said.

"No." Garin didn't want to do that because it would make Schluter even harder to deal with. He still wasn't certain he knew as much as Schluter did and he didn't want to risk the working relationship he had in place.

It wasn't the potential profit so much as it was the promise he'd made to the old woman all those years ago, but there was no discounting the chance for more wealth. He'd never allowed himself to get comfortable like Roux.

"Do nothing," Garin ordered. "Let me have the feed. I'll call you if I need you." He stood and looked at Kikka. "If you'll excuse me for a moment."

She smiled and nodded. "Of course."

Garin left the study and went up the stairs to the second floor, heading for Schluter's private suite. He pressed buttons, bringing up the video stream Gunther was piggybacking from Schluter's signal.

The phone's screen was small, but it was clear enough to recognize Annja Creed as she stepped out into the covered pickup areas in front of the airport. There was even an audio feed.

The men closing in on Annja pulled weapons from under their jackets. Then the sound of automatic gunfire rattled through the tiny speaker.

# 30

"Annja Creed," one of the men called out. He pointed his pistol at her.

Annja's stomach churned as adrenaline sped through her system. Her senses came alive, as sharp as they'd ever been. Time slowed down for her the way it sometimes did when her life was on the line.

Beside her, Stanley was tense and hesitant. He stared at the sound-suppressed pistol in the man's hand.

"Not a fan," Stanley said hoarsely.

"Definitely not a fan," Annja agreed.

Down at the curve leading into the canopied area, a scarlet Alfa Romeo pulled out of the parking space, cutting off a hotel shuttle bus gathering late-night arrivals. Rubber shrilled as all four wheels roared up to speed.

The compact car drifted as the tires ripped free of the pavement. Then it spun around. The driver shifted gears. The reverse lights flared to life, and the car roared backward toward the curb.

"Hang on," Annja said.

The man in front of her turned to point his weapon at the car's driver.

The driver's side window was down, allowing Annja to clearly see Roux seated behind the wheel. He wore a khaki shirt under a dark blue coat.

The man fired the pistol. Bullets chopped into the car, gouging holes in the body and piercing the rear driver's side window.

Annja pulled the sword into motion. Wrapping both hands around the hilt, knowing the man would kill Roux without a second thought, she brought the sword down in an arc that caught the man at the shoulder and sliced all the way through his heart. As quickly as she could, she twisted the blade and yanked it free of the dying man.

"Here!" Roux shouted as if he wasn't already noticeable enough. He shoved a mini-machine pistol through the window and opened fire, sweeping short bursts at the gunmen running toward them.

Stanley Younts had hit the pavement, wrapping his hands over his head.

I guess he has been under fire before, Annja thought. The first instinct was always self-preservation. She ran toward him, caught his arm and yanked him to his feet as a hail of bullets hit the pavement where he'd been. She kept him moving in front of her, a hand in the small of his back.

They left their baggage behind them. Annja saw that the skycaps had escaped without getting hurt. But her new suitcase was riddled with bullets.

"The other side of the car!" Roux ordered, firing again.

Annja pulled Stanley sideways. Until that moment she

hadn't thought that trying to get in behind Roux would have left them open to hostile gunfire that raked the side of the car. On the other side, she opened the door just as a fistful of bullets slammed through the window.

Stanley started inside, staying low. Annja put her shoulder into his back and shoved. They spilled into the backseat as more bullets struck the car. She let the sword fade away.

"Go!" Annja shouted.

Roux tossed the mini-machine pistol into the passenger seat, shoved the car into gear and dropped his foot heavily on the accelerator. The tires shrieked, but the sound was punctuated by gunfire.

"Reload," Roux yelled.

Shrugging out of her backpack, shoving it onto the floorboard behind Roux's seat, Annja sat up and reached over the seat for the machine pistol. Extra magazines for the weapon lay on the seat.

Horns blasted in front of them.

As she worked the reload, Annja realized they were headed into oncoming traffic. "You're going the wrong way." She was surprised how calmly she spoke.

"I know that," Roux replied testily as he swerved to miss a cab pulling out away from the curb. "This was the direction I was headed when I picked you up."

Annja slid the fresh magazine into place and released the slide. "Thanks for coming."

"You're welcome." Roux reached up and adjusted the shattered remnant of the rearview mirror. "We'll talk later. Right now it appears that those people back there didn't just have men on foot. They had cars standing by, as well."

Looking back, Annja saw two sports coupes racing to close the distance between them.

UNABLE TO COMPREHEND what he had just witnessed, Wolfram Schluter stood up. "What the hell just happened, Piccoli?"

"You didn't tell me there would be an outside party waiting to pick them up," Piccoli responded.

"That's because I didn't know." Schluter stood and leaned over the desk, trying to focus on the camera shifts as Piccoli's men moved around.

It didn't help. No one had a camera on the escaping car.

Piccoli kept up a steady stream of cursing.

"Get them!" Schluter ordered. "Get them now!"

"IT'S ALL RIGHT. The woman appears to have gotten away."

Garin paused outside Schluter's door. He heard the man screaming invective inside the room. Despite the tension of the situation, Garin smiled. Annja had always been surprisingly resourceful. However, in the same moment he silently congratulated her for her success, he realized that she was going to be stepping into his sights if she pursued the prize in Latvia.

"Who was in the car?" Garin asked, though he suspected he knew.

"I don't know. He appeared to be an elderly man. A surprisingly quick elderly man."

Garin wished he had someone in Venice to pick up the trail. "Stay with them as long as you can."

"I don't think they're going to get away," Gunther said. "Schluter's men are on their heels."

"THEY'RE STAYING with us," Stanley said. "They're right back there." He pointed, nearly stabbing Annja in the eye as she slid against the backseat to peer through the broken glass.

"I can see that," Roux snapped as he took a hard left and skidded behind a line of traffic to head into an alley.

"Wow, you're really good," Stanley said appreciatively. "I didn't even see this alley."

"This alley has been here for a long time," Roux replied. He kept the accelerator pinned to the floor, roaring through the alley. The walls were scarce inches beyond his side mirrors.

"Don't you think you ought to slow down?" Stanley asked nervously.

"No, I don't."

"Traffic!" Stanley yelped.

"Of course there's traffic, you idiot!"

Stanley reached for the seat belt and tried to pull it on.

"Where did you get him?" Roux demanded.

Annja fired a burst from the machine pistol, but the bullets struck the wall on the right side of the car. Firing from a moving car wasn't her forte. "New York."

"Did you shoot them?"

"I missed."

"It's a car, Annja! How can you miss a car!" Roux shouted.

"Shooting a moving car isn't as easy as it sounds."

Then the darkness in the alley gave way to the neon lights of the tourist district. Roux cut the wheel hard, downshifting to keep power to the transmission as the tires broke loose and he skidded. With the four-wheel drive, he recovered almost immediately.

"That's *really* good driving!" Stanley yelled excitedly.

"I've attended driving schools where bodyguards had to learn to do maneuvers like that."

"You brought your own cheering section?" Roux asked.

"He's not a cheering section," Annja replied.

The car following them through the alley wasn't as fortunate. The driver expertly cut the wheels and threw the vehicle into a sideways drift. It slammed into another car and knocked the other vehicle into oncoming traffic.

Horns blared and tires screeched as the other cars tried to stop. Most of them did, but a few ran into the car, causing an immediate traffic snarl.

"Shoot them!" Roux bellowed.

"There are too many bystanders," Annja replied.

"Let me have the gun." Roux reached back over the seat.

"No. Keep both hands on the wheel."

Roux cursed and grabbed the steering wheel as a truck pulled out in front of him. He steered to the right, cutting through the chairs and tables of an outdoor café. Only a few customers had gathered there. All of them had been watching the action coming up the street and were already clearing the area when Roux swerved in their direction.

The Alfa collected a number of dents as it roared through the furniture. Only scrap lumber and broken glass remained in its wake.

"Wow!" Stanley said.

"Don't you know any other words?" Roux demanded.

Police sirens screamed through the city. With all the buildings around to trap the noise, it was hard to tell what direction they were coming from. Probably all of them, Annja thought.

"Find another alley, Roux," Annja said.

"I know other words," Stanley replied indignantly. "I know a lot of words. I'm a writer."

Roux didn't respond.

"I'm Stanley Younts," the writer said.

Bullets ricocheted off the car's trunk, scattering sparks and tearing through the back glass and windshield.

"Did you say Younts?" Roux asked, squinting into the hanging fragment of rearview mirror.

"Yes."

"An alley, Roux," Annja said.

Roux cut the wheel hard to the right again. His turn wasn't so clean this time. Despite his best efforts, the rear of the car tore loose and the side slammed into the corner of the building. Harsh grating filled the car's interior as he downshifted and kept the accelerator floored.

"I read your books," Roux said.

From past association with him, Annja knew that the old man had a sweet tooth for popular fiction.

"You're one of the better writers out there."

"Thanks," Stanley said.

"You're very welcome." Roux sped across the next street and into another alley.

Annja watched as the two following cars dropped a little farther behind as they crossed the street more cautiously.

"Take the next right and slow down as you go around," Annja said. She gathered her feet on the seat and knocked out the remaining sections of glass to clear the rear window.

"What are you going to do?"

"Try to stop them. We can't just race through the city. If they don't catch us, the police will. Answering a lot of questions all night isn't something I'm looking forward to."

"Agreed." Roux pulled hard to the right, feathered the brake to lose speed and said, "I'm going left twice at the next two streets. Cut through the alley behind us to catch up."

"All right." Out of sight of the following cars for the moment, Annja scrambled through the back glass with the mini-machine pistol in her left hand. By the time she hit the ground, she had the sword in her right.

From the sound of the racing car engines, the pursuit vehicles were almost on top of her.

# 31

The car screeched around the corner. Bright lights stabbed into Annja's eyes. Then she had the pistol up, squeezing the trigger at point-blank range.

The bullets chopped into the windshield, turning it into Swiss cheese. She was vaguely aware of shadows inside the car shifting. Bullets cut the air and tugged at her hair on the left side.

She ran toward the vehicle. The pistol was empty, deadweight in her fist, but she knew she couldn't throw it away. Chances were it would be identified by the police.

They could say they were outrunning a kidnapping attempt. Since she and Stanley Younts were both public figures, she thought that at least would be a credible defense.

At the top of the first car, she jumped just enough to land on the hood of the second. Reversing the sword effortlessly, she thrust it through the windshield and pierced the driver through the chest.

Knowing she was dealing with hired killers stripped her of mercy. Later she would feel badly about taking another person's life, but she was determined not to let it mean her own death.

The car's momentum tore the sword from her grip. She let it go, leaping from the second car as it crashed into the first. They locked up in the alley, leaving long scars down the stone walls.

Landing hard on the ground, Annja looked back at the cars and raised her hand. She reached into the otherwhere and felt the sword. She turned and ran through the alley.

By the time she reached the street, Roux was just bringing the car around the corner. One of the car's headlights was extinguished.

She crossed the street, dodging traffic, and got to the other side before Roux could get to the curb. He reached across and opened the passenger door so she could drop inside.

"Well?" Roux asked.

"Done." Annja handed him the mini-machine pistol. "Now let's get rid of this car."

"I TAKE IT we're not going to the police," Stanley said.

"No," Roux and Annja said in unison.

"Oh."

"There's no reason to spend the evening entertaining them," Roux added as he pulled over into an alley a few blocks from where he had picked up Annja. "Surely you can understand that. The heroes in your novels don't like to be slowed down by law enforcement."

"But this is real life. There are laws. We can't just run away."

"Do you know who tried to kill us back there?" Roux asked as he got out of the car.

"No." Stanley remained seated in the back, seat belt still firmly in place.

"Neither do I." Roux walked to the back of the car.

Annja looked at the old man and said, "I want to know who told you I was looking for Thor's hammer."

"Does it matter?" Roux tried to open the car's trunk but it was jammed. "Help me."

Annja didn't budge.

Roux sighed, exasperated. "Don't be obstinate. The police will come along soon enough and I'd rather be long gone from here."

"Who told you?" Annja hated it when Roux tried to pull the privileged-information card.

Sirens screamed, sounding close.

Roux sighed. "Garin."

"Garin called you?"

"Yes. Is something wrong with your hearing?"

"Well, there was all that gunfire," Stanley said helpfully from the backseat.

"Why did Garin call you?" Annja asked.

"Because he wanted you clear of the situation."

"What situation?"

"Actually, that's my question," Roux said. "I got a phone call from Garin telling me to keep you from looking for Mjolnir, and I didn't even know you were looking for it." He narrowed his eyes. "Why *are* you looking for Mjolnir?"

"Garin didn't ask you to warn me off because he was worried about me," Annja replied. "He was worried I might get to it before he did."

"Perhaps." Roux tugged on the trunk again. "Could you lend a hand? It appears to be jammed."

"Why is Garin looking for Mjolnir?" Annja asked.

"Really, Annja, can you not see this is hardly the time for this?"

Annja stood quietly, waiting.

"I should have stayed in Monaco," Roux groused. "I gave up the charms of a very beautiful woman—a woman who's quite rich, mind you—to get disrespected first on the phone, then while trying to dispose of a getaway car riddled with bullet holes. Does that make any sense to you?"

"I'm still struggling with why Garin is looking for Mjolnir. And why you're not."

"Because the Mjolnir he's looking for is a sham."

"Then Mjolnir *does* exist?" That caught Annja off balance even though she'd been expecting the reply.

"Joan's sword exists. Why shouldn't Thor's hammer?"

"Because it belonged to a god."

"Everybody forgets that the Norse gods weren't gods when it came to immortality," Roux said. "They had to eat the apples Idun kept in order to maintain their youth. If you'll recall the Prose Edda, Loki stole the apples at one point and all the gods aged. The Greek gods had the golden apples they had to eat."

"I suppose some people—and that could be using the term loosely—could lead extended lives. Through some means," Annja said, glancing at Stanley.

Roux grinned at her. "An apple a day keeps the birthdays away."

"Apples?" Annja asked.

"No," Roux answered. "Not apples. The sword. For

however long it lasts. I think. Now, could you help me with
this trunk? I truly don't know any more about Garin's involvement in your current project than you do. I only came
here because the two of you seemed to be on a path that
promised collision."

Annja hooked her fingers under the trunk lid and lifted.
"Garin could have sent those men."

The trunk lid came up.

"He could have," Roux agreed, "but I don't think he
did."

"Why?"

"Because Garin respects you enough that he'd try to do
it himself. Oh, he may not come at you from the front and
may try to stab you in the back, but he'll do it himself."

"Because he was trained that way?"

Roux gave her a sour look, then reached into the trunk
and brought out a quart bottle of bourbon. He grinned as he
hefted the bottle. "Pity. Such a fine distillation, too." He
uncapped the bottle and took a drink, then offered it to
Annja.

Annja politely refused.

"You're taking time out for a drink?" Stanley asked.

"Just a stiffener," Roux said. Then he frowned. "You
need to get out of the car, Mr. Younts."

"I could call my attorney," Stanley offered. "He could
get this whole thing straightened out. We didn't do anything
wrong." He paused. "Well, we didn't do too much wrong."

"Aside from the time factor not exactly being on our
side in this thing," Roux replied, "you also need to realize
that doing our civic duty and going to the authorities will
place us in harm's way, Mr. Younts."

Roux's polite deference to Stanley bothered Annja.

She'd written a few books, tons of magazine articles and been in a television series that was at least partially built around her. He didn't treat her like that.

"How in harm's way?" Stanley asked.

"Because we would be sitting ducks inside a police station."

"Oh." Stanley looked perplexed. "I didn't think about that."

"You did once," Roux insisted. "In *Assault on Ice Station Episilon 2: Revenge of the Quaquod.*"

"I'd forgotten about that." Stanley beamed. "You really do read my books, don't you?"

"All thirty-four of them so far. If I can, I'd like very much to have them autographed."

"Sure."

Irritated, Annja said, "Look, the mutual-admiration society is hereby officially dissolved. We need to be moving."

"Sadly, she's right," Roux agreed. "I've got hotel rooms reserved. We can talk there. But I really need you to get out of the car."

Stanley got out.

"Shouldn't we wipe down the car?" Annja asked. "We've left prints all over it."

"No. This will take care of the need for that." Roux offered the bottle to Stanley. "Stiffener?"

"Sure." Stanley drank from the bottle, swallowing the alcohol with difficulty. "Wow!"

"Wow indeed." Roux smiled affectionately. Then he moved to the car, grabbed Annja's backpack and handed it to her. He emptied nearly all of the remainder of the bottle over the car's interior, saving enough for the exterior and a final swallow.

Holding a lighter a few inches from his face, Roux breathed out the alcohol. His breath turned to flames like a circus fire-eater and ignited the alcohol in the car.

"Wow!" Stanley said.

"Show-off," Annja said.

"Let's walk a few blocks and flag down a taxi. We'll take a water taxi to Venice. Our hotel reservations are there."

AT THE HOTEL, Annja discovered that Roux had rented a suite of rooms. She'd never stayed at the Hotel Concordia Venezia before. Overlooking St. Mark's Square, the hotel was located at the heart of the floating city. Getting to St. Mark's Books in the morning would mean only a matter of minutes on foot.

She left Stanley and Roux waxing eloquently about the author's books, which seemed to make them both happy. But it irritated Annja. They were acting as if they were on a camping trip and happened to end up with great bunk mates instead of being involved in a potential life-or-death situation.

Still, watching them, Annja knew that if Mario had been alive tonight and along for the trip, he'd have been right in there with them. Mario had loved popular fiction, as well.

She walked into the bathroom and saw the marble and mirror walls. The tub was a yawning pit that would hold an ocean of water. She turned on the taps, found what sounded like a soothing bath oil and poured it in. The fragrance, spread by the hot water, filled the room and promised divine deliverance.

Before she could get undressed, a knock sounded at the adjoining door. Reluctantly, she went to answer it.

Roux stood there.

"I swear to you," Annja said, "if you try to pull me into your deliberation on who is the best writer in the world, I'm reaching for the sword."

"My, my," Roux said. "Surly tonight, aren't we?"

"Tired. Cranky. Under-pampered." And feeling guilty because I'm alive and a friend of mine isn't, Annja added silently.

"You lost your luggage at the airport," Roux said. "I know from personal experience that young women appreciate the ability to present themselves well and generally hate dishabille."

"Could we save the flowery speech? I've got a bath and I intend to soak until I look like a raisin."

Roux grimaced. "I could have done without knowing that." He stepped back and pointed at the uniformed bellhop holding on to one end of a transfer cart. "I took it upon myself to provide you suitable raiment."

Annja looked at all the boxes from a clothing store. "But everything's closed."

"I still have a few old acquaintances here who will give me preferential treatment. I simply called in a favor."

Annja stepped back and allowed the bellhop into her room. He wheeled the cart in and looked around. Annja directed him to put everything on the bed. He did, then left.

Mesmerized by the unexpected bounty, Annja opened boxes, finding jeans, tops, underwear, tennis shoes, boots and even three dresses, one of them a simple black cocktail dress. There was even a full makeup case, toiletries containing an assortment of perfumes, and a too-big T-shirt that would be perfect to sleep in.

Everything was in her size. Annja looked at him. "How did you know about the sizes?"

"I've bought clothing for hundreds of years," Roux said. "I know sizes. Do you need anything else?" He eyed the clothes dubiously. "I think I got most everything, but if I missed something, I can still—"

"No," Annja replied, grinning like a loon and unable to stop herself. "This is perfect. Really."

"I'm glad you like it." Roux turned to walk away. "I'll leave you to your bath and bed. We're going to have an early morning."

"Roux."

He turned to face her.

"Thank you. This means a lot."

Roux grinned. "Enjoy, dear girl. It does my heart glad to see you happy." He left.

Annja took new underwear, the toiletry kit and the oversize T-shirt to the bathroom.

# 32

St. Mark's Books was a small shop situated only a couple blocks off St. Mark's Square. Pedestrians, a mix of tourists and residents, filled the sidewalks and alleys. Since there were no automobiles or bicycles, all traffic—except for the canals—was by foot.

After making certain no one was at the bookshop, Annja rejoined Roux and Stanley at the open-air bistro across the street. They'd ordered breakfast and it was waiting by the time Annja took her seat.

"Don't be impatient," Roux advised.

"I'm not impatient," Annja said. It was hard to be irritable with him when she was wearing clothes—really good clothes—that he'd bought for her in the dead of night. "I'm anxious. I keep expecting Garin."

"He's not here." Roux helped himself to a ham-and-cheese frittata, then added another sweet roll, as well.

Annja didn't hold back. Roux wasn't the only one

gifted with a fast metabolism. She piled her plate high. "How do you know he's not here?" she asked.

"He called me last night."

"And you didn't tell me?"

"I knocked. I heard you snoring, so rather than wake you, I thought I'd wait until this morning."

"I don't snore."

"You snore," Stanley said.

Annja shot him a look.

"In a ladylike manner," he added. "A *loud* ladylike manner."

"What did Garin say?" Annja asked.

"He was glad to see that we hadn't been killed. Then he told me he'd be happy to do the job himself if we continued to interfere."

"Where is he?"

"Austria, if his phone number was legitimate. I've heard those can be artificially altered."

"Who's Garin?" Stanley asked.

Annja let Roux field that one.

"A former associate. He's become somewhat disenchanted with us, I'm afraid."

"That's too bad. You guys are a blast to be around. Gunfights. Car chases. Never a dull moment. I've already started fleshing out my next plot. It's gonna be a doozie. It's going to feature a young woman who's struggling to get her independence from her doting archaeologist grandfather, who's kind of a passive-aggressive control freak, only he's gone missing in the wilds of…of somewhere— I'll work that out later—and she's the only person in the world who can find him. Their minds think alike, see?"

"We don't think alike," Annja said.

"And I don't picture myself as a doting grandfather," Roux said. "Furthermore, how can you possibly be both doting and a passive-aggressive manipulator at the same time?"

"If he's never around to share things with her—" Annja shot Roux a glance "—how can he be controlling?"

Stanley sighed and held his hands up, palms out. "Guys, could we take an ego break here? I'm going to be writing a novel, not a biography. Those two characters aren't you guys. They're the people I imagine them to be." He frowned. "You know, this is why writers never talk about their books to their friends. The friends keep trying to see themselves in the plot."

Roux muttered something under his breath.

"And this is novel writing," Stanley continued, "not brain surgery. You can't take fiction too seriously. If it was too much like real life, it would be boring." He looked around. "Although I'll be the first to admit that you guys don't have boring lives."

THE OWNER of St. Mark's Books was a man named Michelangelo DiBenedetto. He was in his late fifties or early sixties, portly and had a habit of running his hand through his longish cotton-white hair. He arrived at ten minutes before ten, put the open sign in the door, and was just setting out a stand of clearance books when Annja approached him.

"Good morning," he greeted in English.

"Good morning," Annja said.

DiBenedetto looked at Annja strangely. "I know you. You're Annja Creed. Mario's friend."

The words hurt. It was one thing to be remembered as the cohost on *Chasing History's Monsters,* which she got a lot—but the association DiBenedetto made reminded her of what had been lost to bring her to this point of her journey.

"You're also supposed to be dead," DiBenedetto went on. "At least, the police keep denying that you are so dogmatically that the media is certain that you are."

"Dead?" Annja repeated.

"In the terrorist attack at the airport."

"They're saying it was a terrorist attack?"

DiBenedetto nodded. "One of those fruitcake fringe groups called in and took credit for it." He looked past Annja and spotted Stanley. A grin split the shopkeeper's face. "You'd be Stanley Younts."

"I am." Stanley was obviously happy to be recognized.

"I would have known you from your picture on the back cover of the books," DiBenedetto said. "Even if there hadn't been all the press coverage this morning."

"Well," Roux said sourly, "I can see that disguises will be in order before we go much further in this endeavor."

They went inside the store, and Roux and Stanley combed the book racks. Both of them wanted to stock up on reading material, and DiBenedetto had some first editions of Younts's books that he wanted autographed.

While they were busy with that, the bookstore owner got the package Mario had left for Annja.

The package was rectangular and five inches thick. Covered in brown paper and secured by twine, it looked unassuming.

"Do you know what it is?" Annja asked.

"No. Mario didn't say. He just asked me to keep it here for him. Until he returned or you came for it."

Annja took her Swiss Army knife out and cut the twine. "Do you know what happened to Mario?"

DiBenedetto nodded somberly. "The family called me and told me. They're going to have the funeral in a couple of days—when they get his body back from the United States. I'm going to shut down the shop and go. He was always in and out of the shop, always talking about things he was researching. I enjoyed our conversations."

The revelation caught Annja's attention. "Had you known him long?"

"Sure." DiBenedetto shrugged. "Since he was a boy. He was my nephew. I married his mother's sister."

Mario had left the package with family. It made perfect sense to Annja then. She unwrapped the contents of the package.

Two books, both leather covered and thick, came loose in her hands. One bore the stamp of the Vatican and looked very old.

"If I didn't know any better," DiBenedetto said, "I'd say that was the genuine article."

"It is genuine," Annja said. The reverent tone in her voice drew Roux and Stanley close. They looked over her shoulder.

An outdated cursive script covered the pages, written in Latin. The first entry was dated January 23, 1209: "Here Opens the Personal Narrative of Janis Ozolini, Town Historian."

"That book is eight hundred years old," Stanley said.

Annja nodded.

"But it's gotta be a fake."

"Why?" Annja asked.

"Because the pages are too white. A paperback has a shelf life of about three weeks and begins to yellow on day one."

"This is the way paper used to be made," Roux said. "The way it should always be made. If you get the chance to look at some of the books that were made six and seven hundred years ago, and longer, I think you'd be surprised at how well they were made, from the paper to the stitching to the binding." He shook his head. "You just don't see that kind of quality anymore."

"I'll take your word for it," Younts said.

"Come to my house sometime," Roux invited. "I'll show you the private collection I've put together."

Annja looked at Roux in irritation. He usually wasn't so generous with his things.

He refused to meet her gaze.

There was a note from Mario in the first book. Annja read it aloud to the others.

Dear Annja,

If you're getting these books from Uncle Michelangelo, then I guess that means something has gone horribly wrong.

I wasn't looking for this story when I found it. But that's the way things are sometimes in our field, isn't it? Looking for one thing and finding another.

Of course, I was looking for embarrassing discrepancies committed by the Holy Roman Church because that seems to be all the rage these days. While doing that in my copious spare time—the job there as an archivist was not only boring, but there wasn't much of it—I started researching the Teutonic order. You know, the German knights in black and white that went forth to smite religion into the heads of unbelievers?

I found this journal—please see to it that Archbishop Morelli gets it back because he is really a decent person who loves books and I didn't exactly tell him I was taking it with me when I left—and the story it contained. It's not really a big secret, but apparently it was enough of one.

It seems there was this Austrian baron, Frederick of Schluter, who got the story of a Viking who lived among the Curonians. As the tale was told, this Viking was named Thor and he had an enchanted hammer that gave him power against all his enemies.

One of the stories involved Thor's untold wealth that he brought with him from wherever it was that he hailed from. No one has said and I haven't found that story. Yet. Hopefully you will.

Apparently Frederick of Schluter was obsessed by the treasure story and went to Riga to find it. He and his men ran roughshod over the local villagers. Ozolini's journal describes the murders the baron committed, as well as the rape and torture of the villagers. Evidently Frederick was cruel and sadistic.

Ozolini, as you'll see, was appalled by the baron's bloodthirsty ways. He documented the atrocities in this journal. I've marked the sections for you. Ozolini states his intention of presenting the case before Pope Innocent III, hoping to get Frederick of Schluter thrown out of the Teutonic order. He sent the journal by messenger while he came back by another route. Evidently he'd told Baron Frederick his intentions.

As you'll doubtless remember from history class, Innocent III's reign was supposed to return the Catholic Church to power during his term. He succeeded and failed. There was enough political infighting going on during those years that the journal arrived and was promptly shelved.

I found a few letters by archivists suggesting the pope take a look at the journal. Unfortunately, Innocent III had his hands full dealing with the fall-out from the Fourth Crusade. He was totally ticked at how the crusaders handled the situation. They were supposed to open a way to the Holy Land. Instead, they attacked and eventually sacked Constantinople.

As a result, the split between the Catholic West and Orthodox East became irrevocable, and the church's power was forever affected. Several more years of accusations and attacks on the church followed.

It's no wonder that this journal was lost. Plus, I think Frederick of Schluter had friends in the church who searched for the journal. The archivist who championed the journal was eventually murdered. I looked him up in the papal histories. His murderers were never caught.

As for Ozolini, he was killed by brigands not far outside the village where he'd lived his whole life. Personally, I believe Frederick of Schluter hired someone or masked his identity while he did it himself. Ozolini's death was recorded in a book kept by the father who kept the church there. I found that out when I visited.

So the only person who's truly following this story now is you, Annja.

On a more personal note, I fell in love with a woman. Believe it or not, I was smitten with her almost as soon as I laid eyes on her. There's something about falling in love at first sight that I never expected. I didn't believe it, either. My sisters tried to explain it to me, but I wouldn't listen. I was too busy chasing the past to live in the present, they said, and maybe they were right.

Her name is Erene Skujans. She's a hedge witch in the community where I was staying. I know you know what a hedge witch is. But she's something more, too. I didn't find out the whole truth until it was too late.

After I'd lived there for a few months, I discovered inadvertently who she truly was. I'd known she'd left the village for a while, but I hadn't known where she'd gone or what she'd done. Her grandmother before her had been the village hedge witch. Erene had been trained to take over for her. She didn't want to, and chose to run away. Personally, I could understand a teenage girl wanting to broaden her horizons.

I met a man in town who told me that Erene was a professional thief and confidence woman. At first, I didn't believe him. But he had arrest records and photographs. The evidence was right there. He told me he was an international bounty hunter there to take her in. He said he'd been a policeman and had pursued Erene for a time, but he'd never caught her.

I may be slow, Annja, and a little off my game when it came to this woman, but you can't ignore an oversight like that. She'd lied to me by omission. You can't take back something like that. One thing living with my family has always taught me is to always be truthful in a relationship.

I left the next day. Erene had shown a lot of interest in the treasure, though I doubt it's there, but there might be other artifacts. I thought she was just excited to see me succeed. But now I don't think that was the case at all. Erene went back home to hide out and regroup after a particularly nasty failure.

I had these books sent in secret to Uncle Michelangelo, then sent a more obvious package to your address in Brooklyn.

Whatever's happened to me, make sure you take care of yourself. This find, if it's Viking treasure, I hope will be significant. But there are other people looking for it.

While researching the facts in Ozolini's book, I contacted Baroness Schluter. She still lives in the family castle outside Vienna. I was surprised she knew as much of the story as she did, but I could also tell she was reticent to share much with me.

Baron Frederick's vile treatment of the locals while in pursuit of the treasure was graphically described by Ozolini. If the story gets out today, there might be repercussions. The Schluter family remains a member of the Teutonic order, but that would probably change given the circumstances of Baron Frederick's service. He did manage to build a church, but he also filled a graveyard with victims.

The baroness told me she'd see me burn in hell before the story of her ancestor came to light. I believed her. She's eighty-something years old and a scary old bat. Not to mention the grandson. Wolfram Schluter is aptly named. There's a hunger and evil in him that you can see. I found out later, while researching the family, that the barony is almost destitute. Greed has always motivated treasure hunters.

As you'll see in Ozolini's journal, when Thor died, the belief is that he was given a Viking funeral. He was put in a small boat in the harbor and set on fire. No mention was made of what became of his hammer or the wealth he'd amassed.

It's there, Annja, and I think I've almost found it. Hopefully you and I will be able to find it together. You were a lot better at site surveys than I was. As near as I can figure, there's a catacomb of old Roman graves somewhere out there that Thor used to hide his treasure.

There was more to the letter, but it was of a personal nature. Annja didn't read it aloud. Mario had intended that part for her only, and she wanted to keep it that way.

Continuing to leaf through the journal, Annja saw the book contained drawings of people and places, as well as maps of the general area. She shifted her attention to the second book.

"Fellini was making a copy," Roux said.

"Why didn't he just photocopy the original?" Stanley asked.

Annja leafed through the second book. She noticed the change from the original notations to extra patches of narrative that Mario had written in.

"Because he was annotating this copy," Annja realized. "Adding in details from his personal observations and on-site fact-finding."

"In Riga?" Roux asked.

"Outside Riga," Annja said. "He said he stayed in a

village he guessed was near the original site where Thor landed and repelled the Vikings." She looked at Roux. "I need some time to read through this."

Roux looked troubled. "We don't have a lot of time. There are others obviously seeking the same treasure."

"They haven't found it yet," Annja reminded him. "We have some time."

"It will take a while to set up a means to get out of Venice and to Riga. You can work en route."

"Terrific," Annja said. "Generous much?"

Roux scowled at her. "Sitting around isn't the way you do things, and you know it. Nor is it how I do things."

"Okay," Annja agreed. "Guilty as charged." She was itching to be on the move herself.

# 33

"What do you call this process again?" Stanley asked as he watched with avid interest.

Seated in the opulent cabin of the yacht Roux had chartered in Venice, Annja stared at the photographs from aerial surveys Mario had accumulated. She had them spread out over the table, moving and shifting them as different points caught her interest.

"It's called an archaeological field study," Annja replied.

"These are geographical maps." Stanley sounded confused but eager to learn.

Annja had heard that tone on several occasions in her career. First as a university student, then again from students in guest lectures or seminars that she had taught at different times.

"Geologists and archaeologists tend to use a lot of the same tools and information," Annja said. "We just interpret them differently. An engineer intending to build a factory or a building would look at everything in another way."

"So would a city planner," Stanley said. "I did a book about a guy who was a city planner chasing a serial killer through the metro area he helped design. I had to learn a lot about building cities."

"So did I." Annja sifted through the photographs and made some notes. "I think I may have found the original site of the Curonian village where Thor was supposed to have lived."

"Where?" Stanley asked.

"Here." Annja placed her finger on the coastline near Liepaja.

"Not closer to Riga?"

"The story that Mario was following has been told several times, and most of them agree that when the Vikings attempted to raid the Curonian village it was in early winter, after the first snows had started coming. Liepaja offers one of the only ice-free ports in the Baltic Sea."

"The Vikings would have known this?"

"The Norsemen would, yes. And they were Norsemen, not Vikings. Viking was an occupation, not a culture."

Stanley nodded. "I try to get it right, but there's just so much to learn, and so quickly, when you're a writer. You have a choice of writing what you know about or trying to expose yourself and your readers to new information. It gets tough."

"Archaeology is the same. I don't know everything. My training allows me to know where to start searching for answers faster than a layman. But I've seen people who have made a time period or a piece of real estate so important in their lives that they knew more than a lot of university-trained professionals."

"So you like Liepaja because of the port."

"I do."

"Why not Liepaja itself?"

"Liepaja didn't exist then. At least, not in name. But it held a large population. Fishing, trade and amber—which couldn't be found anywhere else in Europe—all made Liepaja a major crossroads."

"It wasn't a prize Vikings would have targeted."

"Not a lone crew." Annja pointed to a topographical map. "The physical ground sounds about right." She drew her finger along the map to a mark Mario had placed on the map. Neat handwriting spelled out "Erene's village."

"That's where the girlfriend lived," Stanley said.

"Yes. The elevation in the area is 120 feet above sea level. Plenty of room to put in a catacomb. Or they may be there naturally," Annja said.

"Naturally? I was under the impression that catacombs were graveyards that had been built."

"More often than not, catacombs were put in where caves existed. Excavation made the caves bigger and deeper. By the sixth century, though, most cultures had given up the practice of catacombs and were burying their dead in graveyards."

"Are you looking for a graveyard or a catacomb?"

"The history that Mario turned up indicated the presence of Roman soldiers garrisoned there to protect shipments along the Amber Road."

"I'm not familiar with the Amber Road," Stanley said.

"Amber was beautiful and rare in those days," Annja said. "Kings and queens used it in ornaments and paid a lot for it because it was so hard to get. The Roman warriors were there to keep bandits from hitting the caravans that left Riga and went down to Palanga, Lithuania."

Stanley nodded.

"Mario researched several documents and located the Roman fort." Annja opened the book Mario had copied and appended. "He also found a lot of stories about Roman artifacts that had been found in the area since that time."

"That's important?" Stanley was taking notes on a legal pad.

"When you're doing a field study," Annja said, "you want to consult books and journals written in the area as close to the time that you're researching. Tales that people in an area continue to tell each other and each successive generation are valuable. Other surveys and explorations of the area that might have been done are good. Even if the people conducting those weren't looking for the same things you were. All of those things help an archaeologist decide where to look for answers to a question."

"You have to have a question?"

"You don't have to, but it's better if you do. Then you use aerial photographs," Annja said.

"I noticed there were several of those."

"Mario got some of them from others, but some he took himself."

Stanley looked at the collection of photos Annja pushed toward him. "These look really good. But he only looks like he was a hundred feet or so off the ground. I'm surprised they aren't blurred while flying that close."

"He didn't take them from a plane," Annja said. "He used a kite."

"A kite?"

"You don't always get the equipment you need in the

field," Annja told him. "The actors in movies always seem to acquire ground radar and other high-tech equipment just by making a phone call. In real life, especially when you're on your own, you have to improvise. Mario and I learned to take photographs using kites. A good camera equipped with a timer and you're good to go."

"What are you hoping to find from the air?"

"Shadow marks, crop marks, frost marks or soil marks."

Stanley wrote furiously as Annja searched through the pictures to better illustrate what she was explaining.

"Shadow marks are better suited to finding aboveground features rather than buried ones. I looked for shadow marks, but I didn't find any. Neither did Mario. But he did find crop marks." Annja pulled out a photograph and pushed it over.

Stanley looked at the photo.

"Here. These pictures were taken in the summer. Crop marks show a difference in growth patterns. Places where the ground has been worked or that have buried ditches will hold more water."

"Promoting better crop growth because of the extra irrigation," Stanley said.

Annja smiled. He was a fast learner. "Exactly. Places that have buried structures, or only had the walls left standing when dirt covered it, don't allow the same amount of irrigation."

"The bigger the object, the more it affects the area."

"Yes."

"And what we're looking for is big."

"That's right. Also, it's been partially found."

Stanley looked at her.

Annja took out more photographs. "The Roman soldiers stationed at the fort took advantage of a small cave system located nearby. According to the reports Mario found, the Romans located the caves while digging wells for water. They chose to open the caves and bury their dead."

"They were stationed there long enough to get old and die?"

"Some of the legionnaires were. A posting lasting several years wasn't uncommon. Rome was spread out in all directions. Swapping manpower around was a logistical nightmare. Also, there were bandit attacks and sickness that claimed lives."

"What do you mean it's been partially found?" Stanley asked.

Annja brought out more photographs that showed the excavation of the Roman catacombs. "They were found and explored by British tomb raiders in the 1920s. That's how a lot of the Roman artifacts that turned up in the village where Mario was staying got there. The tomb raiders kept whatever gold and silver they found, then used the trinkets to trade for beer and supplies."

Stanley sat back on the couch. "If the catacombs have already been found, then there's no treasure there."

Smiling, Annja said, "The grave robbers found the Roman catacombs, but I don't think they found Thor's final resting place."

"Why?"

"Because the hammer was never found."

"It might never have existed," Stanley said.

"The problem with archaeology is that you have to believe in something until you prove it or disprove it," Annja said. "Maybe we're just chasing a local legend. But it's been a persistent one. I'm going to believe the story for a while longer because I choose to." She picked up the original book Mario had "borrowed" from the Vatican City archives. "And then there's this, from Ozolini's journal."

Though he will not admit it because he is blinded by his own desperate greed, Baron Frederick of Schluter is a fool. He came here chasing improbable lies and legends of a Norse god who lived among Curonian fishermen and defended them against Norsemen.

The legend says that Thor's people burned him at sea in a captured Norseman's ship. The baron will not hear of that, though. He chooses to believe that Thor was given a grave to sleep away all of time, and his fortune to sleep with him.

I have talked to some who have talked to the Curonians, but not much has been said. They are still a warlike people and not open to friendship, only save enough to maintain trade. My father was alive when they killed the Catholic priests who served the small church by the old Roman fort.

The priests weren't good men, but they were God's chosen. There was talk of forming an army and driving the Curonians from their village, but the Brotherhood of the Sword recently reclaimed that church. Those that were not killed by the German knights died in winter's cruel embrace. Thor may have saved them then, but their hero was not with them ten years ago.

I was with one of those Curonian warriors when he was delirious with fever after taking a German arrow through his lung. My father was the physician and felt no man should be untended. I did not agree with him, but I did not disobey him when he bade me to help. Also, I was curious about those fierce warriors.

The man coughed and spit up blood throughout the night while my father and I tried to care for him as best as we were able. I could tell that my father could do nothing for the Curonian. I had seen that helpless look on his face often enough.

During the warrior's ravings, the Curonian said that he had been one of the men who put Thor in his final resting place. He talked to me as though I were his brother. He told me that the great warrior's treasures are hidden beneath those who are already dead.

Though I am familiar with this area, having grown up here and lived all my life in this town, and I have known of some of the Roman graves that were disturbed, no one has ever claimed the sleeping god's bounty.

Thor and the treasure may never have existed, but Baron Frederick's villainy does. I pray that God is with me on my long journey, for I fear that I have been too vocal in my intolerance of the baron's abuses.

"Even Ozolini didn't believe the legend at the end," Stanley pointed out.

"Ozolini may *never* have believed in the legend," Annja replied.

"Where do you think Thor's tomb is? Beneath the Roman catacombs?"

Annja picked up one of the photographs they'd already looked at. She traced the discrepancy in the ground that Mario's photography had discovered. "Do you see it?"

Stanley peered more closely. "See what?"

"Off to the right." Annja tapped the photograph. "Mario shot this in the winter, on a day that was freezing but the ground wasn't covered with snow. These are frost marks."

"They're like the ones that show the Roman catacombs," Stanley said softly.

"Exactly. But they're hard to see because there's a lot of space open under there."

"You think there's another cave system down there?"

"We're going to find out."

# 34

More than just the ruins of the Roman catacombs and the church remained. A small village was nestled at the bottom of a rolling valley less than a mile away. The people who lived there eked out a subsistence living from the land.

From her earlier trip through the village in the SUV they'd rented after their arrival in Liepaja, Annja knew that the villagers supplemented that income with handcrafts, rugs, blankets and pottery. They'd stared at her with watchful eyes as she drove through the village late that afternoon.

Once at the ruins atop the hill that overlooked a landscape still partially covered in snow, Annja went into photojournalist mode. She was serious about the pictures and used the effort to get a better look at the ground where she suspected the additional cave structure was.

Looking at the widespread frost marks that had sunk into the ground and looked as large as a skating arena, she was more certain than ever of what lay below. Anticipation danced in her mind and made her restless.

The catacombs were sealed and a note in four different languages informed the reader that access should be arranged through the tourism department. Viewings were by special arrangement only. The broken fragments of the church walls that had survived had a similar declaration.

Roux sat in the SUV and looked very much like a doting grandfather as he flipped the pages in Stanley's latest thriller.

"Are you just going to sit there and read?" Annja asked as she downloaded pictures from her digital camera to her notebook computer.

Roux turned a page and for a moment she thought he was going to ignore her. Then he placed a finger between the pages and closed the book.

"If you'll recall," he said, "I suggested that we wait for nightfall after we arrived at Liepaja."

"I'd rather get a look at everything while it's light. It seemed to make more sense," Annja said.

"It does. That's why I came with you. However, knowing how impatient you are, I thought it would be better if we stayed at the hotel with Stanley for a while before coming out here."

Stanley hadn't been happy about being left behind. But even Roux had been adamant.

Annja unhooked the USB cable from the camera and wiped the memory. "Do you think Garin will show up here?"

Roux nodded. "Yes."

"What's his interest in this?"

Shifting his attention to the mound where the Roman catacombs lay, Roux was silent for a moment. "Sixty years ago, Garin fell in love with a beautiful young woman."

Annja grinned. "I'm sure, knowing Garin as I do, that he was over it by the next morning."

"No, and that was sad," Roux said seriously.

"That Garin actually cared about someone?"

"Yes." Roux looked at her. His eyes were hidden by a pair of sunglasses. Clouds blunted the sun, but the snow patches were exceedingly bright.

"Why?"

"You've never lost anyone in your life that you loved," Roux stated bluntly.

Anger twisted knots in Annja's stomach, but pain was there, as well. "I learned early not to get too involved with anyone. I've never had anyone to lose."

"I know. I see that in you. Given your current state, and the burden that sword puts on you, your reticence to commit to a long-term relationship is the best thing that could happen to you."

"From what I've heard of Garin's personal life, he isn't someone who just reaches out, either," Annja said.

"No, but Garin didn't grow up and become as complete as you did. That's why he cherishes material things and power as much as he does. But inside, he still romances the idea of being in love."

Annja silently disagreed with Roux's assessment. Garin was hard and distant, and he wouldn't *ever* care about anyone but himself.

"He grew up in a different time than you did, Annja," Roux said. "Maybe his life was harsh, but he was brought up believing in love—that there would be a woman for him."

"If this was the one, then how did he lose her?"

"Because he saw what would happen if he stayed."

Annja leaned a hip against the SUV. She reached into

the back and took out a sandwich from the picnic basket Roux had ordered prepared for the trip.

"What would happen?" she asked.

Roux smiled mirthlessly. "She would grow old, of course. And die. He would not."

Annja thought about that and realized how sad that would be. She also realized that Roux—and Garin—must have watched many people they loved pass away during the course of their long lives.

"The first time you fall in love," Roux said, "you're so busy falling in love that you don't think about the consequences. Ten or twenty years later, you begin to realize what you've done, and the loss you face."

"Did Garin leave her because of that?" Annja ate her sandwich mechanically.

"No. I don't think he would have left this one. There were others, you see. But none that he felt matched him so exactly." Roux gazed at the western sky. "She was married, and at the end of her infatuation with Garin, she told him to go away. Even though Garin was a man of great means in those days, he wasn't titled."

"The man this woman was married to had a title?"

"Yes."

"And she chose that title over what she felt for Garin?"

"Ultimately."

Annja shook her head. "Maybe she still loved her husband."

"Hardly. The man was weak willed and easily controlled. She chose him over Garin because she felt Garin would threaten her chances of getting a new infusion of money through inheritance. Her father had somewhat exhausted the family holdings."

"But you said Garin had money."

"He was a commoner. She was the daughter of a baron."

"I don't understand what any of that has to do with why Garin is involved in this now."

"The woman is still alive," Roux said. "Her name is Kikka Schluter. Baroness Schluter."

"Oh," Annja said. "And Mario's investigation threatens her family's good name."

"Exactly." Roux pulled an apple out of the basket and bit into it with a loud crunch.

"But it's been sixty years," Annja said.

"I know. But Garin is still involved with her on an emotional level."

Annja ate her sandwich for a moment, thinking. She was involved in the current situation partly because of her curiosity, but mostly because of her friendship with Mario. Most people she knew wouldn't have hung on so tightly to getting to the truth of everything that had happened.

"Did Garin tell you this?" she asked.

"Of course not. Garin would never discuss something like this with me. I have people to keep watch over him from time to time. In those years, so soon after the war, with everything changing around us and so many important artifacts that Hitler had gathered up being on the move, I knew it was in my best interests to know where Garin was."

"And so you think he's going to be here," Annja stated.

"I do. I only hope that we lost all pursuit in Venice."

Annja knew that was possible because Roux had provided new identification papers for everyone. They'd been picked up at sea by a helicopter, then flown to Rome and boarded Roux's private jet to Liepaja.

She ate her sandwich and waited for sundown.

STANLEY WAS on the phone with his agent when the blond man stepped through the doorway of his hotel room. That hadn't been an easy thing to do. In addition to the electronic lock, which Stanley knew could be circumvented, he had also used the dead bolt.

The dead bolt shrilled as it tore out of the doorframe.

The man crossed the room in three long strides, grabbed the satellite phone from Stanley's hand and tossed it against the wall. The phone shattered and fell to the floor.

"What do you think you're—?" Stanley got very quiet and still when the man shoved a big-barreled pistol into his face. Then he recognized the intruder.

Wolfram Schluter grinned at him. "Come with me. Now. And maybe you won't die."

Even though he knew Schluter was lying, that the man probably intended to kill him no matter what, Stanley went. He hoped to live long enough to find out if Annja Creed was right about the dead Viking.

GARIN WAITED out in the SUV. Kikka Schluter sat beside him. He studied their reflection in the window, seeing no changes in himself and what time had done to her.

Is this what it would have been like? he wondered. If I had stayed, if she had let me, would this be what we would have been left?

"You're tense," she said in that husky voice that hadn't changed much.

Focusing on the hotel beyond their reflection in the glass, Garin said, "I'm not used to sitting and waiting."

Kikka smiled. "Your father was like that, too. He would see something he wanted and go right for it."

Painfully, Garin was aware that Roux had always told

him that, too. He'd thought Roux incredibly old when he
was just a boy. Now, with over five hundred years of living
behind him, he realized that he himself was incredibly old
but that his way of handling his life hadn't changed much.

He didn't know whether to be proud or embarrassed.

"Everything will be all right," Kikka told him. She
reached out and took his hand. It felt fragile and cold in his.

Fleeting, he couldn't help thinking. For him time had
stood still, but for her it had marched on inexorably.

Garin turned to her then, remembering how he'd loved
talking to her, how much he'd enjoyed simply holding her
hand. He was surprised at how little his love had faded
over the years.

He smiled at her. "I'm supposed to be the one reas-
suring you."

"Then do so," she challenged him.

"I really wish you had stayed at the hotel," Garin said.
"You would be a lot safer—"

Kikka laid a finger across his lips. "Not another word,"
she said. "This could be my last adventure, and I want it
to be a good one."

Garin's heart melted. It was so easy to look past her appearance. She was still very much the woman she had
been all those years ago.

"All right," he said.

SCHLUTER KEPT the pistol pressed into Stanley Younts's
side as he marched him from the hotel. The writer tripped
and stumbled a couple of times.

The woman at the concierge desk noticed and frowned.
"Sir, do you need help?"

"No, thank you." Schluter smiled at her. "He's just had

a little bit too much of a celebration. When I get him home, he'll be fine."

"I can call a cab."

"I've got a car waiting outside."

The woman waved to the doorman, though, and the door was opened.

"Straighten up and walk," Schluter commanded. "If you don't, I'm going to take you outside of town and put a bullet through your head."

The writer made an effort to stand more strongly. "Why are you taking me?"

"Shut up."

"I don't know anything."

"You know where Annja Creed is." Schluter directed the writer toward the black SUV pulling to the curb.

"I won't tell," the writer threatened.

Spinning the man around, using his body to conceal the pistol in his hand, Schluter shoved the writer up against the SUV and screwed the pistol barrel up under his jaw.

"You'll tell," Schluter said. "I promise you that."

Fear widened the man's eyes behind the glasses.

Garin Braden reached forward and opened the side door.

Schluter shoved the writer inside, then climbed in. Dropping into the seat facing his grandmother and Braden, Schluter noticed that the old woman was holding the man's hand. Schluter cursed and put a foot on Stanley Younts's head.

"Stay down," he ordered.

The writer remained on the floor as the SUV got under way.

Glancing through the window, Schluter kept the pistol

on his lap. Three other SUVs, all carrying his men, pulled into line after them as the vehicle rolled onto the street.

Temptation ate at Schluter to simply lift his pistol and shoot Braden in the head. Nothing could stop him. His grandmother might be irritated, but she'd get over it. And if she didn't…

Then he noticed that although the man's left hand was held by his grandmother, his right hand was hidden beneath his jacket.

Braden grinned at him and nodded.

Disgusted, Schluter directed his wrath at the writer. "Where is Annja Creed?" They had missed her in Venice and Braden had been certain she'd gone searching for the prize.

"I'm not going to tell you," Stanley Younts said.

Schluter hit him in the face with the pistol butt. The writer cried out in pain. When he recovered, Schluter repeated the question.

"Do you have a map?" Younts said.

# 35

Just after full dark had fallen, while Annja was getting her gear from the back of the SUV, Roux grabbed her arm.

"Quiet," he whispered.

Like her, he was dressed in winter camouflage gear that they'd gotten at a military surplus store in Liepaja. The camouflage gear was Russian made and didn't fit very well, but it was patterned in white and brown and would hopefully offer some invisibility in the snowy night.

Annja had pulled the SUV into the trees nearly a quarter mile from the Roman catacombs. No one else had been on the road when she'd hidden the vehicle with Roux's help.

They were still and silent. Just when Annja was about to ask Roux what was wrong, she realized something.

We're not alone.

The thought struck her like a physical blow.

Roux pointed to the left, along the ridgeline of the hilltop overlooking the ruins. "That way," he mouthed.

She could see just well enough in the darkness to read his lips.

They went together, moving silently through the brush. Before Annja knew it, she had the sword in hand. The possibility existed that whoever was closing in on them was purely innocent, maybe inquisitive kids or teenagers wanting some privacy, but she wouldn't have taken a bet on it.

Whoever was coming was approaching stealthily.

Roux knelt in the brush and pulled the lower part of his mask up over his mouth to keep his breath from showing. He had a Russian-made Tokarev pistol in his hand. He'd purchased two of them. Annja had preferred the sword and hoped it wouldn't come to that.

A few minutes later, shadows formed in the darkness and gathered around the SUV. Annja recognized Erene Skujans from the picture Mario had carried in his wallet, but she didn't know the big man with her.

Other men moved in the darkness around them.

Annja pressed herself more tightly against the pine tree at her back.

ERENE SKUJANS SURVEYED the landscape. She laid a hand over the SUV's engine. "Still warm," she said.

Dalton Hyde stood at her side, his pistol visible in a shoulder holster. "They're still here somewhere," he said quietly. "Must have heard us coming. Don't worry about it. We'll find them."

Erene didn't say anything, but she was worried. When she'd woken in the morning after the fight with Ivanov, she'd had a hangover and been in more pain over Mario's death than ever. The violence and the vodka had stripped her of the wall she'd used to dam up the emotions that had lain in wait.

Hyde had taken care of her, helping her through the sickness, fixing her meals and talking to her. It was a lot like it had been in the old days when he'd first agreed to tutor her in burglary.

In the end, he'd asked her why she had come back to the village—besides the botched job she'd been part of. There hadn't been any use lying about it. Mario had left the house covered in the research he'd done regarding the Norse legend he'd been pursuing.

So she'd told him. After that, he'd stayed and they'd talked about what she was going to do when she left the village with him. It had been a foregone conclusion that she would go. There was nothing to hold her there.

Erene thought of the little girl whose arm she'd rebroken and splinted. Erene had told Hyde that she wanted to wait a couple more weeks before leaving, at least long enough to see if the bones were going to knit properly this time.

Hyde had agreed with less of a fight than Erene had expected. But he'd talked about a few of the jobs he was looking into where her skills would be invaluable.

While they'd been in the tavern earlier in the day they learned Ivanov had fled the village and they heard about the chestnut-haired woman who was at the old Roman ruins. Hyde mentioned that she sounded like the picture of the woman he'd seen in one of Mario's albums, and that there had been a lot of pictures shot at the Roman ruins. When they'd shown the photograph of Annja Creed to the man who'd seen her, he'd said it was her.

"You know," Hyde had said, "it would be a shame if Mario told her where to find that treasure."

Jealous and angry, Erene had quickly agreed that they

should investigate. He'd made a call and men he'd brought with him had shown up in the village, fully armed and ready to move.

Hyde broke the SUV's window and reached in to pop the hood. Using a flashlight for just a moment, he reached under the hood with a knife and slashed the spark plug wires.

Then Hyde called to his men and they moved quietly through the night. Erene moved after Hyde, just as she'd done while they'd worked together. Despite the familiarity, though, everything felt different.

So many things had changed since she'd met Mario.

"WELL," ANNJA WHISPERED, looking at the hood raised on the SUV, "we're not going to be driving out of here."

Roux looked up at her. Even though she couldn't see his lower face due to the mask, Annja sensed he was grinning.

"You didn't want to just drive away now," Roux said. "Not when things have gotten so interesting." He nodded toward the men and the woman moving down toward the ruins. "And someone down there is responsible for the death of your friend."

That was true. Annja took a fresh grip on the sword hilt. Watching the big man moving so effortlessly through the night, she thought about Mario's note, about how a big man claiming to be an international bounty hunter had told him of Erene Skujans's past.

"Do we want to wait until they find the Viking treasure?" Roux asked.

"No," Annja answered.

They started through the night together.

WHILE ROUX WAITED to cover her from a dozen paces away, Annja came up behind one of the men without a sound. Still, the man must have somehow sensed her and started to turn at the last moment. She hit him with the sword hilt, crashing it against the back of his skull.

The sound was muffled but it traveled, alerting the man farther to the right.

Annja caught the unconscious man as he fell, lowering him more gently to the ground. She stayed low, moving slowly to take advantage of the brush as she closed on the next man.

The second man called out to his friend twice, then Annja was on him, wrapping her left arm around the man's throat to keep him from crying out and to shut down the blood flow to his brain. She stomped the back of his right leg, causing the man to collapse, and rode him down to the ground. By the time they hit the ground, the lack of blood carrying oxygen to the brain rendered him senseless.

Pushing herself up, Annja nodded at Roux. He held up a circular shape and made a tossing motion. Annja caught it one-handed, then realized he'd thrown her a roll of military friction tape. She used it to quickly bind and gag the unconscious man.

As she stood, she saw lights fill the horizon to the west. In another moment, the lights separated and became the headlights of four distinct vehicles, all traveling at the same speed in a straight line along the narrow, twisting road that led to the village and the ruins.

"It appears," Roux said grimly as he knelt to pick up the AK-47 the unconscious man had dropped, "that our timing tonight lacks."

Around the catacombs, Erene Skujans and her party went to ground, taking cover where they could.

The four SUVs pulled off the road together and charged across the patches of snow, frozen mud and frost. They flared out with military precision, swooping in like predatory birds.

Annja searched the unconscious man's pack and found a pair of night-vision binoculars. She pulled them to her eyes and scanned the arriving vehicles.

Wolfram Schluter got out of the first SUV. Garin Braden followed. Both of them were clad in military combat harnesses.

"Schluter?" Roux asked.

"Yes," Annja said. "And Garin."

Schluter's men advanced cautiously.

"It appears we're about to witness a bloodbath," Roux said. "That could be a good thing. At least that way the odds would be cut down."

Instead of a bloodbath, though, the big man with Erene Skujans suddenly stepped out of hiding. He held a pistol to the woman's head as he walked over to Schluter, calling out a greeting.

Erene was forced to her knees between the two men in the full light of the SUVs.

"That was unexpected," Roux commented dryly.

Schluter and the big man talked for a while. The big man pointed toward the surrounding forest.

"Do you think they'll kill her?" Annja asked.

"I don't know," Roux answered. "Nor is it our problem." He looked at her in the darkness. "We've come as far as we can with this one, Annja. We need to let it go."

Regret washed over Annja. She'd come this far and she wasn't going to be able to find what she'd set out for.

"We can't stay here," she told Roux.

Roux visibly relaxed. "At least we're in agreement on that. Going up against these odds isn't a pleasant prospect. Perhaps they'll claim the treasure, but they're known to us. And it wasn't treasure you were after anyway, is it?"

"No," Annja replied. But she had wanted Mario's killers brought to justice if possible. More than that, though, if some bit of history—*important* history—existed in those catacombs, she wanted Mario to get the recognition he'd always craved.

Schluter stood beside the lead SUV, taking cover there. He raised his voice. "Annja Creed!"

"Ignore him," Roux said. "We're leaving. Erene Skujans and her friends came by some vehicle. Even if we can't find it, we can always walk out of here." He started to slide away. "Come on."

Schluter stepped away from the SUV and reached inside. He hauled out a struggling figure and threw him on the ground in the light pools.

Stanley Younts, his hands cuffed behind his back, flopped weakly on the ground. Blood smeared his face.

Roux cursed.

Schluter pointed an assault rifle at Stanley. "Come out, Miss Creed. You and the old man, or I'm going to kill this man."

"That puts things in a different light," Roux said. "I liked Stanley, and I'll miss reading his novels." He shrugged as he looked at Annja. "Admittedly, it'll be a little harder to walk away from this, but it's still the safest—"

"I can't leave him like that." Annja stood up and started down the hill.

"You're a fool," Roux called after her. Harsh anger stained his accusation.

Annja listened, but she didn't hear him coming down after her. She was on her own. She tried to tell herself that she wasn't disappointed to be abandoned. She'd been abandoned most of her life.

And she couldn't fault Roux for wanting to save himself. She let the sword fade from her hand just before the adjustable searchlights on the SUVs threw her into sharp relief.

# 36

"She's beautiful," Kikka Schluter told Garin as Annja Creed walked down the hill.

"She is," Garin agreed as he watched her. And so foolishly brave, he thought.

Schluter never took his eyes from the approaching woman, but he asked Garin, "Where's the old man?"

"If he's here, he's up in the hills," Garin said.

"Why didn't he come down?"

"Because Roux isn't going to put his neck on the line for anyone." Garin grinned at that. It was one of the things he respected about Roux.

"What if I threaten to kill the woman?"

"He still won't come."

Schluter stepped toward the cringing man on the ground. "I can shoot this man to show him I mean business."

"He already knows you mean business," Garin said. "He got that when you tried to have him killed in Venice."

Schluter looked at Garin then, obviously surprised that Garin knew as much as he did.

"And if you kill that man, after Annja has put her life on the line to save him," Garin added, "she won't cooperate with you." It was going to be interesting to see how things worked out.

Annja halted twenty yards away. "Let him up."

Cursing, Schluter took the rifle off the man and nodded to one of his guards. The man yanked Stanley Younts to his feet.

"What do you want?" Annja made no move to come closer.

"I know the Viking treasure is inside those catacombs," Schluter said. "Your friend here told us everything."

"I didn't have a choice, Annja," Stanley said shamefully.

"It's okay," Annja replied. "Just stay calm. We're going to be all right. All they want is the treasure. Once they get that, they'll leave."

Garin knew that wasn't the truth. Schluter liked killing. He'd seen it that night in the club. Garin felt certain that Schluter would leave their bodies in the caves once the treasure was secure.

"That's right," Schluter said.

"What about Erene?" the big man holding the dark-haired woman asked.

Garin knew Schluter considered ordering her death. But he didn't.

"Bring her," Schluter said.

The big man yanked the woman to her feet, keeping the pistol pressed against the back of her head.

"Bind Annja's wrists," Garin said, knowing she couldn't draw the sword if her hands were bound.

Schluter ordered it done. Then the men pulled Annja over to their leader.

"Now," Schluter announced with a smile, "let's see about that treasure."

TWO OF SCHLUTER'S MEN used crowbars to break the lock on the doors sealing the catacombs. They switched on powerful flashlights and started down the carved stone steps.

Hands bound behind her, the sword out of reach, Annja stumbled as she was pushed into motion. She went down the steps carefully because they were too narrow and steep to be negotiated with any real speed. The fetid stink of death clung to the place.

The stairs sloped but quickly led into the catacombs. The burial area was twenty feet wide and forty feet long. The dead were long gone.

Nearly two thousand years earlier, Roman legionnaires had been laid to rest in small holes dug into the cave walls. Without benefit of caskets or crypts, they'd been left on the bare rock to decompose naturally.

Annja knew they wouldn't have been buried with much. Perhaps a few personal possessions and a few coins to pay for passage with the ferryman across the River Styx. Whatever had been left had long ago been stripped. Now it was only a place where death had once held court.

Schluter commanded his men to look for the entrance to the other cave system.

"There may not be one," Annja said.

"You came here to find it," Schluter said.

"I came here to look," Annja admitted. "There were no

guarantees that the entrance was here. Or that the treasure even existed."

"You came here for a reason."

Knowing it was a waste of time to argue with the man, Annja kept quiet. She couldn't help looking at the woman with Garin. The woman held on to Garin's arm for support. She was so old it was hard to imagine the two of them being in love.

Erene Skujans stood at Annja's side. Like Annja, her hands had been tied behind her.

"You are Mario's friend? The archaeologist?" Erene asked.

"Yes." Even with the woman standing bound beside her, obviously betrayed by someone she'd trusted, Annja couldn't find any sympathy in her heart for the woman. She'd used Mario to get a shot at the treasure.

"You knew about me?"

"Only after Mario was killed." Annja made her voice harsh, thinking of Mario's family and other people who would miss him.

Pain glinted in the woman's dark blue eyes. "I had nothing to do with his death. I didn't know he was leaving the village until he was gone. If I had known, I would have talked him out of it or gone with him. He wasn't trained to deal with men like these."

"Your friend seems to have caught you by surprise," Annja said.

"I was weak," Erene replied. "I thought I could trust him. Dalton Hyde trusted me."

"To be a thief?"

Erene took in a short, angry breath, then said, "Yes. I had no skills. Dalton offered to train me. All I wanted was a chance to live my life and be able to take care of myself. Thieving is a trade. You don't have to hurt individuals with it. I didn't prey on the weak or unfortunate."

For a moment, Annja's resolve was shaken. She wondered what her life would have been like without the training and education she'd received.

The men searched the room, shining their lights in all directions.

"Being a thief has its uses." Erene smiled at Annja in the darkness. "For instance, I practiced getting out of handcuffs all my life, though I never once had to. But tonight? That's a different story. Let me have your hands."

Annja turned slowly, giving the woman access to her cuffs. Everyone in the room was involved with the search.

"Dalton is so obsessed with the treasure that he forgot about my ability with restraints."

The woman's fingers, quick and sure, held a piece of metal that briefly touched Annja's wrists. In the next minute, almost as though she had a key, the cuffs opened.

"Hold them closed until we're ready to make a move," Erene advised.

Looking up, Annja discovered that Garin was watching her with interest. She didn't know if she suspected what was going on. Before he could act or say anything, one of Schluter's men called, "Over here."

He'd lit one of the torches that had been left in one of the crypts. Annja suspected the torches were used during tours, to give a more authentic lighting for how it would have been all those years ago.

The man held the torch up to where the low ceiling met the wall. Gently but insistently, something pulled at the flame. Soot gathered there from the exposure and revealed a hairline fracture in the stone. He continued trailing the flame over the fissure, following it down the wall. When he was finished, he'd outlined a square section almost five feet high.

Given the relative height of the Romans at the time, Annja knew it could have been used as a door. She could also understand how it could have been overlooked. The Romans had buried their dead inside the catacombs and never allowed anyone in. Later, when the graves were robbed, there had been little to take. Most tomb raiders only grabbed what was immediately discernible.

The door, if that was what it was, had remained virtually invisible.

Schluter turned to Annja. "How does this open?"

"Do you see a handle or any kind of release lever?" she asked sarcastically.

"No," one of the men said.

"Then you push." The lack of any way of pulling the block back into place told Annja something more. If the rock had to be pushed back into place, then men on the other side had to do it. That meant that the cave system had a way out.

She thought about it. The Romans had been stationed there to protect the Amber Road. Bandits had often attacked the caravans, and could have attacked the outpost. Having an escape route from the catacombs was strategic.

Three of Schluter's men put their shoulders against the rock and shoved. Grudgingly, the massive stone block slid forward.

A breeze carried into the room from the opening. The smell of dank earth grew stronger inside the catacombs.

One of the men went forward with a lantern. He looked back, the bright orange glow playing across his face. "It's another cave. A bigger one."

Schluter entered the cave, then waved everyone else through.

On the other side of the makeshift door, Annja stared out across the cave. A six-foot ledge ran along the wall. Beyond it was a gaping crevice. The cave ended to the right, but it continued on well past the reach of the lanterns to the left.

Schluter's frustration showed. He shone his light into Annja's face. "Does this cave lead to the treasure?"

"I don't know," Annja replied.

"You knew this cave was here."

"That's all I knew."

"Liar!" Schluter screamed like a spoiled child and crossed the distance separating them. "What did Mario Fellini tell you about the treasure?"

Annja eyed the man levelly. "I'm telling you the truth."

"Where is the treasure?"

"There may not be a treasure," Annja insisted. "It could all be a story."

"Do you have the book?" the old woman asked.

Annja looked at Kikka Schluter standing behind Garin. Her face was grim and severe.

"Do you have the book?" she repeated in a sterner voice.

"The one that describes Baron Frederick of Schluter's torture and murder of peasants in villages in this area?" Annja asked.

Kikka Schluter grimaced and cursed. "My family name means something."

"I can see that. It's why your grandson has turned out to be the same kind of upstanding individual."

The woman's attention turned to her grandson. "Kill

this cow and be done with her. She doesn't know any more than she's told you."

Schluter raised his pistol and took aim.

GARIN MOVED before he'd even thought about it. Roux had always chided him for leaping first and then looking. But he had a pistol in his hand and was pointing it at Wolfram Schluter—intending to prevent Schluter from killing Annja for no good reason that he could think of—when it felt like a sledgehammer hit him in the back three times in quick succession.

The sound of the gunshots rolled through the cave.

Incredulous, he looked down and saw that blood was spreading across the front of his shirt. One of the bullets had gone all the way through.

His arm went numb. Panic filled him when he realized he couldn't breathe. The weapon dropped from his fingertips. In stunned disbelief, he turned to Kikka Schluter and stared at her.

She stood with a smoking pistol in her hand.

He wanted to ask her why, but he couldn't speak.

"No one harms my family," she said almost tenderly. "I'm sorry. You reminded me very much of your father."

Blackness swirled over Garin's vision. The cave floor felt as if it were tilting underfoot. He tried to remain on his feet, but it was impossible. He fell, but he never felt the impact against the ground.

# 37

Annja was in motion even as Garin shoved his pistol in Wolfram Schluter's direction. She slid her hands free of the handcuffs as Kikka Schluter shot Garin in the back.

Schluter stared at his grandmother. As Garin dropped to the ground, Annja had the sword in her hands.

Turning, she saw that Erene was moving, as well. The woman struck Dalton Hyde with a short punch to the jaw and drew his pistol from his shoulder holster before he fell. By the time the big man caught himself on the ground, Erene had the pistol behind his ear. Without a word, she pulled the trigger.

Grabbing Stanley by the shoulder, Annja shoved the writer back through the open hole into the crypt area. He caromed off one of the walls but went quickly enough. For a moment it looked as though he was going to fall, but he kept his feet under him and started running.

Bullets chopped into the stone cube that had been cut through the wall. Annja banged into the rough marks left

by the stone saws that had been used to cut out the
secret door.

Erene was at her heels, pistol blazing in her fist. The
flashes were strong enough to light the narrow stairs that
led back up to the ground level. Stanley fell only once on
his way up. Annja grabbed him and kept going.

Two guards at the entrance had their weapons up, but
made their decisions to fire too slowly.

Annja threw the sword, piercing the heart of one man
while she dived at the other, throwing her feet forward to take
the man's feet out from under him as he fired over her head.

The man fell forward and slammed his chin on the frozen
ground, knocking himself out. Annja grabbed the man's
pistol from his hip holster as she rolled to her feet. Even as
she was standing, she pulled the sword back into her hand.

Erene erupted from the catacombs. She fired the pistol
with rapid but methodical deliberation, taking out three
guards while bullets kicked chunks of frozen earth from
the ground at her feet.

Another pair of guards stood at the nearby SUV. Erene
stopped to reload her borrowed pistol with a magazine she
took from the man Annja had killed with the sword.

On the run, Annja lifted her left hand and fired at the
man in front of her, cycling the pistol empty. Some of the
bullets hit him in the head and shoulders, but most tore into
the front windshield of the SUV.

Then she ran for the man on the other side of the
vehicle, diving past him as he fired his assault rifle on full-
auto, narrowly missing Stanley, who was quick enough to
dive to the ground.

Annja scrambled to her feet almost five feet behind her
opponent. She swung a backhanded blow with the sword.

By the time his body dropped, she was rounding the front of the SUV, heading for Stanley.

She helped the writer to his feet and guided him to the SUV. Looking inside, she saw that the keys were in the ignition. She opened the door and shoved him inside, then started to crawl in herself.

Erene ran around to the passenger side.

Gunfire blasted the windshield to pieces. Bullets cut the air around her. She had a brief impression of the gunner to her left, then he went down under a short burst of fire from Roux's captured AK-47.

"Annja!" Roux called, running up.

"You're still here?" Annja started the SUV. "Don't you think that's pretty foolish?"

Roux looked around. "Where's Garin?"

"Back there," Annja replied. "The old woman shot him."

Roux's face blanched and he swore. Then he bolted back toward the catacombs.

"Oh, now that's *really* stupid," Annja said.

Roux fired, killing at least one of the two men seeking to crawl out of the catacombs. Then he plunged inside.

Annja opened the door and slid out. She turned to Stanley and Erene. "Get out of here. Don't stop until you get to Liepaja."

Then she ran after Roux, stopping only long enough to grab one of the flash-bang grenades she'd noticed on one of the dead men's combat harnesses. She'd seen the grenades in action before and had a healthy fear of them. But they could also be useful. Especially in the dark in small, enclosed spaces.

She ran down the steps leading into the catacombs, but

not before she saw that Stanley and Erene weren't leaving. They were arming themselves.

The idiocy was spreading.

ANNJA CAME UP behind Roux, yelling to let him know it was her as he blasted a man back through the doorway cut into the wall. She underhanded the flash-bang through the door, bouncing it off the stone cube away from where Garin had been and hoping that it didn't carom over the edge.

"Cover your eyes," she advised, closing her own.

The flash-bang went off with a series of deafening detonations and bright flashes that pained Annja's eyelids. Even though she'd had her eyes closed and had turned away from the eruption of light in the other room, spots still danced in her vision.

Roux sprinted forward, slamming a fresh magazine into the AK-47.

I can't believe you're in here for Garin, she thought. But the relationship between the two men wasn't easy to describe. From father and son to mortal enemies wasn't a normal progression, but they'd done it. Either end of that spectrum manifested at the strangest times, though.

She followed Roux into the other cave, listening to the AK-47 roar without mercy.

Most of the men in the room were down. Annja was sure some of them were missing. She wondered if Roux's bullets had knocked them over the side or if they'd fallen over the edge while blinded by the flash-bang.

The old woman was standing against the wall with her small pistol thrust before her. Annja didn't know if the baroness was reacting to the sound of Roux's rifle or still retained some of her vision, but she started firing at once.

Roux fired again. The bullets slammed into the old woman and drove her back against the wall. She dropped to the ground without a sound.

No one else remained around Garin, who was deathly still on the ground. An overturned electric lantern played over him as he lay sprawled there.

Annja knew Garin had to be dead. The old woman had fired at least three times that she had counted, and blood had spread over the stone floor.

"Garin!" Anguish filled Roux's cry. The old man began tearing Garin's shirt open.

Some unnamed sense warned Annja of the men to her left. She turned, bringing the sword up as metal gleamed on an assault rifle thrusting out of the shadows.

Whirling, Annja drew an emergency light stick from her pocket and broke it against the stone cube. Pale blue light invaded the immediate vicinity, drawing four men out of the darkness.

One of them was Wolfram Schluter.

Gripping the sword in both hands, knowing that Garin and Roux were vulnerable behind her, Annja took the fight to her opponents. No matter what, she wasn't going to let them get past her. In his grief, Roux wasn't even paying attention.

Annja chopped through two of the rifles, causing one of them to misfire and the other to blow up in the man's face as rounds cycled through. His face a bloody mess, he screamed in agony and fell over the ledge. His screams lasted for a moment, then ended abruptly.

Ducking low, Annja sliced another man across the stomach, mortally wounding him. Footing became slippery with his blood.

She brought the sword down onto the last man's head,

intending to go for Wolfram Schluter next. But the blade got caught in the dead man's skull.

Schluter fired at her, but she grabbed the heated barrel and shoved it away as it fired the last four rounds in the magazine. Unable to hold on to the superheated metal, Annja released the rifle and abandoned the sword, intending to call it to her again.

Before she could, Schluter reversed the rifle and butt-stroked her in the face, dazing her and driving her back to the edge. He kept up his attack, hitting her once more in the side of the head before she got a hand up.

You can't let him get by you, she told herself. He'll kill Roux.

When Schluter drew the rifle back, Annja shifted and launched a side kick. Her foot drove the rifle into Schluter's face and chest, ripping it from his grip. He reached for the knife at his hip, roaring with rage, then came at her.

Sweeping her left arm out, she blocked the overhead thrust, broke into his overhand strike the way she'd been taught, caught his wrist in her left hand, slammed his elbow with her right hand to make the joint bend, then spun and stepped back under his arm as she twisted the knife to bring it back toward him.

The knife went into Schluter's chest easily, propelled by his strength and hers. It pierced his heart and he crumpled to his knees, looking surprised. He tried to speak but couldn't. When life left him, he fell over onto his side.

Breathing hard, cut and battered, Annja looked around. No one else remained standing except Erene and Stanley at the doorway.

Roux was administering CPR to Garin, working hard in the familiar rhythm.

As she approached him, Annja felt sorry for Roux. He hadn't just lost an enemy; he'd lost a son. Tears tracked his cheeks.

"Roux," she said softly.

"He's not dead," Roux said. "His heart has just stopped. That's all."

"There's nothing you can do. She shot him three times at close range. He never had a chance. He died trying to save me." At least, Annja was pretty sure that was what Garin intended to do.

"He's not dead," Roux growled fiercely. "He was wearing a vest."

Annja leaned in closer then, seeing that Garin had been wearing a Kevlar vest under his clothing.

"But the blood—"

"One of the rounds missed the vest and went through under his shoulder. If I can get him breathing again—" Roux was starting to flag.

"Let me." Annja performed the compressions, then leaned down to breathe air into Garin's lungs. When she did, he kissed her, long and tender, surprising her completely.

Annja recoiled and slapped him hard enough to turn his head.

"What are you doing?" Roux demanded.

"He's faking," Annja said, getting to her feet.

Garin started laughing, but that triggered a coughing fit that almost strangled him. "I wasn't faking," he said weakly. "Not at first. Roux got my heart going again, but I saw you sitting there and I wondered if you'd try to save me, too."

"It was a mistake," Annja assured him. "An aberration. It won't happen again."

"If it takes getting shot to get a kiss," Garin complained hoarsely, "I hardly think it's worth it. You didn't put any effort into it at all."

Annja slapped him again. Then she and Roux helped Garin to his feet.

Garin gazed down at the dead woman. Sadness showed on his face. "At one time, I really loved her. In all my years, I've never met anyone who attracted me the way that she did."

There was no mistaking the pain in his voice, but Annja didn't think it was all from the wound in his shoulder.

# EpiloguE

Erene and Roux tended to Garin. Certain that no law-enforcement people would show up for some time, Annja stared at the ruins of the church. What kept coming to mind was the entry in Ozolini's journal. The part about Thor's treasure being buried under the others.

She walked to one of the SUVs and got a shovel and pick from the back.

"Where are you going?" Roux asked.

"To check out a hunch," Annja replied. "The Roman soldiers buried in that catacomb weren't the only ones buried here. I keep remembering how the Curonians killed the priests who occupied this church."

"They hated them," Erene said. "All the old stories tell of the Germans who came to our lands and tried to subjugate our people."

"But what if they killed two birds with one stone?" Annja asked. "What if they killed all the priests so no one would know they buried Thor *under* their crypt?"

She walked the remains of the church and found where the apse had been. Crypts were usually constructed under the hemispherical section beyond the altar and to the liturgical east.

She broke through the tiles and into the crypt.

IT TOOK over an hour to dig through the bottom of the crypt. She knew where to dig because she'd struck the floor again and again until the sounds turned hollow.

Climbing down into the hidden crypt, using iron handholds mounted into the wall, she found the remains of the Viking who'd chosen to make Courland home.

His mummified remains lay in a small boat. Furs and blankets, leather pouches of food and carved items occupied the boat with him.

Roux, Stanley and Erene climbed down to join her.

"Not much in the way of treasure, is there?" Roux mused.

Garin kept bellowing from above, wanting to know what they had found.

In fact, there was no real treasure. A few silver coins and a bag of amber, which wasn't worth as much these days as it had been when Thor had been entombed.

But he had his amber ax. It was a beautiful piece of craftsmanship.

"Do you think he could call down the lightning with this?" Annja asked.

"I don't know," Roux answered.

"It would be cool if he had," Stanley said. Despite his violent adventures, he still carried a sense of wonder about him.

*"What is it?"* Garin demanded from above.

They ignored him.

"There's something about this handle." Erene's knowing fingers prized at the bottom of the handle. She used Annja's Swiss Army knife to pull the cap from the end. Inside sheets of calfskin parchment were neatly coiled within the hollow space.

Pulse pounding, Annja freed the parchment sheets from the hidden area and used a flashlight to examine them.

*"What is it?"* Garin demanded again.

A smile spread across Annja's face as she looked at the carefully drawn map and Norse ruins inscribed on the parchment.

"This is a map," Annja said. "Thor's trade map." She flipped through the other pages. "And this, from what I can decipher of it, is his life story. Where he went. What he did. How he came to be here." She'd studied Norse runes while at Hadrian's Wall. The Norsemen had left their mark there, too.

"Well done, Annja," Roux congratulated. "It appears that you've made a very significant find."

"Not me," Annja said. "Mario was the one who discovered this story and followed it here. I only picked up the trail he'd left. This is his find. I'm going to make sure he gets full credit for it."

"Mario would have wanted that," Erene said.

"I know," Annja said.

# JAMES AXLER

# DEATH LANDS

## Remember Tomorrow

An earthquake in the Arkansas dust bowls shakes up the warriors, leaving an amnesic J. B. Dix in the employ of the iron-fisted ruler of Duma. Can Ryan and the others save their friend from the most dangerous ville in all the Deathlands?

### *Available September wherever you buy books.*

---

# JAKE STRAIT

## TWIST OF CAIN

### BY FRANK RICH

Jake Strait has been
hired by one of the rich
and powerful to find an
elusive serial killer, who
is handy with a nail gun
and is a collector of
body parts. Except
Jake Strait has been
set up from the start.

**Available in October
wherever books
are sold.**